BENJAMIN FORREST AND THE LOST CITY OF THE GHOULS

ENDINFINIUM #3

CHRIS WARD

"Benjamin Forrest and the Lost City of the Ghouls (Endinfinium #3)"
Copyright © Chris Ward 2018

The right of Chris Ward to be identified as the Author of this Work has been asserted by him in accordance with the Copyright, Designs and Patents Act 1988.

All rights reserved. No part of this publication may be reproduced, stored in a retrieval system, or transmitted, in any form or by any means without the prior written permission of the Author.

This story is a work of fiction and is a product of the Author's imagination. All resemblances to actual locations or to persons living or dead are entirely coincidental.

ABOUT THE AUTHOR

A proud and noble Cornishman (and to a lesser extent British), Chris Ward ran off to live and work in Japan back in 2004. There he got married, got a decent job, and got a cat. He remains pure to his Cornish/British roots while enjoying the inspiration of living in a foreign country.

www.amillionmilesfromanywhere.net

ALSO BY CHRIS WARD

Head of Words
The Man Who Built the World
Saving the Day

The Fire Planets Saga
Fire Fight
Fire Storm
Fire Rage

The Endinfinium series
Benjamin Forrest and the School at the End of the World
Benjamin Forrest and the Bay of Paper Dragons
Benjamin Forrest and the Lost City of the Ghouls

The Tube Riders series
Underground
Exile
Revenge
In the Shadow of London

The Tales of Crow series
The Eyes in the Dark
The Castle of Nightmares

The Puppeteer King

The Circus of Machinations

The Dark Master of Dogs

The Tokyo Lost Mystery Series

Broken

Stolen

Frozen

Also Available

The Tube Riders Complete Series 1-4 Boxed Set

The Tales of Crow 1-5 Complete Series Boxed Set

The Tokyo Lost Complete Series 1-3 Boxed Set

*You may feel certain sensations of hot or cold with no obvious source.
These should be ignored at all costs.*

Extract from *The Pupil's Handbook, Revised Ed.*
Endinfinium High School
(Author unknown)

THE LOST CITY OF THE GHOULS

PART I

A WHITE ELEPHANT IN THE WATER

1
TRIANGULATION

THE SUNS—BOTH OF THEM—WERE RESPLENDENT. The dominant yellow sun hung high overhead, beaming out of a clear blue sky, while its smaller red counterpart hung above the bank of fog and cloud to the east that marked the edge of the known world, casting the surface of the sea with a glittering net of crimson. While it was never truly hot in Endinfinium, it was certainly a pleasant shade of warm, and for once the winds that usually whipped up the front of the cliff on which the school was perched were still.

A team of cleaners—the blank-faced bodies of the reanimated dead—had set up a rickety wooden stage far too close to the edge of the clifftop courtyard for Benjamin Forrest's liking. It was a relief then that he wouldn't need to stand on it for at least another six Endinfinium years.

He stood now in the front row of pupils, with his best friends, Wilhelm Jacobs and Miranda

Butterworth, to his left and right. All three, like the rest of the first-year pupils in their row, wore their best uniform for the event, a light, blue-grey jacket and trousers. Each year wore a slightly darker shade, so from above the six lines of pupils most likely looked like a gradually darkening shadow stretching toward the postmodern glass doors of the school a short distance behind.

'Wilhelm, quick!' Miranda hissed over the back of Benjamin's shoulders. 'Dusty patrol.'

Professor James "Dusty" Eaves had indeed begun another of his casual inspection checks, ambling along the lines of pupils, his hands clasped behind his back, making his hunchback even more prominent. Wilhelm, with one quick movement, reached back and tucked his shirt back into his trousers. As soon as Professor Eaves had returned to the side of the stage, Wilhelm pulled it out again.

'I don't know why you bother,' Benjamin whispered.

'A quiet rebellion grows into a loud rebellion,' Wilhelm said.

'But what are you rebelling against?'

Wilhelm grinned. 'Everything.'

'Can you two zip it?' Miranda said. 'Here we go.'

To the right of the stage, a large canvas-covered drum began to beat itself in a slow rhythm that matched the footsteps of the line of pupils walking slowly from the school's entrance across the courtyard to the stage. At the front walked Professor Robert Loane, the *de facto* head of the teaching staff. He wore a black suit and a tall top hat that didn't quite cover his hair.

The Lost City of the Ghouls

'Look, you can see it,' Wilhelm said. 'The grey patch.'

Benjamin saw he was right—just beneath Professor Loane's left ear, his formerly brown hair had gained a palm-sized patch of grey. Whether through age, stress, or sickness, no one knew, but the pupils were keen to settle on a secret nickname as soon as possible.

'Pebbles,' Miranda sniggered, ducking her head to hide a smile.

'Salt shaker,' Wilhelm said, throwing an angry glance in her direction.

'Is something the matter, Jacobs?' boomed a stern voice from the side of the stage. Ms. Ito, fearsome owner of the chessboard hair and a nose so thin that from front on it was nearly invisible, stomped into view, the overlarge cast on her left leg swinging out and down like a giant white rolling pin.

Wilhelm dropped his eyes and gave a fast shake of his head. Ms. Ito scowled and turned back to watch the graduating pupils making a line across the stage.

'Licorice Loane,' Benjamin whispered. Wilhelm elbowed him in the ribs, and when he subsequently bumped into Miranda, she elbowed him back again. Ms. Ito looked round, and all three of them found their mouths snapping closed hard enough to make their teeth hurt.

The graduating pupils had made two lines across the stage, eighteen in total. Benjamin found it difficult to put names to many of them, but he recognised Terry Wilkins—the head of the rugby club (infamous flusher of Godfrey Pendleton's cohort Derek Bates for a club initiation)—and Sara Liselle, a waiflike girl of indeterminable age: it was said she was graduating purely on duration as a pupil rather than her approximate years of existence. Then there was Andre Bellini, a popular member of the flower-arranging club, and a keen student of Endinfinium's bizarre flora.

A hush had fallen over the small crowd. Benjamin felt the magical hold on his jaw relax, and he gave his mouth a slight flex to test its worthiness. From beside the stage, Ms. Ito offered him the briefest of smiles.

'Opening word,' Professor Eaves said, speaking into a microphone at the edge of the stage. A pair of speakers set up in front crackled; one of them bumped from side to side like an excitable monkey.

Professor Loane took up the microphone.

'Welcome, everyone,' he said. 'On this day, the fourth of estimated-October, on the anniversary—as best as anyone can tell—of the founding of our fine school, we would like to say a thank-you to the current seventh-years and wish them well in their choice of triangulation.'

'Shouldn't it be graduation?' Benjamin whispered to Miranda, after first checking Ms. Ito's gaze was elsewhere.

Miranda shook her head. 'Of course not. This is Endinfinium. Do you really think they would do something normal?'

Benjamin glanced from one teacher to the next, then looked along the two lines of pupils. None of the teachers were smiling, and few of the pupils. Back in Benjamin's school in Basingstoke, England, graduating

The Lost City of the Ghouls

would have been a happy event, but here in Endinfinium it marked a step into the unknown.

Professor Eaves took up the microphone again. 'First, a speech from our headmaster, Grand Lord Bastien.'

A series of whispers circulated among Benjamin's line. None of the first-years had ever seen the Grand Lord this close, and never outside the Great Hall.

'Where is he?' Wilhelm whispered.

Heads turned as the school doors creaked. A line of cleaners emerged, carrying an old-fashioned palanquin that looked dug straight out of the ground. One side was covered in intricate carvings, the other was faded and worn as though it had lain half-buried on a beach for some years.

The cleaners carried the palanquin in front of the stage and set it down. One opened a door, and a heavily robed figure emerged.

'He's so creepy,' whispered Derek from the row of second-years behind Benjamin. 'I reckon he'll melt if he takes that veil off.'

'You can see right through him!' another one hissed.

The veil covered the Grand Lord's face, but as he turned to face first the pupils on the stage, then the rest of the assembled, Benjamin saw the boy was right. At a certain angle, the Grand Lord's pale face was partially translucent.

He remembered Professor Loane telling him once that the Grand Lord was a "disassociated soul". Part of the old man was here in Endinfinium, while part of him was elsewhere, in an old life he could no longer connect with. It was a fancy name; to the kids he was simply a clothed ghost.

The Grand Lord walked across to the microphone. Walking was something Benjamin, who met with the Grand Lord frequently, had never seen him do. Closing his eyes and concentrating, he felt the warmth of the Grand Lord's magic, and knew their headmaster was using his power to move in a way that a lack of physical substance denied him.

'I am honoured to see those who have risen through our ranks,' the Grand Lord said. 'It has been many years since your coming, and your survival alone in such trying circumstances is a testament to your maturity. Now, the time has come for you to leave the protective walls of Endinfinium High. It is time to make your choice.'

The Grand Lord stepped back from the microphone, lowering his head in a gesture to suggest his involvement in proceedings was now over. Professor Loane stepped forward.

'Many years ago, the founders of our school agreed that, for school leavers, three paths exist. This became known as your triangulation. Your choices exist as such. One: you may choose to remain at the school, and become part of its staff. Opportunities exist to study beneath your former professors or within faculties such as administration, catering, or services.'

A few pupils behind Benjamin sighed. Beside him, Wilhelm was trying to untie one shoelace with the toe of his other shoe. Miranda, standing stock straight to emphasise her status as prefect, glared at him like a mother frustrated with a disobedient child.

'Your second choice,' Professor Loane continued, 'is to make your way out into Endinfinium and become part of its wider community. There are small villages associated with the school, and farming and fishing communities. Some former pupils work in the forests to the south, or run guesthouses and study camps. There are many opportunities for you to make a life for yourself where you can find happiness and pride in what you do.'

'And now the third choice,' Wilhelm whispered, grinning at Benjamin. 'That's the big one, isn't it?'

'Shh!' Miranda hissed.

Professor Loane cleared his throat. 'And then there is choice number three. It is the one which brings us in the teaching community a sense of regret, but it is one we nevertheless respect and support. The third possibility of your triangulation is that you decide to leave the protective wing of the school and seek your fortunes beyond the known boundaries of Endinfinium.'

Behind them, Derek Bates made a falling and plopping sound. One of the third-year girls hissed at him to shut up and another slapped him on the shoulder.

'You have been prepared for these choices,' Professor Loane continued. 'Now is the time to make your decision.'

He stepped away from the microphone. Dusty Eaves stepped up to take over.

'Your choices will now be announced,' he said.

'First, I will read the names of those who have chosen to become part of the school's staff.'

With a little cough, the professor reeled off six names, adding which department they would join. After Terry Wilkins' name was read, Professor Eaves announced he would be this year's assistant to Captain Roche in gym class.

Next came the list of pupils choosing to work out in the wider area around the school. Andre Bellini was announced as an apprentice of Alan Barnacle at the Paper Dragon Bay Guesthouse, a study camp a couple of hours north of the school, and a place Benjamin remembered with mixed feelings. Nine pupils had taken this second option, leaving just three who had decided to take their chances. Benjamin wondered how he would feel when his triangulation came, whether he could follow them off into the unknown, or perhaps continue to forge a life for himself at the school.

'Sara Liselle, Timothy Long, and Emmie Bromwich … we are aware that you have had plenty of time to come to this decision. For the past nine years, no school leaver has chosen this third option. Do any of you have anything to say?'

Sara Liselle lifted a slender hand. Benjamin shook his head, and out of the corner of his eye he saw Miranda glance at him, perhaps because more than once he had already tried to take a similar path.

'Yes, Sara. Come forward.'

Her bottom lip was trembling, and when she spoke the amplified voice came out in a tremor.

'I wish everyone here at the school well,' she said. 'As

I'm sure Tim and Emmie do too. This was a decision we came to ourselves, after much deliberation. What is it they say about curiosity? That it's like a cat trying to escape from a box.'

Miranda scoffed. 'Load of rubbish,' she muttered. 'A cat doesn't die if it escapes from a box.'

'Depends where it is,' Wilhelm said. 'Train tracks—ow!'

'Shut up.'

On the stage, Sara cleared her throat. 'Well, I am that cat. Tim and Emmie are also that cat. We might return, we don't know. But we have to look. None of us were born here in Endinfinium, and while we thank the teaching staff and everyone who has helped us from the bottom of our hearts, we have no wish to die here, either.'

At the side of the stage, Ms. Ito rolled her eyes. Captain Roche was rocking back and forward as though caught in a breeze meant only for him, while Grand Lord Bastien was a statue standing at the back, his head bowed, leaving no sign of a person beneath the thick robes.

Sara Liselle handed the microphone back to Professor Loane, who cleared his throat.

'Then, without further ado, from everyone here at Endinfinium High School, we would like to wish you all the best as you make your way out into the world … and beyond.'

2

LIBRARY SERVICE

'Are you coming, Benjamin? I want to see if they chicken out. I mean, they must do, right?'

Benjamin looked up from where he was folding away his school uniform and putting it back into his drawer. Wilhelm still wore his, but his shirt was now fully untucked, his shoelaces untied, and the buttons of his shirt unfastened. He had even added a perfunctory ruffling of the hair to his rebellious look.

'You know, if you're going to be the year's delinquent, you'll need to smile a bit less,' Benjamin said. 'It kind of betrays you, don't you think?'

Wilhelm shrugged. 'As long as I get under their skin, that's all that matters.'

'I imagine you're already there. Buried in deep, like a roach.'

Wilhelm laughed. 'You sound like Miranda. Are you coming or not?'

Benjamin shook his head. 'I'll meet you down on the

beach. I have something to do first.'

'Let me guess? It's a secret.'

Benjamin lowered his eyes. 'I'll tell you soon, I promise.'

'Okay, but you better not have some new friend you're going off to hang out with without telling me.'

'Nothing like that.'

'Or is it a girl?'

'No! That's horrible.'

'Good.'

Benjamin made his excuses and left, already dressed in his secondary uniform, the one used for general knocking about. It would be quicker to head straight to the beach after his appointment rather than come back to change; it was already likely he would miss the departure of the three leavers for the edge of the world. It depended on how hard Godfrey felt like punishing him.

The detention cells were several levels below the surface, built into the solid rock of the headland. As a result, there was little evidence of reanimation—rock being one of the few things for which reanimation happened so slowly as to be undetectable—save for the flickering candles bouncing in the metal holders fitted to the walls.

It was drafty down this deep underground, with much of the headland filled with natural holes and gullies like a giant sponge, meaning chill blasts of sea air could strike you at any moment. Benjamin, wrapped in a woolen cloak, hurried along, his head down.

When he reached the door of Godfrey's detention

cell, he put the piles of books he had brought from the library on the floor and leaned down to look into the small space through which food trays were passed.

Freezing water splashed into his face, soaking him nearly to the waist. Too shocked even to cry out, Benjamin simply closed his eyes as his skin tingled, then wiped it away with one hand, and opened his eyes to find himself staring into the bright green eyes of Godfrey, the school's resident bully, cohort of the Dark Man, and Benjamin's personal nemesis.

'Oh, sorry there, Bennie. I was just changing my bath water.' The sour-faced boy grinned. 'You're lucky it wasn't the slops. That's next.'

'I brought what you asked for.'

Godfrey's smile dropped. 'Did you check they were complete? If I get to the end and find there's a chapter missing, I'll tell on you, you know I will—'

'They're complete. I flicked through each one myself, just to make sure.'

'They'll cast you out if they know what I know. Don't you try me.'

Benjamin sighed. 'I won't. Don't worry, they're complete.'

'Are you sure?'

'Cleat said from time to time storage boxes wash up with the contents sealed inside. No water damage. I got what you wanted.' Benjamin pushed the bundle forward. 'Isaac Asimov. The complete *Foundation*.'

'Which edition?'

Benjamin sighed. 'How am I supposed to know?'

'I told you, I wanted the 1998 reissued edition.

Nothing else.'

'I did my best—'

'Are you sure about that? Do you want to be wandering Endinfinium forever, Forrest? Living life like an outcast? Shunned by everyone you meet?'

Benjamin slammed a fist on the floor. 'I tried—'

Godfrey started to laugh. 'I'm only messing with you, Forrest. My God, you're so gullible. If I called you a scatlock would you try to fly?'

Benjamin said nothing. He pushed the bag closer to the food slot, then waited while Godfrey unloaded the books one by one. When he was done, Godfrey began pushing books he had read back through the slot. The *Earthsea Trilogy*, Gene Wolfe's *Book of the New Sun*, *Ringworld* by Larry Niven, *Eon* by Greg Bear. Some of them had extensive signs of water damage, but at least they were all complete. Godfrey had thrown a tantrum after getting a copy of Stephen King's *Dark Tower 7* which was missing the final chapter. Benjamin, who had read it, had offered to talk Godfrey through the end, only to find a kick aimed through the food slot miss his face by a hair's width.

Godfrey's love of speculative fiction had come as a surprise. If he wasn't such a mean-spirited, generally evil git, they could have been good friends.

Godfrey sat on the floor and went through the books one by one. Benjamin waited with his face pressed to the floor. Finally, Godfrey looked up.

'You're still here?'

'Yeah. I was just wondering if you can remember anything more about this shifting castle place.'

Godfrey threw the book down. It landed, open-sided, on a puddle of water. 'So that's it, is it, Forrest? You're fishing for information? Trying to find out if I'm lying or not about you and the Dark Man being one and the same? Oh, you're so shallow.'

Benjamin shrugged as best he could for someone lying on the floor. 'Of course I believe you. I was just wondering. And, you know, you don't get many visitors down here.'

Godfrey glared at him. 'I'll tell you what, Forrest. You've been pretty good at finding things so far, so let's give you a test. If you pass, I'll answer your questions.'

'Okay. What do you want?'

'A bottle of fizzy pop.'

'What?'

Godfrey sneered. 'See, not so easy now, is it? I've told you what I want, now get to it. And just to make things more interesting, if you don't find it, I'll start spreading the word about you and the Dark Man. How's that for a challenge?'

'You're a sod.'

Godfrey laughed. 'Bye-bye, Forrest.'

As Benjamin sat up, Godfrey called out again. 'Wait.' The book—a copy of *Prelude to Foundation*—crashed against the small opening and flopped half through like a dying bird. 'You've ruined this one now. Get me another.'

Benjamin sighed and picked the book up. He didn't bother to say goodbye to Godfrey as he walked back up the gloomy corridor, but he could hear Godfrey's laughter echoing in his ears.

3
DEPARTURE

MIRANDA APPEARED TO HAVE SWALLOWED A thundercloud. As Benjamin scrambled down the final steepest section of path to where the other pupils and teachers were assembled on the beach, she tapped the invisible watch on her wrist and hissed, 'Where have you been?'

'Says the girl who vanished on me the first time we met,' Benjamin snapped back, unable to help himself. Immediately he felt guilty, but Miranda's bony fist snaked out and cracked him on the arm before he could start to apologise.

'At least I had a good reason. What's yours?'

Benjamin patted his stomach and grinned. 'Bad lunch.'

'Well, at least you didn't miss anything.'

Further down the beach, the three departing pupils were climbing into a rickety boat that didn't look capable of crossing a road on the back of a truck let alone an ocean. Cleaners loaded cases for them, which contained as much food and provisions as the school could spare. The teachers stood in a rough circle around the boat, with the pupils behind them. Formalities had been forgotten. The pupils were now dressed in gym or casual wear, and were talking among themselves. The teachers, their faces glum, were making one last attempt to persuade the three leavers to stay.

'No decision is ever final,' Ms. Ito was saying. 'Not unless I make it.'

Sara Liselle shook her head. 'Thank you for everything,' she said.

'Well, send us a postcard,' Professor Eaves quipped. 'Or a fax, or whatever it is you can send when you get there. Perhaps a carrier pigeon.' He raised a hand to give a brief wave, then turned and walked back up the beach. As he passed Benjamin, he muttered, 'Hell, throw a message in a bottle for all I care. Huh. Seven years of schooling literally thrown off a cliff.'

'Are you ready, Professor Caspian?' Professor Loane said.

Standing next to a wooden crate a little way up the beach, Edgar Caspian nodded.

'Well, fire away.'

Edgar, unsmiling, leaned into the box, then stepped back. With a sudden whistle, a rocket burst up into the sky and exploded. It was quickly followed by several more. While it wasn't quite dark enough to make the firework display beautiful, with the red sun now below the line of the cliffs to the north, the multi-coloured sky took on an eerie brilliance.

The Lost City of the Ghouls

Most of the pupils whooped and cheered. Benjamin was wondering where the teachers had found working fireworks when he felt the faint heat of Edgar's magic and understood. The teachers had found old, damaged fireworks, and a little bit of reanimation magic had turned them into a passable explosion. For Benjamin, who still struggled to control his magic, even under the watchful instruction of Grand Lord Bastien, it was quite the display of skill.

With the three pupils aboard, the boat moved gently out into the bay. Far out on the horizon, something huge rose from the water and then dived out of sight. Benjamin frowned, but all three pupils were facing the beach, waving at the friends and teachers they were leaving behind. All three looked happy. Benjamin, who had been to the edge of the world and barely survived, struggled to share their enthusiasm. Neither Miranda nor Wilhelm were smiling either.

'Well, good luck to them,' Miranda said. Then, turning to Benjamin, she fixed him with a glare. 'Don't you ever dare leave me standing on this beach while I wave you off on some stupid boat. I'll swim out there and drag you back with the anchor tied around your neck to hold you down.'

'Would you tie an anchor around my neck?' Wilhelm asked.

Miranda scowled. 'I'd tie you to the bow of a cruise-shark to give you a swimming lesson at the same time.'

Wilhelm smirked. 'You're going to make a great teacher one day.'

'I know. Not like there's much else to do, is there? Other than become a chamomile farmer.'

'I thought I might set up a water-skiing school.'

'Well, make sure you don't fall over the edge.'

'You can talk—'

Benjamin put up a hand. 'Can you two be quiet? I want to watch.'

With the fireworks display over, the pupils waved as the boat drifted out into deeper waters. From time to time, strange beasts surfaced alongside it, eyeing it with curiosity, but it passed beyond the headland unharmed. Some of the other pupils were talking about going onto the cliffs to watch it fall over the edge of the world, but Professor Loane ordered everyone back to the school for dinner. The last Benjamin saw of the little boat was it disappearing behind the rocky cliff.

In honour of the triangulation ceremony, dinner was almost special. The new members of the teaching staff sat alongside their more celebrated counterparts as the cleaners dished out the usual plates of bland vegetables topped by a slightly sweet custard sauce, but tonight served with a side bowl of fruit jelly filled with shiny red strawberries.

Benjamin gave one a tentative prod with his fork, suspicious, as always, of anything never served before.

'What do you think it's been fused with?' Wilhelm asked. 'Plastic buckets and spades? Old party balloons?'

Miranda pushed Benjamin's hand away, speared the

strawberry, and popped it into her mouth before he could begin to protest.

'You know they won't serve us anything that's been reanimated,' she said. 'How about a little trust? It tastes fine to me. If you'd grown up eating what I had to eat, you'd be more thankful.'

'What did they make you eat?' Wilhelm asked. Benjamin leaned over to hear better, interested as always in where his friends had come from, even though, like most pupils, they didn't talk about it much.

'Nothing. We were fed through a tube that was inserted into our stomachs.'

'Sounds gross.'

Miranda shrugged. 'You got used to it. Once a day, at breakfast. On special occasions we were allowed to eat with our mouths. Birthdays, for example. They made a big cake and we all got a small piece.'

'We got porridge in the orphanage,' Wilhelm said. 'Pretty much every day. It never tasted quite the same but it always had the same thick consistency. One of the other kids found out why one day.'

'Why?'

'We were eating food donated by a local supermarket. Each evening a truck would pull up and unload a few crates of leftovers which would do us the following day. To save time cooking it, the whole lot was poured into a giant blender.'

'What did your friend do when he found out?' Benjamin asked.

Wilhelm grinned. 'He cut the blender's cord with a pair of scissors, then thieved some money out of one of the security guard's bags. He sneaked out and got fish n' chips. Brought a couple of bags back for the rest of us. Tasted like gold. Problem was, we were still kids, you know. Didn't think about the smell. The stiffs got us the next day.'

'The stiffs?'

'Yeah, you know, the management. We wouldn't own up to who did it, so they got out the cane.'

'The cane?'

Wilhelm held his hands out two feet apart. 'About so big. It was this thin piece of flexible bamboo that one of the stiffs bought on holiday somewhere posh and exotic. They'd crack you across the back of the legs.'

'Ouch.'

'Yeah. No one said anything, so we all got it. Tag-teamed it. Us verses the stiffs, that's how it all went down.'

'In an orphanage?' Benjamin frowned. 'Isn't that a bit barbaric?'

Wilhelm shrugged. 'It was more of a young offenders' home really.'

Miranda, who had sat quietly listening to the exchange, lifted an eyebrow. 'And what exactly was your offence?'

'Well, that's another story….'

Before Wilhelm could launch into a new dialogue, he was interrupted by garrulous laughter from the next table. Derek Bates pushed back his chair and grinned.

'You two gullible idiots. Do you believe everything that comes out of his mouth?'

'Can it, Derek.'

'Make me.'

Wilhelm pushed back his chair and stood up. He grabbed a half empty bowl left on the table nearby and sent it flying into Derek's face. The older boy coughed as the dregs of another boy's custard spattered into his eyes and hair.

'I'll do you for that—'

'Jacobs!'

Derek ducked low in his seat as Professor Eaves jumped to his feet. He glared across the room at Wilhelm, who still stood, arm held out in the follow-through of his throw.

'I think we need to have a talk about violent behaviour,' Professor Eaves said. 'You know bullying won't be tolerated.'

'I didn't start it!' Wilhelm protested. Benjamin and Miranda added their voices of agreement, but Professor Eaves waved their protests away.

'It doesn't matter who started it. It takes a stronger person to finish it. One thousand cleans.'

Wilhelm groaned. 'You've got to be joking.'

Professor Eaves narrowed his eyes. 'You can make a start straight after dinner.'

As Wilhelm turned back to his food, shoveling it into his mouth like an angry kid looking for a buried toy in a sandpit, Benjamin watched Derek and his friends. While his friends were sniggering, Derek was cleaning himself up, but the custard was removing itself from his face and clothes with far greater precision than any cloth could manage, peeling back and combining neatly into larger pieces which then dropped into his bowl.

Benjamin closed his eyes and felt for the heat of magic. It was there, but none of the boys seemed to be using it. He glanced at Professor Eaves. The old man was nodding slowly as he stared at Derek. At the other end of the table, none of the other teachers had noticed. They were deep in conversation with their new junior teaching assistants.

Wilhelm grumbled under his breath. Miranda, beside him, had finished her dinner and was watching him intently.

'Benjamin and I will help you, don't worry. We stick together, don't we?'

'It's that….'

'And don't worry about them.'

Wilhelm shrugged. 'I'm not. I was telling the truth. I think.'

'What do you mean, you think?'

Wilhelm puffed his cheeks and let out an exasperated sigh. 'I mean, it starts to get vague, doesn't it? Don't you think so, Benjamin?'

Benjamin turned. 'What does?'

'The old life.'

Benjamin frowned. He had been in Endinfinium for nearly a year by his best guess, and while he could still remember much of his life before, certain details had faded, never to return. His phone number. His address. The colour of his father's car. The names of his goldfish. His brother's favorite food. It was slipping away, piece by piece, as though the jigsaw puzzle of his past was slowly turning blank. He had overheard older kids talking about not remembering anything, being left with just a vague outline of what had come before, but none seemed concerned. More than anything, most kids who had arrived in Endinfinium had left behind a life they wanted to forget, even if they could no longer remember why.

'I still remember everything,' he said, looking from one to the other, defying them to challenge him. 'And I won't forget it. One day I'll find a way to go home.'

Miranda glared at Wilhelm. 'Look what you've done. You've started him off again.'

Benjamin shook his head. 'It's okay. Let's go and play checkers or something up in the dorms. I'll be fine.'

Miranda stared at him. 'I hope so,' she said. 'I'm worried about you.'

'I'm fine,' he repeated, feeling anything but.

After dinner, Benjamin made an excuse about getting some books from the library, then ran off to find Edgar Caspian, the formerly exiled science teacher who had become their close friend. Edgar had left the dining hall early and Benjamin found him in a little office adjacent to the science classrooms on the school's third floor.

'Benjamin!' Edgar said, giving his pointed beard a tug. 'How nice to see you. I imagine it was quite an emotional day. Your first triangulation. They get easier, trust me. Watching those kids sail off, though, that always hurts.'

'Do they really think they'll find a way home?'

Edgar shook his head. 'I think they're just hoping to find something,' he said. 'Answers of some kind.'

'Can I ask you a question?'

Edgar smiled. 'Sure.'

'I'm worried that I'm forgetting my past.'

Edgar nodded. 'That's what makes you different. Few of us had pasts worth remembering. Sometimes—like the three who left today—we cling on to an idea of home, but the details, for most of us, are easily let go.'

'Do you remember?'

'About before I came here?' Edgar smiled. 'Yes and no.'

'How do you mean?'

'If you really want to hold on to your past, write it down. By the time you reach your own triangulation, it's likely you'll remember you came from England, and that you had a family, but little else. And wait ten years after that, and you might have nothing left except a vague notion that you weren't indeed born here. Just be careful to keep a hold of the record.'

'What do you mean?'

Edgar smiled. 'Mine reanimated and flew away. I never recovered it.'

'And you lost all your memories again?'

'I wrote down what I remembered of that first journal, and I have kept that one. But another layer of detail was lost.'

'So you remember nothing of your true past?'

'I remember what I wrote down about it, and I trust myself that it is true.'

Benjamin sighed. 'And what you remember, was

it good?'

Edgar shook his head. 'Like many, my awakening in Endinfinium wasn't unwelcome. I rejected the place, but not the circumstances. I seek to understand this new world, but I don't seek to return to the old one. Not … as the boy I was.'

Edgar would offer no further explanation. Benjamin couldn't be sure the old magician even had the answers as he brushed off Benjamin's questions, but Benjamin headed back to the dorms feeling even more confused than before.

He had spent longer with Edgar than he realised. The corridors had darkened, the animated candles burning in their braziers flickering only with a dim glow. With the pupils returned to the dormitory and the teachers to their apartments, Benjamin heard only the occasional distant shuffling of a cleaner.

The school, a vast, sprawling castle part hewn from rock, part built from concrete, wood, and even plastic and glass, had whole floors hidden from view and great labyrinthine wings rarely used except by brave—or reckless—kids playing hide n' seek. Some stood silent and empty, others were filled with recovered goods that groaned and creaked with the slow onset of reanimation. While most pupils and teachers stuck to the often-traversed routes, Wilhelm had taken it upon himself to learn as many ways around the school as possible and taught Benjamin and Miranda about the best ones he found. One particular route was a shortcut back to the exit leading to the dormitory via a winding wood-walled corridor that snaked through an area of meeting and storage rooms, none of which were in current use.

Dark and gloomy, the constant creak of the wood as it gradually came to life spooked Benjamin worse than any graveyard could, but a quick, five-minute head-down rush saved twenty minutes of walking back to the school's main entrance and then up the stairs to the higher floors. Pausing at the entrance to the corridor, he made up his mind, hugged his arms around himself and went for it.

He was halfway along when he heard voices.

Stopping dead in his tracks, he started to turn back, sure it was ghosts or ghouls or something hideous he was yet to learn about, when he recognised one of the voices.

Professor Eaves.

'In here. They're waiting for you. Let me find the key a moment.'

And then the reply sent chills through his blood. 'Hurry up, won't you? Before someone sees me.'

Benjamin steeled himself and peered around the bend in the corridor, in time to see a heavy door closing.

He ran up to it and looked for a keyhole he could peer through, but whatever the key fitted into was well hidden. He closed his eyes a moment, feeling for magic, and from inside came a wave of cold so terrifying it made hairs stand up on his arms.

Losing his nerve, he hurried on, heading for the dorms, wondering what he could do, who he could tell.

And most of all, wondering why Professor Eaves had let Godfrey out of his cell.

4

THE FERRY MASTER

Standing with her hands planted so firmly on her hips that she could have been a mathematical instrument, the ferry master was a tall, muscular woman called Tania. So tall, in fact, that she looked rather ridiculous standing next to the unnaturally wide Captain Roche, like a pencil beside an eraser. To look at her, the captain had to fully swivel his oversized head upward, until his ear was buried in his neck.

'Welcome,' she said, clapping her hands together hard enough to break bones. 'The captain tells me you're taking a field trip over to the Haunted Forest.'

A few pupils nodded and muttered, 'Yes.' Tania smiled. Beside her, a tall dog, unlike anything Benjamin and his friends had ever seen before, sat back on feet that were completely hidden by thick blue-brown fur. Benjamin had seen show dogs in magazines from time to time that had a vague resemblance, but it looked literally made out of carpet, right down to the coloured beads it had for eyes that swiveled to watch them as it fidgeted from foot to foot.

'Tania has been minding the ferry here for more than twenty Endinfinium years,' Captain Roche said, again swiveling to look up at her as if still surprised by her height. 'As this is the first time for most of you to cross over into the Haunted Forest, I've asked her to give you a talk on health and safety.'

Tania nodded. 'First, a little history. The ferry here was established about a hundred years ago. By all accounts, there used to be a bridge, but no one is old enough to remember, and documentation has a habit of rewriting itself, as you might have noticed.' She gave a little laugh, but no one seemed to get the joke except Benjamin, who didn't find it particularly funny anyway.

'It's believed that the bridge, itself a product of some bizarre reanimation, was washed away during a junk storm. Don't know what one of those is? It's when a particularly heavy load of rubbish comes floating down the river. They say that Source Mountain turns into a kind of chocolate fondue of chaos.'

Again, a little laugh. Only Benjamin and Wilhelm of the assembled pupils had ever been to Source Mountain, so Tania received mostly looks of confusion. Benjamin gave her a smile he hoped was encouraging, but she had turned to stare back upriver.

'Most such deluges are merely legend. Perhaps the only one I've ever seen myself was when the twisted remains of a rollercoaster came floating past.' She grinned. 'That was quite something. It was like the skeleton of a futuristic dinosaur. No doubt it lies at the bottom of the ocean somewhere now, slowly reanimating into something incredible, like a serpent or giant snake.'

Most of the girls tittered with revulsion. Only Miranda didn't react. Beside Tania, Captain Roche raised one slug-like eyebrow and gave a slow nod, as if remembering something similar.

'In any case, the ferry is available for operation whenever someone wants to cross. Which, admittedly, is rare. There are ferry stations on either side of the river, and one can be signaled from the other using a set of mirrors.' She pointed behind her at a tall metal frame with something flat and square attached to the top that was angled upward, so all that could be seen was an underside of fittings and framework.

'Angle it so that the mirror on the riverbank opposite begins to flicker,' she said. 'When that happens, it causes a bell to ring in the ferry station below. Clever, isn't it?'

A couple of pupils mumbled agreement. Beside Tania, the dog gave a sudden musty bellow, causing a cloud of dust to plume around it.

'Now, now, Crokus,' Tania said. 'It's not dinnertime yet.'

'Its name's Crokus,' Wilhelm sniggered.

The dog gave another wheeze. The pupils at the front started to cough.

'You'll have to excuse my dog,' Tania said. 'He's been hungry for several days. He only eats what we find in the Haunted Forest, so until someone needs a ride over to the western bank he goes hungry. You might have noticed that he's not a regular dog.'

'I didn't think so,' muttered Snout, once a member of Godfrey's gang, and now president of the Traffic Cone Appreciation Society, a group that did exactly what it said on the tin—collected traffic cones washed up on the beaches, and … appreciated them. As none of Benjamin, Miranda or Wilhelm was prepared to even consider a guest visit, they had no idea what the club actually entailed.

'His parents were reanimated shag-pile rugs,' Tania said. 'Crokus was the oldest of a litter of five.'

'There are more of those things?' Miranda whispered.

'What does it eat?' Wilhelm called out.

Tania turned to him and grinned. One over-sized hand patted the dog on the head, causing another plume of dust to engulf her.

'A good question,' she said, giving Wilhelm a wink. 'He eats ghouls. He gobbles them up like boiled candy sweets if he's ever lucky enough to encounter one. Yummy, aren't they, Crokus?'

∾

The ferry had a little bio-fuel engine with a rusty year stamp of 2065 on the side, fifty years in the future from the year Benjamin had arrived in Endinfinium. From the way it creaked and groaned as it bobbled in the water, it had clearly been in service some years already, confirming what Benjamin suspected about time in Endinfinium. It worked differently to Earth. Miranda, for example, had woken up in Endinfinium three months before Benjamin, but had been born in the year 2875. Wilhelm, they both suspected, was from some time in both of their pasts, although Wilhelm claimed not to remember.

'Don't worry,' Tania was saying to Tommy Cale, Benjamin's timid classmate. 'Every time it gets a little rickety we let it reanimate for a while, fix itself up.'

Tommy Cale didn't look convinced as he peered over the side at the choppy water, his face as pale as a bleached rag.

Tania steered the ferry upriver into the current, making a gradual arc around to the far bank. Here the river was a clear two hundred metres across, a churning mass of grey filled with every kind of imaginable rubbish. From simple plastic bags and water-damaged pieces of newspaper to beds, fridges, even old cars, all sorts of junk bobbed past them. Twice Tania screamed for them to look over the side, once to see an articulated lorry slink past barely an arm's length away, and then again for the massive corrugated iron roof of a grain silo.

With the kids whooping and ahhing each time some monstrous piece of rubbish came within near-touching distance of the little ferry, spinning them in its slipstream, they chugged and spluttered across the river. Tania brought them expertly in to a stumpy pier on the far bank, identical to the pier on the school-side.

'Thanks for journeying with us today,' Tania said from a pontoon above the main deck. 'Unless we have any other customers—unlikely—we'll be waiting right here for your return journey.'

Captain Roche waved at the pier as Tania threw a rope around a mooring post. 'Right you lot, get moving,' he said. 'Anyone lagging behind might get mistake for a ghoul. I don't know about you, but that dog looks hungry.'

5
DECISIONS

'Take care, now,' Tania said from outside the little cottage that made up the ferry station. 'Make sure you haven't forgotten anything.'

Huffing and puffing, Captain Roche led the line of pupils up a path to the top of a hill. All around them, long grass swayed in the breeze. Just beyond the brow of the hill, however, the meadow abruptly ended at a wall of gnarly trees.

'That woman gave me the creeps,' Wilhelm said, walking between Miranda and Benjamin. 'And what about that crazy dog? Can you believe it eats ghouls?'

'I think that was just a story,' Benjamin said. 'I can't see that thing eating a bowl of milk, let alone a ghoul.'

'Appearances can be deceiving,' Wilhelm said. 'Right, how are we going to prank Captain Roche?'

Miranda turned on him. 'You aren't serious?'

'Why not?'

'Because of all the teachers, barring Ms. Ito, he's the one I'd least dare to prank.'

'He'll see the funny side.'

'No, he won't. He'll put his eye on you again.'

Wilhelm shrugged. 'So? I'll just put it in my sock drawer like last time. He didn't believe me, but what could he say? I told him it fell off.'

Benjamin grinned. 'And he gave you a thousand cleans to make up for it.'

Wilhelm's cheeks reddened. 'A technicality.'

Captain Roche stopped near the top of the hill. 'Okay, gather round,' he said, spreading his huge arms wide enough to make half of a circle on his own. 'Just a couple of pointers about your personal safety.'

The assembled pupils gathered into a rough circle. Benjamin, Miranda, and Wilhelm stood at the back. In front of them stood all the rest of the second and third years. At currently count there were fifteen second years and twelve third years. Locked up in his basement cell, Godfrey made unlucky number thirteen.

'We're here for two reasons,' Captain Roche said. 'Firstly, to pick up any stray cleaners. Secondly, to avoid ghouls.'

'That's not really two reasons,' Miranda whispered to Benjamin. 'A negative reason actually shouldn't count.'

'Be quiet at the back there, Miss Butterworth,' Captain Roche called. 'You can talk to Master Forrest about embroidery when we're back on the ferry.'

The rest of the pupils laughed, some turning to point and cast throwaway insults. Benjamin stared at the floor, his cheeks burning, despite not even being sure what embroidery was.

Captain Roche lifted a third fat finger. 'And there's a third reason. Did I mention that? A very special reason. Usually we wouldn't entrust such a thing to a bunch of irresponsible kids, but Professor Loane thought it would be a good idea. He figured it might mature you a little bit, even though I tried to talk him out of it.'

There were a couple of murmurs of excitement. Professor Loane was known as the most forgiving of the teachers, and therefore the most likely to let them do something dangerous. 'As you might have noticed,' Captain Roche continued, 'you recently graduated to a new year at our wonderful school. Wondering where the new first-years are? Well, one of them is supposed to be somewhere in this forest right at this moment. Grand Lord Bastien had a *dream*.'

Captain Roche's tone suggested his opinion of such a thing was preposterous, even if he had experienced it multiple times before. He turned and waved at the line of trees.

'Stay on the paths. I repeat: do not leave the cut paths. Do I need to say that again? And stay in pairs or threes. No splitting up. All sorts of horrible things live in this forest. It can be very dangerous. Stay to the higher ground to the north and west.'

As the pupils broke off into small groups, Benjamin turned to Miranda and Wilhelm. 'If it's so dangerous, why are they letting us go in there?'

Wilhelm grinned. 'It's not dangerous. He's just trying to scare you. He'll be keeping a ward of magic on all of us to make sure of where we are and that we're safe. Can't you feel it?'

Benjamin frowned. Wilhelm had always been more sensitive to the warmth of other magic users than he. It wasn't something you could feel on your skin, but rather in your heart. And as a result, it took a different kind of susceptibility to notice it. Miranda always said it was because Wilhelm's heart was a lump of black coal, so any heat was easily noticeable over the usual extreme cold.

'I can feel it,' Miranda said. 'It's slight, but it's there.'

'It's not actively being used,' Wilhelm said. 'He's just thrown it out there like a net. For a magic-denier like the captain, he's remarkably adept at using it.'

They took the nearest path into the forest. Almost immediately gnarly tree boughs closed in overhead. Up close, the trees no longer resembled regular trees. Infused with various levels of metal, glass, plastic, and other materials, some of them were barely trees at all, but the frames of lost machines overgrown with vegetation.

The path, at first wide, quickly faded into a barely discernible animal trail almost succumbing to the gallant undergrowth that looked a mixture of regular plants and some bizarre hybrids. Plastic straws with dandelion heads popped up in clumps beside the path, while regular vines wound their way up tree trunks angular with embedded steel frames. Further back among the trees, something bulbous and round that looked like an upturned ceiling light pulsed like a miniature volcano ready to erupt.

'So basically we wander around until we get bored, then go back?' Wilhelm said. 'Some field trip.'

Miranda grinned. 'Why don't we cheat a little? See if we can find something interesting?'

'How?'

She closed her eyes and stood stock still, her hands at her sides. Benjamin and Wilhelm exchanged a glance. 'What's she doing?' Wilhelm mouthed.

Miranda's eyes snapped open. One arm rose straight to point ahead. 'There,' she moaned in a hypnotic monotone.

Benjamin shrugged. Wilhelm turned to look where she was pointing, and at that exact moment Miranda screamed, 'Yaaah!' and jumped on Wilhelm's back. Wilhelm's yelp of terror was sharper than most bird calls.

'Pranked!' Miranda shouted.

'You're a sod.'

Benjamin, still tentatively feeling around him with his magic, turned as a pulse of heat came from behind.

Captain Roche marched through the trees, boughs and undergrowth parting around him as though he were an elephant in human form.

'Pack it in!' he snapped. 'Five hundred cleans each. You think this is a laughing matter? Keep to the paths and stay quiet unless you see something.'

As the captain stomped off, Wilhelm glared at Miranda. 'Nice one.'

'I didn't know he was right there.'

'Look, we'd better do something to make him go easy on us,' Benjamin said, feeling a conflict of guilt at his frustration with Miranda, despite enjoying the prank. 'Come on, follow me.'

'Where are you going?'

'South.'

'But Captain Roche said—'

'Five hundred cleans. Might as well round it up to a thousand.'

As he led them away from where Captain Roche had told them to stay, Benjamin wondered where the sudden act of rebellion had come from. Since trying to escape Endinfinium a few months ago, he had been on his best behaviour. Partly because he feared that Godfrey would reveal his secrets to all who would listen, and partly because he had drunk his fill of the unknown, come up choking, and decided enough was enough. Now, though, the unknown was calling him again like a child lost in the dark.

Help me, Benjamin.

A child that would forever be his little brother.

6

DISCOVERY

The ground sloped gradually downhill, until the yellow sun to the north was hidden behind the rise, leaving them surrounded by shadow. Miranda scowled at Benjamin between occasional protests, but Wilhelm seemed infused with the spirit of adventure and kept jogging on ahead.

'You're doing it again,' Miranda said, as they reached a fork in the path where Benjamin automatically took the way heading further downhill.

'Doing what?'

'Chasing danger.'

'What's that supposed to mean?'

'There's curious and then there's you, Benjamin Forrest. Why do you keep shaking your hand?'

Caught off guard, he said, 'I think I stung it on a nettle.'

'Really? Did you see what the nettle looked like?' Wilhelm asked. 'Just so we don't run into any others.'

'I didn't see it,' Benjamin said, squeezing ahead on the path so Miranda wouldn't see his face. She had noticed what he was trying to ignore, that a strange chill was coming from the back of his hand, making him clench and unclench his fingers. It wasn't wholly unpleasant, but it radiated out from the thin line of the old scar, from when the reanimated statue of a cat had scratched him nearly a year before, and as they walked deeper into the forest it became stronger and stronger.

'What was that?' Wilhelm said.

'Where?'

Benjamin stopped and looked back. Miranda and Wilhelm were pointing off through the trees.

'There it is again. Something pale. Benjamin, did you see it?'

Miranda's face lit up with excitement. 'It has to be a cleaner. Come on, let's follow it. If we bring one back, Captain Roche will have to let us off those cleans for sure.' She took one step into the trees, and then paused. 'But he said not to leave the path....'

Wilhelm moved in front of her. 'Look, it was only just over there. He's probably got a watch on us with his magic anyway. And Benjamin's a Summoner. We have nothing to be afraid of. He can just blast it.'

Benjamin looked back up the path, back the way they had come. He felt like he had crossed a line and there was no way back.

'Come on,' he said. 'Let's at least see what it is.'

With Benjamin in front, they headed off into the trees. Miranda walked a couple of paces to his left, with Wilhelm, who had picked up a fallen tree branch and held it like a club, just back to the right. The forest floor sloped gently away to the south. The pale thing had headed around the side of the hill.

'I think it's gone,' Wilhelm said. 'Maybe we should—'

A scream broke the stillness. As it died away, leaving Benjamin stunned and Miranda clutching her ears, her mouth hung open as though she had uttered it, the scampering of multiple pairs of feet came from just out of sight around the curve of the hillside.

'Not good,' Wilhelm said. 'Not good at all—'

A pale form appeared, ragged clothing hanging off a skeletal form which was moving unnaturally fast, zigzagging through the trees on bare feet.

Miranda said, 'That's Sara Liselle—'

The shape tripped and landed face down on the springy turf. A scratched and bruised back heaved with exertion through the remains of a shirt. Hair slick with sweat stuck against the girl's face as she looked up, wild eyes meeting theirs.

'Run!' she hissed. 'We found it. We found the lost city. The others … trapped.'

Benjamin jumped back as her face glowed orange. In an instant the colour was gone. He started to kneel down.

'Benjamin, look!'

Through the trees behind Sara came a host of ghouls, running hard on human legs, faces porcelain animal shapes with glowing orange eyes. Serrated teeth clacked where mouths shouldn't have been, and arms that were everything from steel poles to tree branches pushed through the undergrowth as they raced to catch the girl.

'Get behind me,' Miranda cried. 'Wilhelm, help!'

Miranda had stepped in front of them, her arms raised, a trickle of sweat running down her face and her eyes filled with tears. Benjamin felt the heat of her Channeller magic rising, but they both knew it wouldn't be enough to hold off so many. He stood up, but Miranda shook her head.

'You can't control it like I can. It's too dangerous.'

'We don't have much choice.'

'We do. Stay back.'

'Help me,' Sara whispered, reaching up to grip the front of Benjamin's shirt. 'I've been running for … days.'

Benjamin crouched down. 'What happened?'

'We found it … a week south. We thought … oh no, the others—'

'They're coming!'

Benjamin stood up. The nearest ghouls were closing. Miranda reached out for Wilhelm's hand. Benjamin felt an uncomfortable sense of jealousy as they stood together while he stood apart, but Wilhelm was a Weaver, incapable of using reanimation magic on his own. In contact with a Channeller, though, he had great strength.

'Push and pull,' Miranda muttered under her breath. With a howl, the nearest ghoul exploded into a puff of orange dust.

Despite Miranda's warning, Benjamin couldn't let

his friends fight alone. He gritted his teeth and felt for his own power.

Draw from the air, Grand Lord Bastien had always told him. *Draw from what is around you, but never draw too much.*

Trees, soil, air, the tiny creatures that lived in all of it … Benjamin felt overwhelmed by the sources he felt as he built up his strength. His scarred hand felt leaden at the end of his arm, a block of ice. His balance felt off, and the power like a weight about to slip out of his arms. Miranda turned to glare at him again, to warn him, off, but a thrown rock struck her shoulder, knocking her sideways.

She screamed, her hand slipping out of Wilhelm's. A tree exploded, showering them with woodchips. At their feet, Sara screamed at them to run, but the ghouls were too close, serrated porcelain teeth snapping, hands reaching to maim and tear—

'Back!' Benjamin screamed, lifting his arms.

Heat flooded through him and the air exploded with orange and green. A roar like falling water blocked out sound. He had a sense of Miranda screaming but couldn't see her as his body tumbled sideways. Something itchy like the fiberglass his father had used for loft insulation was all over his face, and as he screamed again, the whole world went black.

7

LIES

'Help me, Wilhelm. Oh Benjamin, what have you done?'

He opened his eyes. A bare patch of hillside sloped away. Dotted with tree stumps and seared grass, it was sprinkled with a fine orange dust. Clouds had appeared in an otherwise clear sky, and rain was falling around them, slowly washing the dust back into the earth.

'Help me get him up.'

Wilhelm had a cut down the side of his face. He wiped away blood with one hand as he pulled Benjamin into a sitting position.

'Your face? What happened?' His voice felt strangely distant, as though he were speaking underwater.

Wilhelm shook his head. 'It's nothing. I hit a tree. Not hard.'

Pieces of twig filled Miranda's hair, but she looked otherwise unharmed. 'You destroyed them,' she said.

The Lost City of the Ghouls

'You destroyed them all.' She clicked her fingers. 'Just like that.'

'And half of the Haunted Forest with it,' Wilhelm said, a curl of his lips suggesting an attempt at humour.

It was an exaggeration, but the seared patch was still the size of a decent swimming pool. A couple of strange birds alighted on the jagged remains of tree stumps and pecked tentatively at the exposed innards of the trees.

Benjamin tried to sit up. His body tingled with pins and needles, as though he had lain inert for several days. Only his scarred hand felt different, but the unnatural coldness was slowly fading.

'Where's Sara?'

Miranda looked around her, as though the girl had vanished too. Benjamin felt an incredible sinking feeling, then Wilhelm shouted, 'She's over there.'

Sara was sitting up against a tree by the line of the undisturbed forest. Her eyes were open but glazed over as she stared straight ahead. Benjamin climbed to his feet, leaning on Wilhelm's shoulder for support. Even before he reached Sara's side, he knew something was terribly wrong.

The skin on Sara's face had partially melted away. Knobs of bone poked through, while beneath the rags she wore, parts of her body were the same: skeletal, half decayed.

'She's a cleaner,' Miranda whispered.

'No.' Benjamin shook his head. 'There must be a mistake. She was alive. She was talking to us.'

Wilhelm opened his mouth to speak, but only a stutter came out. 'Be—be—before….'

Benjamin scowled. 'You don't need to say it. I will. Before I used my magic.'

'It was an accident,' Miranda said. 'You were protecting us.'

'I killed someone.'

Wilhelm shook his head. 'No, no. She's not quite dead, is she? Just … mostly.'

Sara's mouth opened and she let out a low moan. She looked up, and her lips parted over the skeletal remnants of teeth to form a Jack o' Lantern smile.

'Sara, can you hear us?'

The thing that had been Sara Liselle turned to stare across the clearing. For the briefest of moments she gave a slight frown, as though remembering some past life, then she looked up again and repeated the same ghastly smile as before.

'Forrest! Butterworth! Jacobs!'

Captain Roche's voice cut through the stillness. All three jumped up, looking around them for the approach of the captain.

Miranda's eyes flared. 'Quick, what do we say?'

Benjamin sighed. 'We tell him the truth.'

Wilhelm shook his head. 'No chance. You'll be cast out at worst, or at best you'll be down in the cells with Godfrey, or cleaning to all eternity.'

'You can't lie for me.'

Wilhelm gulped. 'We were all here. We're in this together.'

Benjamin wanted to refuse, but the sincerity in Wilhelm's eyes swayed him. Guilt chewed at him like a great black bear, but he still didn't understand for sure what had happened, and he needed time to figure it out.

'If there's a fallout, I'm taking it. It's all on me, you got that?'

Miranda shook her head. 'Look at her. Look at Sara. If you didn't know that was her, would you have any clue?'

'We can't—'

'There you are, you abominable fools. Where on Endinfinium have you been?'

Captain Roche pushed through the undergrowth like a buffalo. Behind him came some of the other pupils, among them a small boy with wild hair whom Benjamin had never seen before, who stared at everything as though he had just woken up in a strange, dreamlike world.

Tania, the ferry master, stepped out from behind Captain Roche. She raised an eyebrow, then smiled. 'What's this then? Looks like a doggie feast.'

Crokus, squatted at her feet, gave a squeal of delight then bounded past all of them, up to the nearest scattering of orange dust. With a great carpet roll of a tongue, he began lapping at the ground.

Benjamin forced a smile as he pointed at Sara. 'We found one,' he muttered, his throat dry, the withering gaze of the captain like a hot laser boring into his skull, cutting out the answers one by one. 'We found a … cleaner.'

Captain Roche nodded. 'Huh. And so you did.' He looked up. 'And what exactly happened here?'

'I—'

'We saw some ghouls,' Miranda blurted, pushing in front of Benjamin. 'They looked hungry so I blasted them.'

Some of the other kids were muttering about sorcery. The school kept reanimation magic quiet as best it could, Benjamin remembered, so many of them had only a basic understanding of how it could be used. What skills the pupils had were carefully controlled too, partly by lack of education, and partly by careful wards the teachers placed around them.

Captain Roche turned on Miranda, and in his dinner-platter-sized face Benjamin saw the forming of a desperate, elongated lie.

'Don't run your mouth to me, Butterworth. You won't be gaining any cred points with your friends and you certainly won't be getting me on side. I know exactly what you did. You and your foolish friends started a fire. You did, didn't you? You just didn't realise that these trees burn a little differently to the types you might remember.'

There were ahs of understanding from the assembled pupils. Captain Roche's face screamed a million cleans if Miranda dared defy him.

'Yes….' Miranda sighed and lowered her head. 'We just tried to cook some mushrooms we found….'

'You picked wild mushrooms?' It was difficult to tell if Captain Roche's incredulous expression was genuine or if he had picked up on Miranda's attempt to expand the lie. 'How many times have you been told to never, ever, *ever* eat anything you find out in the wild?'

'More than once,' Miranda said.

'Multiple times,' added Benjamin.

'Between ten and fifteen times,' Wilhelm said. 'Possibly as many as twenty.'

Captain Roche let out a sigh long enough to empty most lungs. 'You fools just never learn, do you? While foolishly picking something that could have done far worse than just poison you, you could have damaged this cleaner, and it's a miracle you didn't burn down half the forest.' He shook his head, and then a corner of his mouth turned up in a smile that only the three of them could see. 'Five thousand cleans each.'

Laughter came from the pupils assembled behind them. Benjamin, Miranda, and Wilhelm said nothing. When the captain turned away to give instructions to the other pupils, Benjamin risked a glance at Wilhelm. His friend gave him a look containing both puzzlement and pity.

Benjamin swallowed. No words were necessary. As he watched Tania and Captain Roche help Sara to her feet, a single thought ran back and forth in his mind, like a hamster stuck in a jar.

Less than ten minutes ago, Sara Liselle had been a battered and exhausted but coherent person. Now she was a mindless monster in a state of permanent decomposition, capable of little more than washing dishes and carrying reanimating objects down to the locker rooms.

As a human being she was, to all intents and purposes, dead.

And Benjamin had killed her.

8
CONSULTATION

'I'M WORRIED BENJAMIN'S GOING TO TRY TO LEAVE again,' Wilhelm said to the gnarly tree stump that rose above his head, and rivaled Captain Roche for girth. He gave the floor another swish with the broom. 'He's in a perpetual funk. It doesn't help that the cleaner that used to be Sara was assigned to lunch duty. He has to see her every day, and that reminds him of what happened.' He sighed. 'She usually does the broccoli counter. It's the most popular, since it actually tastes like real broccoli.'

The air filled with the sound of fluttering leaves as a gust of wind got up. When it was strong enough to whistle through the holes and cavities in the stump, it came together to form words.

'Young Master Forrest bears too much weight upon his shoulders,' said the stump, whose name was Fallenwood, a name shared by all the reanimated leaves, twigs and discarded animal food within this part of the forest south of Endinfinium High. 'He suffers from a feeling of being out of place, even here.'

Wilhelm brushed a patch of decomposed humus into a corner, exposing paving slabs beneath emblazoned with faded tree designs.

'He thinks he shouldn't be here. That he's a mistake.' Wilhelm shrugged. 'I get it, but what's he supposed to do?'

As he worked to slowly clear the floor of the old botanical society building's main atrium, Fallenwood slowly shifted after him, moving on the severed stumps of ancient roots that shuffled him along the floor. High above, the yellow sun shone down through a glass ceiling partly destroyed and partly coated with moss, mould, and a blanket of fallen leaves, painting everything with a rainbow of different greens.

'To understand him, it helps to look inward,' Fallenwood said. 'Your own arrival, for example.'

Wilhelm shrugged. 'I never knew my parents. For as long as I can remember, I was in a home with thirty or so other kids, kept under lock and key. I was a prisoner before I even knew what being a prisoner meant.'

'Then you woke up here?'

'I woke up half buried in the earth at the foot of a tree in the Haunted Forest,' Wilhelm said. 'A group of people stood around me, all eyes agape and hands up like this, in this kind of poster surprise. And there in the middle is this strange man who's almost as wide as he is tall. I screamed and tried to run, but they tackled me.' Wilhelm laughed. 'Captain Roche never has forgiven me for calling him a monster.'

Fallenwood shifted from side to side in a gesture Wilhelm had come to know as a shrug. 'It's understandable. But here in Endinfinium, are you happier than you were before?'

Wilhelm grinned. 'Define happiness.'

Fallenwood's voice became a long, reedy whistle, an indication of a sigh. 'Don't be difficult.'

'I'm not. But happy? I don't know. I'm not upset to be here. It was a bit of a challenge at first, being expected to go to a bunch of stupid lessons. I mean, much of a muchness, isn't it? But I wouldn't go back, if that's what you're asking.'

'Explain to me why not.'

Wilhelm rolled his eyes. 'Is this really necessary?'

'Do your best.'

'I didn't have any control over anything. I was told where to go, what to do, what to say. Here, I'm in a school. As long as I show up to classes, I can pretty much do what I want. Sure, it's all a bit weird, and I'd like to know what's going on as much as Benjamin would, but you get used to it.'

'And what else?'

'What?'

'Your explanation is too short for a being as old as I. Continue.'

'What is this, therapy?'

'Humour me.'

'You're a tree stump that talks. It's not difficult.'

Fallenwood shifted from side to side again. Wilhelm took a deep breath.

'Okay. Yeah, don't make me blush, and don't tell

anyone, but I feel like I have friends here. You know, actual people who like me, rather than just feed off me or hide behind me. Stupid, isn't it?'

'Not at all. But do you see why Benjamin might be struggling?'

Wilhelm nodded. 'Among everyone I've spoken to, he is the only one who truly misses home. He had nice parents, his own bedroom, a brother he liked, friends, all of it. And then he wakes up here, and finds out some guy no one's ever seen is trying to kill him.'

'You can understand his feelings, can't you?'

'Yeah, of course. And now this with that girl. He blames himself, says he killed her. You know he can't have, can he?'

'It is not for me to know. My only advice is to be careful. Stay close to him. Be a friend. Listen.'

Wilhelm nodded. 'I'll do my best.'

'And have you found any more members for the botanical society yet?'

Wilhelm laughed. 'No. I'm working on it. I'll make a pitch to the new first-years at their official welcome ceremony in a few weeks.'

Fallenwood rocked quickly from side to side in a gesture of happiness. 'You are a wonderful curator. An old stump like me and his minions couldn't have asked for more.'

The reanimated stump fell silent for a while. Wilhelm continued his clean-up work, gradually clearing the decomposing material away from the floor in the main atrium and the adjacent growing rooms. Since the Fallenwoodsmen were the reanimated dead parts of trees, dampness, rain, and bugs were their main enemies. The ancient botanical garden society building, in the years since it had been abandoned, had provided the shelter for the community to thrive. However, as the windows cracked, the walls crumbled, and the forest began to reclaim the manmade structure, the civilization Fallenwood had created was forced back into the corners.

'Have you acquired funding in order to fix the roof?' Fallenwood said.

Wilhelm shook his head. 'I can't ask the teachers. These woods are out of bounds as it is. Miranda thinks she can do it with her magic, but she's tried practicing and she hasn't got it yet.'

'We are approaching rainy season.'

Wilhelm nodded. He was yet to see any kind of rainy season in the year he had been in Endinfinium, but Fallenwood always warned of its coming as though it were the botanical equivalent of the Four Horsemen of the Apocalypse.

'I'll do what I can,' Wilhelm said. 'Look, I'd better get back before I'm missed.'

'Would you like transportation?'

Wilhelm hesitated at the offer, but shook his head. 'I'll walk back along the cliffs,' he said. 'I need to think about some stuff.'

'As you wish.'

Wilhelm propped the broom in a corner by the old doors, and headed back to the school, following a forest path that led out to the cliffs. From all around came the creak and groan of the fallen brush beneath the trees, a sign that Fallenwood was watching him, keeping him safe. When he emerged from the forest onto the clifftop, he felt an uncanny sense of loneliness.

Where would he find Benjamin today? His friend was becoming harder and harder to locate during downtime outside classes. During class, he cut a distant figure at a desk, staring off into space, going through the motions, but as soon as the bell rang he was gone, disappearing into the corridors of the school, easily foiling Wilhelm's attempts to follow as though he could turn into a puff of smoke at will.

From the clifftop, the edge of the world was a meandering line between three and ten miles out to sea as a crow flew, a jagged jawline of rock slowly building itself. A bank of cloud swirled and toiled there, hiding whatever—if anything—might be beyond. Wilhelm paused, watching it a while, wondering why so many pupils chose to take a risk and sail for it. An end generally meant an end in his view; there was no reason for it to also be a new beginning. If they wanted adventure, they should have headed south, or inland, toward the High Mountains and the Dark Man in his castle.

South beyond the gaping mouth of the Great Junk River, the land was mostly uncharted. The sea stretched as far as the eye could see, and the land was thickly forested. Endinfinium's width was relatively well explored, but its length, less so. Now, however, as he gazed south, something caught his eye.

A great cloudbank had rolled in off the edge of the world and obscured the sea, but unlike regular fog, which was common during warm evenings, lightning flickered within it, as though a microcosm storm was bouncing on the surface of the sea.

He wiped clammy hands on his trousers. There was something sinister about the ball of cloud that it took him a moment to place.

When he did, he turned and began jogging for the school, wishing he had taken up Fallenwood's offer of transportation after all.

The lightning flickering in the cloud's midst shone a deep, threatening orange.

9

SOCIETY

'Where have you been these last three days? You know I was literally waiting for the next teacher to show up before I exposed you. Time's ticking, Forrest. Don't leave me waiting again. My generosity has limits.'

Benjamin suppressed a sigh and pushed the bag of books through the hole at the bottom of the door.

'Did you get me anything good?'

'Robert Heinlein omnibus.'

'Huh.'

'*Animals of Farthing Wood* complete series.'

'What do you think I am, five?'

'*Atlas Shrugged*. Complete and unabridged.'

'Honestly, Forrest, if you're playing games with me….'

'And seven books in a series called *Harry Potter*. You won't have heard of it yet.'

'What?'

'About a boy wizard.'

'An autobiography?'

Benjamin could sense Godfrey's cruel smile. 'No.'

'Shame. What else?'

'That's it. I found some other stuff, but there were too many water-damaged pages.'

'You're useless.'

Benjamin nodded but didn't answer. He sat down with his back against the door and waited for Godfrey's mouth to take on a life of its own. Starved for conversation and company, it never took long.

'He was going to kill you. Turn you into one of his hideous minions.'

'He said that?'

'Probably.'

Benjamin sighed. Godfrey's truths came layered in blankets of lies and deceit.

'You know they'll come for you. I don't know why, but he wants you more than anything. He commands thousands of ghouls at a time. He clicks his fingers and they just appear out of the ground. I'm amazed you can close your eyes at night.'

Benjamin had already closed his eyes. Recently he found sleep easy, as though his body had given up on staying awake. He fell asleep at dinner, in class, and he struggled to get up each morning. Wilhelm had to drag him out of bed, only for Benjamin to climb back under the blankets as soon as his friend had gone to the bathroom.

'That castle of his, it's an incredible place. The reanimation runs riot. You never see the same room twice. It's a nightmare to get around, but he seems to have no trouble. It's as though he flows through it, like it's part of him. Do you get what I mean? Runt, are you still awake?'

'Sounds fantastic,' Benjamin said, trying not to let his voice slur, to give away how tired he felt.

'There were no cleaners, just weird little creatures that acted like servants. No people either. And you know what? You could see the school from the high towers. Do you know how far it is to the mountains from here? It must be hundreds of miles. How was he distorting distance like that? That kind of power, it's unbelievable. He could wipe us off the face of Endinfinium.'

'Why doesn't he then?' Benjamin muttered.

'How am I supposed to know? He's stuck in there for some reason, but if he knows why, he wasn't telling. Why would he tell me? He thought I was just some kid, and he used me for a tool so he wouldn't have to do his own dirty work. Still, at least he was straight up about things, unlike the teachers here. It's all lies, Forrest. All lies.'

Benjamin nodded as Godfrey prattled on, the boy's words a mixture of half-truths, distorted memories, and speculation, but he would need to sort through everything in his own time to try to get a picture of what was real.

If only he could remember everything.

~

The braziers had gone out, and the corridor was in complete darkness. Benjamin jerked awake at the sound of approaching footsteps. From behind the locked door came the sound of Godfrey's snoring, a low gravelly rumble that echoed down the corridor.

A circle of candlelight appeared at the corridor's far end. Benjamin scrambled across the cold stone and slipped behind the open door of an unused cell opposite. He crouched, shaking sleep out of his eyes.

The newcomer reached the door. An old body leaned over the lock and twisted a thick key. With a squeal like nails on a blackboard, the door swung open.

'Are you awake?'

Benjamin froze. The voice belonged to Professor Eaves.

'I was sleeping. Can't you knock next time?'

'Come on. The society is waiting.'

Godfrey groaned. 'Could we not do this at a better time?'

'No. If we're found out, we'll all be expelled. Myself included.'

'They can't force us out. We're too powerful. If they try, we'll throw them over the edge of the world.'

Professor Eaves shook his head. 'Not yet we won't. We don't have enough strength. You know that.'

'Give it time. The city is coming. He can't come here himself, so he's sent it instead.'

Benjamin frowned. *What city?*

Professor Eaves helped Godfrey up and together they headed back up the corridor. Benjamin followed at a distance, staying back in the shadows but keeping the circle of candlelight in sight. They talked quietly as they walked, their heads close together. Benjamin could only pick up a few words, but none gave him confidence that their liaison was anything other than a threat to the safety of the school and everyone in it.

'… the Dark Man is waiting….'

'… ghouls in their hundreds….'

'… a trap … the net is closing….'

'… soon, Professor. Soon….'

They headed up through the dark, silent corridors to the same room Benjamin had seen them enter before. This time, a tall, cloaked figure was waiting for them, holding the door until they went inside, then following them in. The door closed, a lock turned. The sound of voices already muffled became impossible to overhear.

As he had before, Benjamin closed his eyes and concentrated, feeling for the use of magic. From the room emanated an unnatural coldness. To get a stronger sensation he moved a few steps nearer, only for his hand to begin to ache, the old scar throbbing with a chill that made him shiver.

Only dark reanimation magic could make him feel this way. What were they doing inside?

From his knowledge of the school's layout, he knew these rooms bordered an outer, windowless wall. There was no way to approach from the other side. Above was a toilet block where the creak and groan of reanimating pipes would make it impossible to overhear what was being said.

Which left underneath.

This section of the school was supposedly built on a slope of rock, so as you descended to the main entrance each corridor was itself the ground floor of its part of the slope, unless—

He hurried back the way he had come, heading for the dining hall. The classrooms were silent now, the pupils long gone back to the dorms, and the cleaners, having finished their duties, returned to the locker room to help sort through the junk waiting for deanimation.

Sneaking inside the dining hall, Benjamin located the table where he had first found his way into the mysterious realm known as Underfloor. While there were entrances all across the school, most of them were difficult to locate, and if he wasted magic searching for them, someone might find out.

With the pupils gone, a tiny pull on his magic revealed the lines in the floor indicating the secret trapdoor. Benjamin pressed on the wood and the door popped up. He swung his legs around and climbed down into the tight space, then pulled the trapdoor closed over his head.

Beneath the dining hall's floor, he crawled through the tight, dusty space until he reached a staircase heading down where he could stand up straight again. Not long after, rooms began to open out to either side, secret places, an entire labyrinth that existed behind the walls of the regular school.

From ahead came the sounds of music and laughter. Benjamin turned a corner and found himself on a balcony looking down on an old ballroom.

Reanimated objects twisted and turned in bizarre expressions of dance, while on a stage several others were playing a variety of instruments, both conventional and bizarre. A reanimated kitchen cabinet was banging cupboard doors twisted into arms against an upturned metal drum, while the tangle of metal poles and blue plastic cord of a reanimated clothesline was playing a conventional piano, the use of more than two dozen fingers creating a sonic soundscape that no human could ever hope to match.

'I'm looking for Moto,' Benjamin said to a reanimated table that was leaning over the balcony and tapping two wooden stumps together in time with the rhythm. 'Have you seen him?'

The voice that answered came from the sliding together of hundreds of tiny pieces of wood. It had taken Benjamin many tries to understand the voices of some of the reanimates, but over time it had gotten easier.

'Casino,' the table said.

Benjamin hurried along the balcony then back into the corridor, past rooms where groups of twisted furniture items watched old movies on reanimated TVs, played board games, even cooked food none of them ever needed to eat.

At the end of a long corridor, Benjamin found a room full of old slot machines. A casino table stood in the middle, with a reanimated casino sign acting as the card shark for the group of reanimates sitting or standing nearby.

Moto, a reanimated Honda road bike, turned away from the table as Benjamin entered, standing up on his rear wheel, a human-like face moulded out of tyre rubber revolving as his front wheel spun in greeting.

'Benjamin! What a nice surprise. Don't worry, you're clear. Gubbledon's gone back to the dorms.'

At discovering the only reanimate who would punish him for appearing in Underfloor had left, Benjamin let out a sigh of relief. 'Sorry to show up at this late time.'

Moto's face-wheel spun in a gesture of amusement. 'You know we care nothing for time. You're welcome whenever you like. Any time you need a little respite from all their rules upstairs, you can visit. Would you like some cake?'

Benjamin smiled. 'Maybe later. I had a favour to ask. I need to get to a section of school on one of the upper floors. I need to spy on some people.'

Moto's wheel spun with more amusement. 'Spy? Like in a book?'

'I think they're up to no good. I want to know what's going on.'

'Tell me where, and I'll find out if Underfloor extends that way.'

Benjamin explained as best he could the location of the corridor, and Moto nodded. 'I know it. There are rooms up there, but they're unused. Let's go.'

Benjamin followed the reanimated motorbike as Moto rolled through the corridors, bumping up and down steps, taking his time so Benjamin could keep up. Finally they reached a ladder rising up through a thin shaft.

'A bit difficult for me to get up there,' Moto said. 'We're in a ventilation shaft, but if you turn left at the top, you'll find a crawl space that goes under the rooms you want. Be careful—it's tight. We used to use it for storage, but one day the floor reanimated and all our stuff was crushed. Now it's unused.'

Benjamin nodded. 'Thanks.'

'Good luck. I hope it all goes well.'

Moto waited until Benjamin had begun to climb, then headed off, no doubt keen to continue his poker game. The loneliness that had enveloped Benjamin in the days since the incident with Sara Liselle returned, but he understood Moto's feelings. The reanimates of Underfloor wanted nothing to do with the meddling of the humans who lived beyond their walls unless their own existence was threatened. While Moto would advise him if asked, the reanimated motorbike was far happier embarking on a life of leisure that few previously inanimate objects ever got to experience.

Moto's instructions were right. From the top of the ladder, the ceiling of the tunnel quickly closed down. Soon Benjamin was shuffling on his back, kicking with his legs to push himself forward into an increasing cloud of dust. Guessing his location by his knowledge of the layout of the school, he was sure the ceiling and floor of the tunnel would converge long before he reached the classroom he wanted.

He was just considering risking a slight use of his magic when he heard voices from above. The space was so tight that when footsteps passed over where he lay, the wooden floorboards flexed enough to press against his forehead.

'We will try again,' came Godfrey's voice, moving across the room. Benjamin knew the boy was pacing back and forth. 'We need to be ready when the city reaches us. You saw what happened last time. We cannot risk another failure.'

'But what you suggest is impossible.'

Benjamin frowned. A girl's voice. He tried to place where he had heard it before, but failed.

'I have stood in the presence of the Dark Man.' Godfrey's voice again. 'I have consulted with him on the best course of action, and his conclusion is final. The school must be destroyed. It is all that stands between Endinfinium and its destiny.'

'What can we do?' said a voice Benjamin didn't recognise. He held his breath, straining to hear more clearly.

'We must continue practicing our skills in secret, under the tutelage of the professor. And when the time comes, we must strike from within. The Dark Man has promised me that everyone who aids him will be rewarded with a share of this world's destiny.'

A cackle of laughter. Someone else said, 'Remind me again what's on offer, Godfrey. Just so I can dream well tonight.'

Godfrey uttered a long, sinister laugh. 'Ultimate power, eternal life.' A cheer rose from the group. 'The ability to restore life to those who have none … and to take it from those who resist us.'

10

INVESTIGATION

'Show me. Where?'

Wilhelm pointed. 'There. You see it?'

Miranda nodded. 'Looks like fog.'

'But we both know it isn't. So what do we do about it?'

Miranda shrugged. 'I don't know. Tell the teachers?'

Wilhelm scoffed. 'Are you crazy? When has telling the teachers ever done anyone any good in the history of mankind?'

Miranda pouted. 'Well, I wouldn't know. I didn't have the luxury of going to school like you did.'

'I didn't go to school. I went to prison.' Wilhelm shrugged. 'Kind of.'

'So what do you suggest?'

'Whatever we do, we mustn't tell Benjamin.'

'Why forever not?'

'You know why.'

Miranda sighed. 'Because he'll run off looking for a way home.'

Wilhelm took his hand off Miranda's shoulder and felt a little jolt as the connection between them was broken. In front of them, the telescope they had reanimated to better see the cloudbank accumulating out on the sea far to the south shuddered as Miranda released her grip. As always, Wilhelm felt a strange jostling loneliness when their union was broken. He would never admit it to her face, but being a Weaver had proven more enjoyable than he might have expected.

Together they headed down from the roof of the lighthouse. Two headlands away to the north, the first lights of the school were coming on as evening approached. They needed to hurry to get back before dinner, but Wilhelm had been desperate to tell someone about what he had seen. As he followed Miranda back to the pair of battery-assisted bicycles they had sneaked out of the school's transportation store, he wondered what Benjamin would say if he found out what they were keeping from him.

'I still think we should tell the teachers,' Miranda said, climbing on her bike and pushing it to get the automatic motor to start. 'We're just risking something bad happening if we say nothing. How about we compromise and just tell Edgar?'

'He's still a teacher.'

'Yeah, but he's not only a teacher,' Miranda said. 'He quit the teaching staff, remember? Over the denial of reanimation magic? What do you say to that?'

'Noble,' Wilhelm said, 'but ultimately it makes no difference. He'll shop us out if it comes to it. And then, just like usual, we'll be sent off to the locker room.' He held up his hands. 'Honestly, I must have cleaned every piece of junk in that school five times over.'

Miranda glared at him. 'Well, I think you're being ridiculous. Edgar's always helped us.'

'Only because it's suited his purpose. Look, I'm not denying he's a good guy, only that I think we need to proceed with caution. If you're interested, I've got a better idea.'

'What?'

Wilhelm grinned. 'You got time for a little excursion? You don't really like the food they serve, do you?'

'It's healthy and nutritious and safe.' Miranda grinned. 'But equally it's devoid of all taste. What did you have in mind?'

'A quick reconnaissance mission. Come on, let's go.'

∽

They found Lawrence, Edgar's faithful snake-train, curled around a rock on the foreshore of the beach just below the school's headland. A locomotive followed by five carriages of discarded Italian express, he was more of a lizard these days than a snake, with wheels partially turned into feet that could propel him over almost any terrain at speeds nothing else in Endinfinium could. As Wilhelm and Miranda approached, Lawrence lifted his massive locomotive head and gave a deep whine that sounded uncannily like the purring of a giant metal cat.

'Long time, no see,' boomed a foghorn-like voice.

'Have you been swimming recently, Lawrence?' Wilhelm asked. 'We were wondering if you could do us a favour.'

'What do you need?'

'Just a lift somewhere. It's not far.'

The great head nodded. 'Climb in,' Lawrence said.

With Miranda and Wilhelm strapped into the two seats closest to the wide screens at the front that also acted as Lawrence's eyes, the snake-train crawled down the beach and slid into the water. Headlights switched on, illuminating a mixture of regular ocean filled with regular fish, as well as all manner of unusual swimming and growing objects that were descendants of reanimated trash. Most items were tiny, like pulsing plastic bags with their handles outstretched like the tentacles of jellyfish, or flapping books that moved through the water like underwater butterflies. From time to time however, something huge would rush past that left them both gasping with terror and clutching the seat armrests. Lawrence, for his part, acted like one of the greater predators, darting at anything that came too close until it turned and fled. On the only occasion where they came across something bigger—a monstrous rotating object like a great grey dome—Lawrence switched off his headlights, then in the resulting darkness, turned and raced away.

They had been travelling for about an hour when Lawrence turned upward and headed for the surface.

Miranda had been complaining about getting in trouble for missing dinner, with Wilhelm reassuring her that they could cover their backs by going straight to the locker room, when they broke the water's surface to find the massive cloudbank right in front of them, looming up grey and dark in the evening's gloom.

'Wow, it's thick,' Wilhelm said. 'You know how you usually see fog as this big white cloud, but when you get to it, you can't really see the edges? Well, it's not like that, is it? It's solid.'

'We should go back,' Miranda whispered. 'We're a long way from the school, and that thing scares me. I'm cold, Wilhelm, and it's coming from in there.'

'Don't you want to take a look inside? Lawrence, can you go a little closer?'

The snake-train shook from side to side. 'Master Wilhelm's request is unsupported,' he said. 'Lawrence would prefer to return to the school.'

'But if we go back now, we've got nothing to tell anyone. It's only a big cloud. Can't you go underneath and have a look?'

Miranda glared at Wilhelm, but Lawrence reluctantly pulled back into the water and switched on his headlights again. He spiraled downward, then turned south, moving beneath the fog's boundary on the surface above.

'There's something up ahead,' Wilhelm said. 'Just a little closer, Lawrence. Then we can turn back.'

Miranda punched his arm. 'Wilhelm, no! I don't like it! It's not safe!'

Lawrence raised the beam of his headlights. In the

shaky underwater glow, the angles and curves of something metallic appeared, like the underside of a partially crushed ship, only much, much bigger than anything they had ever seen before.

'There! Did you see that?'

'What?'

'That orange spark.'

'Where?'

'Over there!'

Lawrence inched closer. The metallic underside of whatever was above them was encrusted with sea-life: coral, weed, fat, pulsing anemones, while what at first looked like fish darted among them. As they got closer, they saw they weren't fish at all, but tiny reanimates, living off the reef that had grown up on the outside of the giant, rusting metal thing.

'Another one! Wilhelm, we have to go back!'

Something moved in front of Lawrence's eyes. Three or four metres long, it was deep red and moved awkwardly, as though swimming were a reluctant pastime.

'A reanimated sofa,' Wilhelm said. 'Where's it going?'

A flash of light burst out of the metal surface, striking the sofa midway. It wriggled and shook, rolling over in the water, then went still.

'It shot it!' Miranda gasped.

Lawrence had already begun to withdraw, but in his headlights the sofa-fish's colour switched to a dark orange. It pulsed once more, then drifted closer to the metal thing and pressed against the surface, sticking tight.

'Go, Lawrence!' Miranda screamed, loud enough to shock both Wilhelm and the snake-train. 'Go, now!'

Lawrence began to turn, but a burst of light flashed out from the surface of the metal thing and struck the snake-train somewhere along the side. Lawrence whimpered, and his internal lights flickered and then went dark, leaving only the headlights illuminating the side of the great metal thing as it slowly came closer.

'Swim! Come on, Lawrence, swim!'

'Sleepy….'

'No!'

Wilhelm stared out of the windows as Lawrence drifted closer, passing all manner of strange creatures that had stuck to the sides of the metal thing. All around them, Lawrence's metal walls and ceiling had taken on an eerie orange glow. Wilhelm shouted at him, but Lawrence would no longer answer. Beside him, Miranda was wild, screaming and hitting the armrests as though they were the root cause of all the evil in the world.

'You did this, you stupid idiot. I told you we should have stayed away. Now look what's happened!'

Lawrence came to rest against the side of the giant metal thing with a loud metallic clang. Lights came on again, but this time they glowed only orange. Wilhelm looked at Miranda, whose anger had dissipated into a look of terror.

'It's caught us,' she whispered. 'What do you suggest we do now?'

11

MISSING

'I can't help you unless I know what you're looking for,' said Cleat, the ancient librarian who more closely resembled a zombie than most of the cleaners. 'If you can perhaps provide me with a few keywords....'

'City,' Benjamin said. 'Ancient city.'

'History section,' Cleat said. 'There are all manner of dirty, half-destroyed books on the likes of Atlantis, Byzantium, Babylon, Damascus, and Troy, enough reading to fill any heart with the dusty warmth of ancient history.'

Benjamin shook his head. 'I'm not sure that's quite it. It's got something to do with Endinfinium. A city that's here.'

'There ain't no cities here. If there were, don't you think someone might of seen one? It's just the school, and a few quiet towns where most of what they do is just grow chamomile that gets ground up for spray.'

'But could there have been an old one that somehow got lost?'

'How do you suppose to lose an entire city?'

'Well, Atlantis got lost.'

Cleat grinned, his weathered face crinkling up like an old rag. 'That's assuming it was ever there in the first place.'

'There's loads of books on it,' Benjamin said. 'Of course it existed.'

'I can see why you keep getting into trouble,' Cleat said. 'I mean, you've got some imagination even for a kid shown up in a place that could of been built for it. Sometimes you just have to accept what you're told.'

'Like you did?'

Cleat grinned. 'I ain't never accepted nothing these people keep telling me. I just got old, is all. Not that easy to run off on crazy escapades when you can barely walk up a flight of stairs now, is it?'

'Well, is there anything you've discovered over the years that could help me?'

Cleat shrugged. 'Might of,' he said. 'Ain't got the greatest of memories, but I'll have a root around.'

'For what?'

'For me notes.'

'Notes?'

'I always kept me a kind of diary. Wrote down everything I came across that had some meat to it. Anything that might help me get out of this forsaken rubbish bin of a country.'

Benjamin lifted an eyebrow. 'Where is it?'

Cleat shrugged. 'Who knows? Left it behind in one of the stacks. Couldn't find it. Probably buried now.'

'I'll help you look for it.'

Cleat grinned. 'I appreciate your keenness, lad, but it ain't something that happened recent. More like forty years back, as the mossy wheel rolls.'

Benjamin sighed. 'How old *are* you?'

Cleat grinned again. 'Old,' he said.

'Well, if you find it, I'd appreciate any help. I'm looking for information on a lost city somewhere in Endinfinium. I heard of someone who claims to have found it.'

Cleat shrugged one shoulder. 'And what do you hope to find there?'

'I think a couple of people might be trapped.'

'Oh?'

Benjamin nodded, unsure what else to say.

'Well, I'll keep my eyes open.'

'I appreciate it.'

Benjamin headed up from the library to the dining hall. He was already late, and when he reached the back of the queue of fifth-years taking their turn, he received a stern glare from Ms. Ito, standing on dinner monitor duty with her leg cast sticking out in front of her like a trap for late pupils.

Inside the dining hall, most of the second-years had already finished and gone back to the dormitory. Only Godfrey's sometime-cohort Snout still sat alone, the notoriously boring boy staring intently into his dish as he chewed slowly on carrots, broccoli, and lumps of soggy potato like a cow standing at a feedbox.

Benjamin wanted to sit alone and contemplate both his own misery and what he might be able to do about it, but he was caught by that awkward sense of either sitting with the weird kid or making an obvious show of dislike. In the end, his compassion won out, so he pulled up a stool opposite Snout and sat down.

'The red sun never sets,' Snout muttered by way of greeting. 'Why do you think that might be?'

'Hey, Snout,' Benjamin said. 'Food good today?'

Snout—so called because of his slightly upturned nose, a nickname that while inherently unkind he didn't seem to mind—gave a wide grin. 'It's great,' he said. 'Just gets better every day.'

The food, a mixture of conventional vegetables and some odd-tasting new ones, all covered in a custardy sauce, was almost exactly the same every day. Once in a while something new would appear on the plate, but the general wisdom was that only tried and tested foods were used. From time to time seeds or cuttings washed down the Great Junk River which could be grown and cultivated in the fields around the school, but anything that might have descended from some reanimated product was off the menu for fear of what consuming it might do.

'That's nice.'

'I was thinking that like Earth's moon, it might be affecting the tides,' Snout continued, returning to his previous topic. 'They're a lot shorter here, aren't they? I mean, the foreshore is rarely revealed on any of the beaches south or north of the school.'

'That's pretty much what I was thinking,' Benjamin

said, throwing a longing glance at the tables of fifth- and sixth-years, where they were engaging in seemingly interesting conversation.

'I've been thinking about this a lot,' Snout said.

'I don't doubt.'

'In fact, I'm not convinced it's a sun at all.'

'No?'

'No.'

Snout seemed done with the subject. He went back to his chewing, staring into space uncomfortably close to the side of Benjamin's face.

'Have you seen Miranda and Wilhelm?' Benjamin asked after a long pause.

Snout nodded. 'I saw them in maths class earlier. You know, I was a little lost on simultaneous equations this morning, but I asked Mistress Xemian after class and she set me straight.'

'Fantastic.'

Snout nodded. He glanced at Benjamin as though just remembering he were there, then ran one hand over the tabletop. 'Is this mahogany or teak? I'm unfamiliar with hardwoods.'

Benjamin smiled. 'I think it's oak.'

'You're sure?'

'Wilhelm told me. You know he runs the botany society now.'

'Ah, yes. I was thinking of joining.'

Benjamin suppressed a laugh. Unable to resist the opportunity to partake in a little mischief, he leaned close to Snout, and said, 'You know, I'm sure he'd love a few new members. He was just telling me the other day how he thought you'd be a perfect—'

The words cut off in Benjamin's throat as the cleaner who had once been Sara Liselle ambled through the tables in a beeline for theirs. He gulped as her eyes met his, then when he feared her tongueless, gap-toothed mouth might recover the ability to speak, she veered away, turning to collect empty plates that had been left on the adjacent table.

'Um, I was saying, if you just tell me the start time and what room they usually meet in, I'll be sure to attend.'

'What?'

'I would have asked Wilhelm himself, but he didn't show up for dinner.'

Benjamin dragged his focus away from Sara, who was heading back to the kitchens, her partially decomposed arms laden with used plates and bowls.

'What do you mean?'

'Perhaps he took dinner in the locker room with Miranda.'

'Miranda? She didn't show up for dinner either?'

'No. There was some talk, but as you were late, and the three of you were in such trouble after last week's excursion, the general consensus was that you had already gone to the locker room.'

Benjamin started to shake his head, then paused. 'Yes, that's exactly it. I finished early and was allowed back up, but they stayed down there.'

'You clean quickly.'

'Yes, I … yes, Snout. Anyway, I have some homework to finish.'

'Me too.'

Benjamin stood up. 'Great. Anyway, nice talking to you.'

'Sure. I'll see you back at the dorms?'

'Can't wait.'

Before Snout could respond, Benjamin hurried for the kitchens, carrying his plates over to the depository where all pupils were supposed to put them but few ever did. Behind the shelves, he saw Sara wandering through the kitchen units, carrying a pot of custard. Her eyes stared straight ahead. He put down his plates and ran before she had a chance to turn toward him.

He dreamed about her at night. Sometimes he only saw the cleaner she had become; other times it was the frightened girl he had destroyed. Worse was when he saw both, chasing him through a forest, one screaming, 'Help me!' and the other, 'Look what you've done!'

Only he, Wilhelm, and Miranda knew what had really happened. Benjamin trusted his friends, but knowing they were protecting him made his heart ache. He couldn't let them shoulder his failings forever; he had to find out how to fix what he had done.

And now they were missing. Captain Roche had kindly divided their latest punishment into blocks of one hundred cleans to be carried out after dinner each evening, but Miranda loved dinner, and while Wilhelm always grumbled about it, he never missed it either. Perhaps Snout was right: his friends had taken their dinner down to the locker room with them—something many pupils did. After all, he had spent the hours after classes were done for the day in his own funk, avoiding everyone except Cleat in the dusty confines of the library.

Something was wrong; he could feel it. As he headed reluctantly for a planned meeting with Grand Lord Bastien, he wished they would just appear from somewhere, give a big smile, and put his mind at ease.

12

RECOGNITION

GRAND LORD BASTIEN WAS STANDING BY THE ONLY window of his tower room when Benjamin entered. As always, the school's headmaster was heavily clothed in a long flowing robe with a hood that covered his face. Hands clasped behind his back were similarly hidden by rolls of sleeve, and no feet were visible beneath folds of cloth that bunched on the floor around him.

The window faced inland. A fog had come in over the afternoon, strangling the view, leaving only the nearest rolling hills visible. On a clear day, the Grand Lord's window had a view over the Great Junk River a few miles west as far as the Haunted Forest beyond, but today that view was severed by an impenetrable wall of white.

'Benjamin,' the Grand Lord said, his voice framed by a peculiar hiss that always reminded Benjamin of a radio station slightly off-tuning. 'In the week since we last met, have you thought much on what was said?'

'I have.'

'And?'

'I have decided that while I will never consider Endinfinium my true home as others have, I will do my best to be a productive member of the school.'

The Grand Lord turned. As always, Benjamin had to suppress a flinch at the first view of the ghostly, translucent face beneath the hood. Even after multiple meetings, it got no easier to speak directly to the Grand Lord without displaying some degree of discomfort. He had seen all manner of nightmarish creatures during his time in Endinfinium, but they were all somehow less terrifying than what was essentially a ghost.

'Your knowledge continues to grow. It is good.'

'Thanks to your teaching.'

'You humour me. But like most people, I enjoy being humoured. How has your memory been? Do you still think often of your family?'

As always, the Grand Lord wasted no time. Benjamin sensed the headmaster was attempting to toughen him to life in Endinfinium, but talk of his family only reminded him of what he had lost.

'I can no longer remember the colour of my father's car,' Benjamin said. 'It's been two weeks since I could remember the name of our street.'

'And you wrote down what you could?'

'Yes.'

'That is good. But my advice to you is not to dwell on them. Do not read them over and over. You will forget; it is inevitable. Most do. If you try to hold on, it will only bring you more pain.'

'I don't want to let go.'

The Grand Lord's gaze fell to the floor. 'Believe me, when you become old, you will. I stand across two worlds, Benjamin. I remember strange details of my old life. I no longer recall the town in which I lived, yet I remember with absolute clarity the crack in the pavement in front of my old antiques shop, and the way the rain would run from the gutter into the drain during a storm.'

Benjamin felt a growing sense of frustration. 'You could leave, you know.'

The Grand Lord shook his head. 'I have been here for decades. I fear what my body has become in the world I once knew.'

It was the first time the Grand Lord had given Benjamin a time. While he had mentioned his life as an antiques dealer before awakening in Endinfinium as a ghostly memory of his former self, he had never mentioned how long in Endinfinium years he had been here. Benjamin knew that time didn't work here as it did everywhere else, but if the passage of time was equal, what remained of the Grand Lord's body, perhaps comatose as his brother David had once been, would be surely ancient.

'And your skills with reanimation magic, what of those?'

Benjamin felt his cheeks redden. 'I … haven't practiced with it since the … um, incident.'

Grand Lord Bastien nodded. 'Captain Roche gave me his report.'

'Oh.'

'I am aware that you were protecting your friends. However, your control is still erratic. And *erratic* is a word that often morphs into *dangerous*.'

Benjamin thought of Sara Liselle's dead eyes. 'I know. I panicked. When I saw those ghouls coming at us, and one of them hit Miranda … I panicked.'

'And your hand?'

'It ached.'

'Now?'

'Less so. The longer I ignore the magic, the less it hurts.'

The Grand Lord nodded. 'I have thought long and hard on this,' he said. 'I fear you have some kind of taint. The teachers, as always, wish to keep to the Oath, at least on the surface. Beneath it, they are concerned. They fear he is watching you too closely.'

'The Dark Man?'

'Yes. They fear another attack on the school, and….' The Grand Lord trailed off. His eyes darted back and forth from the door to the window, as though afraid someone might be eavesdropping.

'What is it, sir?'

'I hesitate to tell you what concerns me,' the Grand Lord said. 'I am but an old man despite how I appear. I have the same distrust of my own feelings as everyone. Hmm. We will talk again soon.'

Grand Lord Bastien turned back to the window. He glided over to the ledge and stood peering out at a light rain that had begun to fall.

'Thank you for coming today,' he said. 'I will see you again one week from now.'

Benjamin left feeling more frustrated than when he arrived. He headed back to the pupils' dormitory building out on the clifftop, avoiding the kids sitting in groups in the common room, and straight up to the small bedroom with a sea view which he shared with Wilhelm.

Unmade as it had been when they left for classes this morning, Wilhelm's bed gave no indication that he had ever returned. His shoes were missing too, and in the drawer left half open, Benjamin spotted his casual evening uniform.

On the floor below, at the other end of the corridor, Miranda's room was also empty. Benjamin went back downstairs, but neither was in the common room. Gubbledon Longface, the reanimated racehorse who acted as the pupils' housemaster, was leading a reluctant group in a game of monopoly. Another group was playing cards, while several kids were lounging on beanbags and sofas, reading books or comics. Snout was sitting alone at a table, doing his science homework.

Benjamin went back out, slipping quietly across the narrow path along the cliff face that led back to the school. After the yellow sun had set, the school building was mostly dark, with only a few reanimated candles at rare intervals along the corridors. The non-teaching staff all went back to their rooms in the teachers' tower at seven p.m., leaving just the odd teacher on night duty. With some clubs operating after school, plus an allowance to visit the locker room to carry out one's punishment, it wasn't unusual to find people wandering around, but in a school so vast that even after nearly a year there were whole floors and wings Benjamin had never even visited, as soon as Endinfinium's excuse for night had fallen—a perpetual twilight orchestrated by the dim red sun, which never rose far above the horizon, but did a complete circuit of the known world during a full twenty-five-hour period—the only way to describe any journey through the school was as foreboding.

From the side entrance leading to the dormitory, the long concourse to the main entrance was as reminiscent of Benjamin's old school in England as Endinfinium High could be: concrete walls with wooden doors leading to quiet classrooms. The main entrance itself, however, with its high atrium and glass front that faced the sea, could have come from a modern office building. Behind it, though, things changed. Stone and wood-paneled corridors led off in haphazard directions, while below the level of the main entrance the corridors and classrooms were cut from solid rock.

Endinfinium High perched on the edge of the cliff like a giant boil. At its rear rose dozens of towers—most of which were off-limits to the pupils, deemed unsafe due to uncontrolled reanimation. On a clear day, from the fields behind the school you could see some of the towers shaking back and forth like rockets preparing to blast off.

Benjamin headed straight for the stairs leading to the basement levels. The locker room was on the fourth level down, one level below the library and a series of musty archive rooms, two above the incinerators.

The sin keeper, a reanimated suit of Samurai armour, stood guard outside the locker room door.

Benjamin, who still had eight hundred cleans hanging over his head but had a free pass to complete them by the end of the semester, claimed a smaller punishment of fifteen in order to get inside.

'I yawned in Professor Loane's history class,' he muttered to the sin keeper's empty helmet while a polished crossbow pointed at his chest. 'I mean, I didn't care about the Boer War when I lived in England, so why should I care now?'

The sin keeper, as impassive as ever, waved him through the door.

The line of cubicles, each with their own door, faced the endlessly revolving conveyor loaded with objects from around the school which had begun to reanimate. Cleaners, moving with careful deliberation, collected buckets of deanimated objects from outside the cubicle doors, checked them, and then replaced the buckets. Three cubicles were currently occupied. Closest to the conveyor entrance, where you could take your pick of all the easy-to-clean items like rulers, cups, and pencils, the two closed doors suggested pupils who knew the system. The other, five spaces along, where you were left with the awkward stuff the closer pupils left, obviously belonged to someone who had never been down here before.

Benjamin, his hopes rising that he would find Miranda and Wilhelm working in tandem, went up to the first door and quietly opened it to peer inside.

Derek Bates sat inside, his head lowered, hands frantically polishing at something Benjamin couldn't see.

Suppressing a sigh, he closed it again without the

The Lost City of the Ghouls

boy knowing he was there. He had a feeling Wilhelm and Miranda had gone somewhere together, but he checked the other cubicle anyway, finding Cherise, a third-year, and one of Miranda's haters. The ticker on the wall read 347. Benjamin wondered what she had done, but it could have been anything. With so many items constantly requiring deanimation, and with nowhere near enough cleaners to do it, many teachers would invent elaborate punishments just to help meet the quota. Particularly in what Endinfinium called a summer, everyday items reanimated at frightening rates, and Wilhelm still told the story of the evening he had come down to carry out a punishment and found Captain Roche—the teacher who had set it—crammed into one of the cubicles, frantically scrubbing away.

Just in case, Benjamin checked the third occupied cubicle, but a fourth-year he didn't know sat inside. His ticker read 36, perhaps a punishment for forgetting his notebook.

Once inside the locker room, unless allocated a punishment broken into installments, there was no way back past the sin keeper until you were finished. With a sigh, Benjamin went into the third cubicle from the conveyor entrance and pulled the door shut behind him. The ticker on the wall automatically flicked to 15.

Benjamin remembered the very first time he had come to the locker room. A novice, he had picked up a small cat statue only for it to scratch the back of his hand. Now, nearly a year later, the scar was all but invisible, but often, when near to ghouls or dark reanimation magic, the scar would throb and his hand would go cold. None of the teachers knew why, and even Grand Lord Bastien was unable to fix it. Benjamin, for his part, had begun to treat it as an early warning system for when danger was near, but as a precaution against it happening again, any cat statues he saw sliding past he left for someone else.

Neither Cherise nor Derek was working particularly fast. A handful of pencils slid past so Benjamin grabbed them all at once. One quick squirt of the deanimation spray and a hard rub with the cloth and the tiny shuddering things went still. Satisfied he was already half there, Benjamin dropped the newly inanimate objects into the basket at his feet.

With the practiced skill of someone who had been punished many, many times, within a couple of minutes fifteen items sat in his basket. He was done, barring the checking of a cleaner. He carried the basket to the cubicle door and set it down, waiting for a cleaner to appear.

By some system that he could only imagine, they seemed to know when a basket was ready for collection. A door opened at the end of the line of cubicles and a cleaner stumped out, hair falling over their face, the movements slow and careful. Benjamin had long ago lost his fear of them, but looking into the mindless faces never got easier. As the cleaner reached him and squatted down for the basket, he braced himself for the inevitable smile.

The cleaner's hands closed over the handles of the basket. As he or she went to lift the basket back up, the cleaner looked up into Benjamin's face.

He shivered. It was her.

Sara.

Cleaners were the mindless shells of the reanimated dead. Capable of a few simple tasks which could be taught, they had no emotion or initiative.

Sara cocked her head. Dead eyes looked into Benjamin's own. Then, what remained of her cheeks rose, giving her a slight squint.

Then she was gone, turning back to the door, the basket held in front of her. Benjamin, his heart thundering, stared at the door as it closed behind her, and was still staring at it when his ticker flicked over to zero and a ping sounded, meaning he was free to leave.

As he headed out of the locker room and back up to the dorms, he played her expression over and over in his mind.

She had recognised him.

13
LOST BOOKS

'Don't you ever sleep?' Cleat said, stomping out from behind the cluttered library desk as Benjamin came through the door.

'I'm a lazy boy,' Benjamin said with a grin. 'I get a lot of extra homework because I'm always sleeping in class.'

'I find that difficult to believe,' Cleat said. 'That Jacobs boy you hang around with, I could see it, but not you.'

'Why not?'

'You're a … what's the word you kids use? A swot.'

Benjamin scowled. 'Thanks. I think.'

Cleat shrugged, as though it had not been intended as a joke. 'What can I help you with today, Master Forrest?'

Benjamin took a deep breath and smiled. 'Chemistry.'

'Huh?'

'I want to look at the section of chemistry textbooks. Specifically, future ones.'

'Why?'

Benjamin felt a certain level of kinship with old Cleat. The old librarian had no love for the authoritarian figures in the school, and outside Wilhelm and Miranda, knew as much about Benjamin as anyone.

'I figured it out.'

'What out?'

'Reanimation. They refuse to acknowledge it as magic, right? The teachers all call it a science we haven't yet discovered. Well, at some point back in England someone must have figured it out and written it down.'

'So? Don't mean it's here.'

'And at some point the so-called science must have become banal and ordinary, perhaps taught in schools the same as other sciences.'

'Hear that clicking sound? That's me old brain running to keep up.'

'So what I need are chemistry textbooks from as far ahead as you have them here. And there, I think, I'll find out what's going on.'

'Well, let's go take a look,' Cleat said, shuffling around in a circle. Benjamin trailed the old man as he headed deep into the rows of shelves.

'It's around here somewhere,' Cleat said, his neck creaking as he craned his head into every alcove they passed. 'I know I put those here somewhere. Was it next to physics? Or was it earth science?'

The tall shelves became taller, denser, and more closely packed. Cleat lit a frighteningly dangerous candle off another in a light fitting on the wall, then leaned into stacked shelves so overloaded they looked set to fall at any moment. Benjamin hung back behind the ancient librarian, wondering if the crackle and fizz of Cleat's creaking bones would alert someone of authority to their plight.

'Here,' Cleat said, squeezing into an aisle full of dusty books that overhung their shelves like an undercut cliff. 'Chemistry.'

Benjamin put a hand on the nearest books to make space to squeeze in behind Cleat, but jerked his hand away, ringing his fingers.

'Wow! They're freezing. Don't they reanimate?'

Cleat shrugged. 'Oh, they did. You can see how they tried to get out, the pesky little mites. They must of got tired. Let's have a look now, shall we?'

He squatted down and began pulling ancient, weather-beaten books off the shelf, opening their first pages to look for dates. Whenever he found one, he called it out loud: '1926 … 2003 … 1975 … 1981 … wow, 1889—I bet that's full of useful information.'

'Aren't there any newer ones? It was 2015 when I came here, so specifically I'm looking for books written in the fifty years or so after that.'

Cleat shrugged. 'You know time don't work here like it does there, don't you? Something from 1850 might show up brand new next week, while something from 2100 might have been sitting on these shelves for donkey's years.'

'Exactly. But why aren't they? I know Miranda is from eight hundred years ahead of me, and I've found these weirdly written novels from close to then, but where are the textbooks?'

Cleat pointed at an empty section. 'Could of been here.' He squeezed a little further along and ran a finger over the empty section of shelf. 'Not even dusty. Must of gone to archives. One of the cleaners must of done it.'

'The cleaners?'

'Yeah. They're not all that bright but from time to time they show evidence that there's a spark in there. Books might of been too old, falling to bits—who knows? They only go two places from here. Down to the lockers, or to the archives. From the lockers they come back. From the archives … they don't.'

Benjamin shook his head. 'What if the book I'm looking for has gone to the archives?'

Cleat shrugged. 'Read another book.'

'But I need something specific.'

Cleat managed to find room in the tight space to turn around. 'Look. Lots of books here. Hundreds get washed up on the beaches every day. There are drying rooms you've probably never seen. That's where most of the cleaners are at any given time. Unfortunately, we can't keep everything. In with the new, out with the old.'

'But doesn't anybody check? There could be important information in some of the books you send to the archives.'

Cleat grinned. 'Ah, there could. But do you think anyone really wants to know? And most of them lot upstairs, they spend all their time spraying stuff to keep it quiet. Not enough time for reading. And even if they did … most of them, you know.'

'What?'

'You'll understand one day. Most of them up there, they've got to or a point in their life where they've given up. Resigned themselves to die here, as most do. How do you think they'd feel if they found out there was a way back? A door, say, that was a one-way ticket home, and that door could lead to any point in history. You might have the nerve to step through that door, Master Forrest, because you're still young. You ain't built your life yet. But once you have, would you dare?'

'So you think that somewhere in these books there's an answer to this place?'

Cleat grinned again. 'Of course there is.'

'So how do I find the archives?'

Cleat's grin vanished. 'Well, it's not that hard to find them, but … well, they're a bit of a mess. The books, they go down a chute. And the door, well, I'm not sure anyone's ever opened it. Nothing is expected to come back out, and it's all kept there for possible incineration if we have a cold spell.'

'Can you at least show me the door?'

Cleat looked increasingly uncomfortable. 'Sure. I can, but I really wouldn't advise….'

'I really need those chemistry books.'

Cleat gave a reluctant nod. 'Well, you insisted. But you might want to wear a crash helmet.'

'Um, why?'

'Well, by all accounts, the archives are in a bit of disarray. The, um, books got a little angry with each other.'

14

THE ARCHIVES

Cleat leaned over the map, gnarled old hands pointing. At first, all Benjamin could see was a dirty square with a few lines drawn across it.

'Here's where the chute comes out, right in this corner.' He turned and gestured over his shoulder at the top of a metal pipe sticking out of the floor. Padlocked wooden doors covered the opening, behind them a space just large enough for a human to squeeze through.

'All the newly archived books will be in this corner, underneath the chute's opening. There'll be a decent pile, so just don't let go of the rope and you'll land nice and soft. Find the books you want, put them in your bag, and give the rope a tug. I'll pull you back up.'

'What happens if the rope breaks? How do I get out then?'

Cleat shook his head. 'Don't worry, it won't break. I have a couple of little tricks to stop that happening, if you know what I mean.' He tapped the side of his head, and Benjamin felt a sudden heart-warmth. Cleat, it appeared, was a Channeller like Miranda.

'What happens if I can't find them?'

'You will, trust me. But if they've moved at all, the books you're after will have gone right, over here. Moved to the battlelines. I suggest that if you need to run over here, you do it very quickly indeed.'

'The, um, battlelines?'

Cleat nodded. 'There's no easy way to tell you this. The archives have been involved in a civil war for as long as anyone can remember. Fiction versus non-fiction, by all accounts. Getting books out of there just to incinerate is a humungous challenge, so some long-ago group of teachers did the only easy thing—they sealed the doors and washed their hands of it all.'

'They just left the books alone?'

'Left them to fight it out for all eternity. They're books; they don't die and they don't feel pain. I've never been in there myself, but at night, when all's quiet, you can open up these little doors and hear them down there, fighting away.'

'Sounds intense.'

'It is. Which is why it's very important that you don't let go of the rope. Are you really sure you want to do this? It's a bit much for a bit of homework, don't you think?'

Benjamin gulped. He held Cleat's gaze a moment. 'I think we both know this isn't just for homework. It's a bit of an, um, self-study project.'

Cleat gave a knowing sideways nod. 'Then I imagine you want to get it finished as soon as possible. Let's go.'

The old librarian was shaking his head as he led Benjamin to the chute entrance. He unlocked the doors and left Benjamin standing for a few minutes while he went to fetch a rope. Benjamin leaned close to the opening, listening for sounds from below, but heard only the gentle whistling of the wind.

'Right, this should do it,' Cleat said, returning with a coil of thick rope. He tied one end into a loop which he wrapped around Benjamin's arms, before tying the other end around a pillar. 'Brace your feet on the sides and abseil down. I imagine Captain Roche has put you through your paces.'

Miranda had always loved Captain Roche's climbing classes on the steep cliffs around the school, but Benjamin was now glad he had paid attention. As he climbed into the chute, he found the wooden sides had good purchase, making it easy to gently lower himself down.

'How far is it?' he asked, when his whole body was inside. He felt like he was looking at Cleat from a submarine's periscope.

'Far enough,' Cleat said. 'Good luck, Master Forrest.'

Within a few steps, the light from the chute entrance above was too dim to make any difference. Benjamin found himself in a tight hardwood shaft smelling of ink and sea water. He had expected the drop to be sheer, but he found that instead it curved and twisted like a water slide, perhaps making a path around other rooms on lower levels in the school. At one point he found himself crawling through a bed of fluttering pieces of paper ripped out of books on the way down, before the chute abruptly steepened.

The last section was a vertical drop. By now Benjamin was unsure how far he had travelled, but he was beginning to worry that Cleat's rope would run out when he saw light below his feet.

The chute exited in the corner of what felt like a vast room, even though only a small area around the exit was illuminated, lit up by creaking spotlights high up on the walls that revolved slowly in their fittings as though trying to break free. The rest of the room was in shadow, but Benjamin got the impression that he was in a massive, subterranean sports stadium. Hewn out of stone, tall bleachers rose around him, their stepped rows of seats piled high with heaps of shredded paper, among which lay the remnants of countless books.

The chute entrance was ten feet off the ground. Benjamin braced himself, pulling on the rope until it was taut, then lowered himself, landing on a heap of books that completely covered the floor. He untied the rope, leaving it dangling from the chute, and looked around him, taking stock of his surroundings.

He had never been inside either a recycling centre or a paper mill, but he guessed this could be a representation of both. Around him were mounds of pulped and shredded books several times his own height, great paper barricades that looked to have been cut and sculpted into shape. Other smaller mounds lay scattered all around, ant hills made out of crushed novels, school textbooks, dictionaries, picture books, religious texts, and even some old newspapers. In pieces, their words scattered, they were all as worthless as each other, a memory of knowledge now lost. Benjamin picked up a picture of a spaceship lying at his feet, but two paragraphs in it died with the line, '… and at the start of a war that had already lasted forever….'

Near the bottom of the chute, some piles of books were in far better condition than the shredded majority. He crawled over to these recently archived items and began picking through them, the flickering overhead lights illuminating the titles of novels Benjamin had never heard of and likely never would again: *The Gathering, Wicked Shores, The Tube Riders: Underground, Silent Storm, Airbrushing, A Man's Folly, Dust and Trees, A Little Book of Victory* … the list went on. Benjamin gave them only a cursory glance before tossing them aside, looking for the old chemistry books that must have fallen somewhere among them.

He was beginning to despair when he noticed a rough trail heading to his right, a parting of paper and bits of book as though a box had been dragged through them. His eyes followed the line to the edge of the light, where a lumpy thing appeared to be moving.

It looked like a snowball made from tightly packed books.

Benjamin began clambering through the piles of book pieces in pursuit of the slowly rolling ball. Paper shifted around his feet, at times taking his footing out from under him, at others allowing him purchase on hard, stone floor.

He had closed to within a couple feet, when the ball

shifted to its left, giving Benjamin a clear view of a book embedded in its top.

Dark Reanimate: Is this the End? (20th Anniversary Edition)

While the title was an obvious oxymoron, it looked substantial enough to begin providing answers. Benjamin stretched for it. His fingers closed over its top edge and jerked it free.

The paper ball gave a fluttery squeak and broke apart, spewing the remains of other textbooks around his feet. Benjamin, his hands shaking with eagerness, opened the front cover and stared at the title page:

Dark Reanimate: Is this the End?

(20th Anniversary Edition)
with a new foreword by the author

Dr. Benjamin Forrest, Ph.D

AMMFA Publishing Ltd
LONDON
2045 (First edition)

His hands trembled. His cheeks flushed, and his heart pounded so hard he felt blood pumping in his ears.

And then he felt a sudden shifting beneath him, like the suck of a spring tide.

He nearly dropped the book as a siren sounded, a bizarre sound formed from the rustling of thousands of sheets of paper. Lights came on, illuminating the whole enormous arena, a space piled from end to end with mountains of shredded paper that were now shifting, forming into distinct shapes, ones with arms and legs and heads, feathers and wings, wheels and catapults and great crushing hammers.

Something struck Benjamin from behind, knocking him over. He looked up from a mattress of shredded paper to see paper creatures rushing at each other, slamming like giant sumo wrestlers and breaking apart, only to reform in different shapes and throw themselves back into the fight. The room filled with the roar of battle as volleys of books flew through the air, and huge, paper war machines rumbled to the attack.

Benjamin stared, unable to believe what he was seeing. It was impossible to identify who was fighting whom, but across the arena faces formed from thousands of books stuck together howled with pure hatred.

Even up on the bleachers, smaller paper creatures were slamming and crashing against each other, ripping each other apart, launching volleys of book missiles into their opponents' midst. As one enormous creature crashed down not far from Benjamin, spraying him with shredded paper, some of it hard and sharp like the chopped covers of hardbacks, he realised there was nowhere to run except back to the chute.

It was only thirty paces, but with paper creatures rushing into the fray all around him and volleys of books fluttering past his face, it felt like a mile. With the textbook tucked under his arm, he staggered through the paper apocalypse, ducking and dodging to avoid being hit in the crossfire.

The rope still hung from the chute, but when he was almost within reach, it began to shake.

'No!' he screamed. He battered at the obstacles in front of him with his free hand, kicking piles of paper aside, but by the time he reached the chute, the rope lay in a coiled pile at his feet.

Benjamin gasped. He looked up, and his heart sank. The entrance to the chute was right above his head, but, out of arm's reach, it might as well have been a million miles away.

15
ESCAPE ATTEMPT

Cleat had tied the rope to a pillar. There was no way it could have come free unless someone had untied it. Now, though, it lay uselessly at Benjamin's feet, his escape route gone.

He turned. Two massive paper creatures slammed against each other in the middle of the arena, ripping and tearing limbs off each other like savage shredding machines. All around, smaller creatures crashed together in a battle with no obvious sides, no clear winners or losers.

Something hard struck his shoulder, making him stagger. Too shocked even to cry out, he rubbed the sore place while a flapping hardback fantasy book with a fierce dragon on its cover shook and shuddered at his feet.

'I could die in here,' he muttered. Sara Liselle's decomposing face appeared in his mind, and he wondered if a death in Endinfinium might actually be worse than a death back home.

The battle between the two paper factions took up most of the arena's main floor. Up on the bleachers, rows of smaller creatures flung projectiles at each other. Volleys of flapping paperbacks led the way for cannonball-sized lumps of shredded paper, hard enough to smash apart anything they struck.

Benjamin squatted down in a trench-like dip. Both factions were inflicting heavy damage on each other, only for the broken and smashed remains of destroyed paper creatures to form new monstrosities which stumbled back into the fray, hacking and slashing with a savagery Benjamin had never witnessed outside of a book.

Above him, one of the huge spotlights flickered off. A couple of creatures nearest to it paused, peering up, then as it flickered back into life they resumed their battle.

The arena lights had reanimated. Perhaps only in darkness did the creatures pause their endless battle, but he had no way to turn out the lights long enough to get across the arena to where he supposed were the main entrance doors.

Or did he?

At the very thought of drawing on his magic, his heart filled with a sorrow that brought tears to his eyes. His foolishness had condemned poor Sara Liselle to a future as a stumbling, mindless cleaner, a fate of eternal purgatory, perhaps truly worse than death.

He remembered what he had overheard Godfrey

say, and squeezed his elbow against the book held under his arm. Then, peering up at the spotlight closest to the edge of the arena on his left, he concentrated his gaze on the glowing light itself, and drew from the reanimated paper around him, pushing the force inward.

The bulb popped. A corner of the arena went temporarily dim. As the creatures in that area slowed their assault, Benjamin scampered for the far wall, clawing his way over mounds of shredded paper.

Cowering in the shadows below the bleachers, he targeted the next spotlight on his side of the arena and repeated the previous process. Eventually the lights would reanimate, but for a few precious minutes the battle slowed enough for him to find a way through, and gradually, one spotlight at a time, he made his way along the side of the arena.

By the time he reached the far corner, farthest from the bottom of the archive chute, his scarred hand was throbbing, the skin cold, fingers tingling. He had taken a couple of blows that had drawn blood, but had avoided all the cannonballs that might break him up like a piece of driftwood on a stormy shore.

But he was tired. Cleat had said the teachers had sealed the archives doors, so he needed to get them open somehow. His strength was failing, and he crawled into a corner near the wall, where the fighting was lightest, in order to rest.

The middle of a warzone was no place for reading, but Benjamin couldn't resist turning the book over in his hands, looking over the title page, one that bore his name. How could he have written this book? It was impossible.

On the first page inside the cover he found the copyright information. It had been water-damaged, but there near the bottom, he found it:

Copyright 2045, Dr. Benjamin Forrest, Ph.D. All rights reserved.

Thirty years from now, he would write this book, and somehow it would end up in the library at Endinfinium High before he even arrived.

He didn't even try to understand. He flicked over the next page, to the very start of the book, and read:

To disrupt the natural order of the world could be called a bad thing. But what if one is only righting the wrongs of previous generations? Surely in such circumstances, a clean-up act might prove necessary?

Benjamin wrinkled his nose, wondering how he could have written something so boring. Surely this was some kind of a joke? As he skimmed over the next couple of paragraphs, he struggled to understand what some unfamiliar future version of himself was talking about.

Then he stopped, one finger tapping on the page. A book like this, there would be a biography. It would tell him what he needed to know—who he would become, how he could possibly end up writing this book when he was trapped here in Endinfinium. In such books it was often on the back cover or just inside.

With shaking hands he turned the book over.

He caught a single glimpse of a photograph of a

man before a shadow loomed over him, obscuring it. He looked up, the book suddenly warm.

Something huge and monstrous was growing out of the mounds of shredded paper. A torso and massive arms appeared, then the outline of a face: angry eyes, a mouth drawn wide in a snarl.

The book in his hands was shaking, as if wanting to get away, and Benjamin realised his mistake.

He had brought a non-fiction book into fiction territory—enemy territory. He was trapped.

The door was to his left. He stumbled for it, the book tucked again beneath his arm, but the paper around him drew back, sucked up into the monster, pulling Benjamin's feet out from under him.

Bare stone floor surrounded him as he reached the doors. Twice as tall as a man, they were made of solid hardwood embossed with metal, like the doors of a medieval keep. He tugged on a handle, but they were sealed tight, and time had sealed them tighter. He turned to face the monster as he searched for his magic, aware he couldn't both fight it and open the door at the same time.

'Come on,' he muttered, feeling for the air around him, searching for something to draw upon. In his hands the book had become so hot he thought it might catch alight, his arm and side stinging from its touch.

The book itself! A strange sense of power emanated from it, but he risked destroying it should he draw too much.

He turned back to the door just as a volley of books

landed around him, flapping like stranded fish. Benjamin lifted his hands—

The doors flew open. Wind struck his face, knocking him back. His hand jarred against the floor and the book spun free.

A figure stepped through the open doorway. Curly, jet-black hair framed a sour face, out of which beamed startlingly green eyes that reminded Benjamin of a snake.

'Godfrey—'

The other boy lifted his hands. 'You'll learn, Forrest,' he said. 'One day you'll learn you never should have crossed me.'

A powerful wind lifted Benjamin off the ground and sent him spinning through the air. He slammed into the body of the great paper creature, plunging into its dark, spongy depths.

The last thing he saw before the hole he had punctured in the creature sealed over was Godfrey picking the book up off the floor, then striding out of the arena like a gladiatorial champion, the dark, amorphous shadow still looming at his shoulder like a bad aura.

Then the paper shifted and Benjamin found himself squeezed, the last air expelled from his lungs in a sudden jolt.

16

SURVIVORS

'So what do we do now?' Wilhelm said. Before Miranda could reply, he put up a hand. 'While I imagine your preferred course of action would be to scold me to the end of the world, I believe that such a route would prove counterproductive.'

Miranda scowled. 'I'll save it for later. Do you have any kind of plan, or is that it?'

'That's it.'

'Well, we can't just sit here, can we? We need to go and find out what's trapped us. And if possible, find a way to free Lawrence.' She turned to address the snake-train. 'Lawrence, how far underwater are we?'

'Twenty metres,' came the reply.

Wilhelm shook his head. 'We'll never make it. That's almost the length of a swimming pool.'

Miranda lifted an eyebrow. 'And I thought you were the brave one. Don't be so chicken. I'm going out there, with you or without you. Do you want to protect me, or do you want to sit in here looking at the fish swimming past the windows?'

Wilhelm glared at her. 'I didn't say I wasn't coming. I was just pointing out that it was dangerous.' He stood up and marched over to the wall. 'That's why we need these.'

Set into Lawrence's wall were several inflatable lifebuoys Edgar had installed due to Lawrence's liking for a swim. Wilhelm pulled the emergency handle and opened the glass door. He picked out one of the red circles and turned it over in his hands. 'We blow into the tube and it inflates. Then we can just float to the surface.'

Miranda took one and hooked it over her head. 'Now we just need to figure out how to get out without getting drowned.'

'Easy,' Wilhelm said. He turned to Lawrence and explained his plan. The snake-train agreed, his stuck head shuddering as he tried to nod.

With the lifebuoys around their necks, Wilhelm and Miranda went through the interlocking doors and down to the end of the train. Lawrence had five carriages behind his locomotive head, so they went to the last one then locked the door into the rest of the train.

'Right, here goes,' Wilhelm said. 'Remember, straight up. We need to stay close to the edge. If you float off, you might never find your way back.'

Miranda nodded. 'I hope it's not too cold,' she said.

Wilhelm grinned. 'I bet it's freezing.' Then, taking a deep breath, he called, 'Okay, Lawrence, open the windows.'

All the side windows slid down at once, and the sea rushed in. Benjamin and Miranda scrambled to blow into the plastic tubes which inflated their lifebuoys as the chilling water rose up their bodies, gurgling around their waists.

Wilhelm turned to Miranda. 'This might be a good time to say that I, um, think you're not bad,' he blurted. Then, with a smile, he added, 'For a girl. For a boy you'd kind of suck.'

Miranda opened her mouth to snap something back, but the water was already past her neck. Instead she settled for a weak, water-resisted punch on the arm.

Then they were underwater.

Wilhelm opened his eyes to a blur. Already his lungs burned, but the inflated lifebouy was lifting him off his feet. He scrabbled for Miranda's hand, finding only her sleeve as she floated up to the ceiling, and pulled her toward the open side windows.

The water was colder than water should be allowed to be. Wilhelm's body tingled, his senses weakening as his orientation became confused. He was no longer sure where the windows were as his hands touched the ceiling, and he fought down a rising panic. Then Miranda's other hand grabbed his, and he felt a sudden weightlessness.

Free from the snake-train, they rose up along the crusted metal edge of the strange object, unable to see it clearly underwater, but feeling it every time something hard and trapped bumped against them. Wilhelm's head felt like it was going to explode, but the pressure was slowly lifting.

It felt like they were rising through the water forever, and finally he could no longer stand it. He kicked out at something nearby, feeling resistance underfoot, and dragged Miranda toward the surface.

They burst free beside each other, coughing and choking, both gasping down desperate breaths. More out of relief, Wilhelm pulled Miranda close to him and hugged her. To his surprise she hugged him back.

'Quick,' she gasped. 'The edge. Before we float away.'

They had surfaced a short way offshore, and Wilhelm already felt a current trying to pull them along the metal thing's side and into its wake as it cruised slowly north. He kicked out, thankful for the buoyancy of the lifebuoy as the water twisted him around, and managed to get a hold of a metal protrusion.

He had caught an old mooring hook, and climbed out onto a rusty metal platform. Miranda crawled out of the water beside him.

'We made it,' she gasped, coughing up a mouthful of water. 'I'll say, you never stop surprising me.'

'Happy birthday for next year,' Wilhelm muttered. 'Do you like your present? I got you an, um, lost world.'

Miranda shook her head. 'No. You took me to a theme park. Look.'

Through a thinning haze a short distance back from the water's edge, a road appeared, its end jagged as though the whole island had been dug out of the ground. And there, standing over the road, was a faded sign above a rusty, half-collapsed gate:

WELCOME TO SUNSHINE LAND
The world's most northerly theme park

'I didn't bring any money for a ticket,' Wilhelm said.

'I think we're good,' Miranda said, pointing at the tumbledown ruin of a ticketing office just inside the gate. I think the park's closed.'

Beyond the sign, the road became a wide concourse between two lines of buildings. The once gaudy facades of shops, restaurants, entertainment galleries, and amusement arcades had faded to grey and fallen into disrepair. Wisps of fog drifted through the air, but it was apparent that the vast fogbank had been to keep the island hidden.

'What do we do now?' Miranda asked. 'It's pretty cold here, and we're both soaked. I think we'd better find some way to warm up.'

Wilhelm was trying not to let his teeth chatter, but Miranda was right. The best thing for both of them was to wring out and preferably dry their clothes before trying to figure out what was going on. They only had an hour before dark, and surrounded by a cloud of fog, Wilhelm wasn't optimistic about their chances of survival.

They walked a short distance up the main thoroughfare, the silence broken only by the occasional rustle of wind, the creaking of faded signs, and the rumble of the sea hidden in the fog.

'There,' Wilhelm said. 'Madame Light's Accessories. There's a picture of a t-shirt in the window.'

The door's lock was a block of rust, but at some

point in the relatively recent past it had been broken off its fitting and now lay in a patch of unenthusiastic grass by the roadside.

'Someone else is here,' Miranda said.

'Let's hope we don't run into them. Can you feel any magic?'

Miranda shook her head, her eyes glazed, almost trancelike. 'Nothing. Just … cold.'

'Can't you punch me or something? I'm getting a little nervous.'

Miranda looked at him as though seeing him for the first time. Then, with a nod, she gave his forearm a tentative tap.

'Um, thanks.'

Wilhelm went first, easing through the doorway, holding what remained of the door back for Miranda. The light through a grimy window was poor, but it was enough to see the wreckage inside.

Little remained that appeared usable. Shelves had been pulled over, their contents spilled across the floor. Among all manner of smashed knickknacks and tourist souvenirs, Wilhelm pulled free a couple of shirts with AT SUNSHINE LAND THE SUN ALWAYS SHINES written around the outside of a smiling sun character. They were threadbare and moth-eaten, and when he tried to put one on, it fell apart in his hands.

'This whole place is a giant piece of junk,' Wilhelm said. 'I guess that explains why it's here in Endinfinium.'

'This stuff should burn,' Miranda said. 'Let me try to start a fire.'

'How are you going to do that?'

She shot him an angry glance as she squatted down. 'Be quiet. I need to concentrate.'

Wilhelm nodded as Miranda scooped a few ancient souvenir items into a small pile. Wilhelm watched her for a couple of minutes as she frowned and occasionally grimaced, her hands held around the pile as though trying to trap a spider. Finally, bored, he wandered over to the windows and peered out onto the boulevard.

It was still empty, but there was a sense of being watched that he couldn't shake. Like Miranda had described, when he closed his eyes he could feel no magic, only a subterranean chill. There had to be magic here, because the whole island had reanimated enough to float and drift against the natural current, but what kind of magic, and where it was originating from, were secrets the island refused to reveal.

The sky overhead was darkening, black clouds threatening rain. Wilhelm leaned out of a broken window to get a better look at the street, but as he twisted his shoulders, he caught a glimpse of a shadow moving quickly across the street further up. A moment later it was followed by another, ducked low, arms hanging down, carrying something.

He turned. 'Miranda—'

A glow lit her face. 'Look, I got it started.'

A small fire cracked between her hands.

'Um, I'm not sure it's such a good idea. I just saw some people.'

'Where?'

'At the end of the street. Just shadows, but they were definitely people.' He came to crouch beside her, the warmth of the small fire enough to remove any thought of extinguishing it now it was lit. Miranda's face was expectant, so he did his best to explain what he had only seen for a brief moment—two people who were no more than shadows, running from one side of the street to the other, one perhaps carrying something.

'Where were they going?'

'No idea.'

'Did you see what they were wearing?'

'No. Unless they were wearing black.'

'They were wearing black?'

'I don't know. It's almost dark, and it looks like it's going to rain.'

'What do you think—' Miranda began, but Wilhelm held up a hand.

'Look, there's nothing else to tell you. I definitely saw them, which means we're not the only people here. If you ask me, we should hunker down here for the night, try to get our clothes dry, and in the morning go looking for them. They might know how to get off this thing.'

'Then why are they still here?'

Wilhelm shrugged. 'Adventure?'

Miranda shivered. She dropped a lump of wood that had once been a carved paperweight on to the fire and watched it begin to crackle.

'You know, I didn't realise how comforting the dorms at the school were until we ended up stuck here.'

Wilhelm grinned. 'You reckon? Did you ever get up in the night for a glass of water in the kitchen downstairs? Gubbledon's a reanimate, so he doesn't need to sleep. I went down there one time and he's there in the common room, making these striding gestures like he's reliving one of his old races. Damn near scared the skin off me.'

Miranda laughed. 'I appreciate your attempt to take my mind off our predicament.'

Wilhelm shook his head. 'It's not a joke. I was half asleep as I came round that corner at the bottom of the stairs and the red sun over the horizon lit up his face like something demonic. I actually wet myself.' As Miranda wrinkled her nose and punched him, he added, 'And you know what? He was wearing a monocle.'

Miranda snorted. The flames of the small fire flickered, but she cupped them quickly and they hung on.

'Quick, throw some more tourist tat on there. I was enjoying being warm.'

'Do you think Lawrence is cold?' Miranda wondered, as she poked the fire with a stick. 'I mean, being stuck underwater.'

Wilhelm shook his head. 'Reanimates, from what I can gather, get to experience such things only by personal choice. If Lawrence doesn't want to be cold, he won't be. I imagine he's bored out of his mind, though.'

'We need to find a way to free him.'

'We will.'

They stayed by the fire for a while. Wilhelm took off what clothes he could and laid them out to dry. Miranda was more reluctant, taking off only her outer jacket, a top and her socks, preferring to dry the rest of her clothes on her body, periodically shifting position to warm herself at a different angle. Wilhelm, poking at his drying clothes with a stick, would possibly not have noticed their next problem until Miranda brought it up.

'I'm hungry.'

'I saw a bunch of restaurants further up the street. Maybe they have some food kicking about. Perhaps a hotdog stand has reanimated or something.'

Miranda cocked her head. 'You think?' She picked up the holey remains of a scarf and tossed it on the fire. 'How long does it take something to get like that? Two hundred years? A thousand? You think any food will still be edible?'

Wilhelm shrugged. 'They might have good freezers. Or the food could have reanimated and made itself delicious again.'

Miranda wrinkled her nose. 'I guess if we have no choice.'

'We could try fishing.'

They lapsed into silence for a while. Wilhelm continued to poke his drying clothes, and Miranda to turn in a gradual circle.

At last, Wilhelm said, 'Where do you think this place came from?'

'I don't—'

From outside came a thunderous boom, making the walls and ceiling shake. Puffs of dust came cascading down, fizzing on the fire.

They looked at each other, then both scrambled to their feet and ran to the window. The sky above was still dark, but far to their left, beyond the end of the boulevard, an orange glow lit up the clouds from beneath.

'Oh, not good,' Miranda said, heading for the door.

'Where are you going?'

Miranda turned back and smiled, but there was no humour in it, only a dutiful reluctance. 'Get your clothes on. We're going to find out what it is.'

17

ACCUSATIONS

Benjamin's head was aching when he awoke. He was lying on a bed with a blanket draped over him, but from the way the light fell across his face, he immediately knew he wasn't back in the dormitory.

He sat up. The light came from a single skylight high in the roof. The room was no more than a couple of paces across, and aside from a little washbasin in one corner, was empty of all fixtures and fittings.

The stone floor was cold underfoot as he hopped across to the heavy wooden door.

Locked.

He gave it a shake, but it was solid. Closing his eyes, he concentrated, feeling for his magic. Unpicking locks was one of the first things he had learned to do. When the essence of reanimation magic was pushing and pulling, it was relatively easy to pick even a complex lock, lifting and pressing the lock mechanisms like piano keys.

Here, however, he found the lock immobile, even though he could feel his magic attempting to work it. A ward. Someone had trapped him inside.

'Let me out!' he shouted, pounding on the door. 'Is someone there?'

No one answered. He banged on the door again, but got the same result. Frustrated, he went back to the bed and sat down, kicking his heels against the floor. He was a prisoner, but where was he? With nothing else to do, he lay on the bed and tried to doze, as the block of light from the skylight made its way slowly across the floor.

It had nearly reached the wall, indicating evening, when the lock rattled. Benjamin sat up as the door swung open. A cleaner stepped inside, carrying a tray of food. Vacant eyes watched him, then a slow smile spread over Sara Liselle's dead face as she set the tray down on the floor and retreated.

'Are you haunting me?' Benjamin muttered, wanting to shout it, but aware of the shadow at her shoulder that became Ms. Ito. With a scowl, the teacher with the permanent plaster cast on one leg limped into the room.

'You're awake, boy. About time. Been three days. We were starting to wonder how hard you hit your head. Did you have any interesting dreams?'

'Can I go back to the dorms?'

Ms. Ito's face, made horrifying by the mixture of straight black and curly white hair that attacked her features from all sides, cocked to one side.

'No … is it not obvious that you've been placed in a restraining cell?'

'Oh. I thought it was the nurse's room.'

Ms. Ito glared at him. 'Are you giving me backtalk? You know what folly that is.'

He remembered a time she had thrown Fat Adam against the wall for talking while she was writing something on the board. Fat Adam, the biggest boy in the class. And she had actually thrown him. Not with magic, but with her hands.

'I thought this was the new nurse's room….'

'You are pathetically mistaken. Are you aware of what you did?'

'I just wanted to retrieve a book that was lost.'

'Is that what you call bashing Cleat over the head and then breaking open the archive doors? It took two full days to get those creatures back inside and the doors secured. No one is sure quite what's going on with you at the moment, Master Forrest, but we've reached a point where we have no choice but to enact an ancient school rule giving us the authority to restrain a pupil with an overly destructive streak.'

Benjamin rubbed his head, frowning. 'I didn't do any of those things. I remember Godfrey—'

'—pulled you out of there. After you blew out the doors, one of the paper creatures caught hold of you. According to Professor Eaves, Godfrey ran inside and broke you free. The boy is a hero.'

'What? That's an absolute lie!'

Ms. Ito shook her head. 'That's not a good way to talk about another teacher,' she said. 'Think carefully before you accuse someone of telling lies.'

'But it's not true!'

Ms. Ito gave a sad sigh. 'Godfrey, escorted by

Professor Eaves, was on his way to an audience with the Grand Lord,' she said. 'They overheard a disturbance and went to investigate. Godfrey's actions were witnessed not only by Professor Eaves but also by Captain Roche and his new assistant, Junior Professor Wilkins.'

Benjamin sat back. While he could argue that Professor Eaves was in league with the Dark Man, Captain Roche had always seemed on their side, albeit reluctantly. If both he and Terry had also seen Godfrey help him, then they were either all in it together, or….

…he was losing his mind.

'I think I need a lie down,' Benjamin said.

Ms Ito arched a manicured eyebrow. 'You've been lying down for three days. How much rest do you need?'

'Three days'?'

'You took a bump on the head, but whatever.'

Benjamin frowned again, trying to recall the events leading up to his attack by Godfrey and calibrate it with what Ms. Ito was saying.

'Cleat—'

'Is still unconscious.'

Benjamin felt a wave of white heat wash over him. 'No.'

'If he dies, boy, you will find yourself in a whole higher level of trouble. We do not allow murder here in Endinfinium High. Not at any time, not by anyone.'

'I didn't hit him.'

'You were seen going to the library. The archive chute was open. There was a trace of reanimation on the lock. Everyone knows how good you are with locks. You came top in Professor Loane's class on the subject.'

Benjamin shook his head. 'It was Cleat. It must have been.'

'Why would Cleat need to do that? He's got a key.'

The evidence, whether circumstantial or not, was building up. Benjamin could tell from Ms. Ito's eyes that she was convinced, and like a truck with its accelerator jammed, there was no stopping her.

'Is there anything else I can say to defend myself?'

Ms. Ito shook her head. 'It doesn't look good for you, I'm afraid, boy. Within the teachers' circle we have always given you preferential treatment because of the Dark Man's unusual focus on you, but it seems you're more trouble than you might be worth.'

Benjamin felt a sudden urge to cry. The injustice of Ms. Ito's words stung like an angry wasp. 'No one believes me. I was just looking for a book.'

'Don't you get it, fool? This is Endinfinium. You don't just "look for a book". You do a thousand other things, and when everything's connected, you end up in a mess. Survival here is a fine line. You have to work to stay on it. At times I don't think you even know where the line is.'

Benjamin shrugged. His cheeks burned and he found himself unable to look at her.

'Find that line again and you'll have a chance. Until you're ready to confess and apologise, though, enjoy the view.'

'What view?'

Ms. Ito rolled her eyes as she hobbled to the door. 'Someone will come to see you tomorrow.'

'I won't change my story, because it's the truth.'

Ms. Ito shook her head and gave a long sigh. 'Oh, why can't you be more like Godfrey? Such a good boy.'

For a few seconds her gaze became erratic, her eyes darting around the room as though watching the dust mites.

'Are you all right, Miss?'

Ms. Ito's head snapped around. 'What? Yes. Get some sleep. It might help you with your memory.'

She reached out to close the door, but Benjamin lifted a hand. 'Wait!'

'What? Come on, boy, I'm in a hurry for class.'

'Are Wilhelm Jacobs and Miranda Butterworth around? Is it possible I can see them?'

Ms. Ito's countenance darkened. 'I'm afraid it appears they have gone on a little adventure. You wouldn't know where they are, by any chance?'

Benjamin shook his head.

Ms. Ito sighed again. 'Well, if you happen to remember something, we would most like to know.'

Before he could say anything else, the door slammed shut and the lock clicked. Benjamin stared at the closed door, feeling emptier than ever.

18

AWAKENING

'Come on,' Miranda said, jogging up the street in the direction of the light. 'It's right over there.'

Wilhelm was huffing as he struggled to keep up. 'Can't you slow down a bit?'

'I don't want to miss what's going on.'

Through the fog, the glow from the red sun was barely brighter than the orange glow in the sky, but as she became accustomed to the light, Miranda found it relatively easy to navigate. The boulevard ended in an open square filled with heaped junk, while in front of her was a towering fake mountain with the rusted metal frames of an ancient rollercoaster weaving in and out of tunnels on its side. The glow was coming from just beyond it, so she jogged through the heaps of trash with Wilhelm close behind.

Several wide avenues led off the courtyard, cutting between fake trees and blocky buildings with the signs advertising their old rides lying in the dirt in front of their busted-open entrances.

'Which ride do you want to check out first?' Wilhelm quipped from behind her, the humour stolen from his words by his ragged breathing. 'Do you want to ride the ghost train on the right, or the one on the left?'

'Look, it's right ahead,' Miranda said, ignoring him.

She came to a stop by a sign at the start of a tree-lined path winding between two fences. It angled downhill to a fake ornate arch.

'Open air theatre,' she said. 'Let's go.'

She smelled the fire even before they reached the gate. Lifting a hand to stop Wilhelm running through, she paused in the deepest shadows and leaned out, eyes searching the bowl laid out below them.

An amphitheatre had been dug out of the earth, but in the middle of the stage was a gaping hole perhaps as long as a bus. Miranda couldn't see how far down it went, but the fire raging within it washed her face with heat even at this distance, dark orange flames reaching for the sky.

'That's one hell of a barbeque pit,' Wilhelm said.

'I can see someone standing beside it,' Miranda said. 'Look.'

A tiny black-clad figure stood close to the pit's edge, robed, its face hidden. It leaned on a staff which could have been wood or metal.

'Let's go take a closer look,' Miranda said. 'He must be practically cooking up that close.'

'How do you know it's a he?'

Miranda sighed. 'Because … a girl wouldn't stand

that close to a fire for fear of singing her hair. Trust me, I know these things.'

'I didn't realise you were a real girl.'

Miranda gave him a light punch on the arm. 'I am when I choose to be.'

'Well, some boys aren't as brave as girls, so I think we should stay here, just in case he's dangerous.'

Miranda looked at him and grinned. 'Come on, you want to know what he's doing. Don't pretend you don't.'

Wilhelm sighed. 'All right then. But let's be careful. Much as I don't care if you fall in that pit, I don't want to have to explain it to Benjamin.'

Miranda led as they crept forward. The remains of ancient trees lined the path meandering down to the middle of the amphitheatre, shrouded in cobwebs and dusted with ash like grey snow. Piles of junk lay in among the trees, some of it burned beyond recognition. When they reached an extended viewing gallery that looked down over the lower area, Miranda paused. She squatted down and crept to the edge, peering over a stone balustrade at the scene below.

'Can you feel it?' Wilhelm asked. 'It's making my heart feel strange, like I just woke up after only two hours' sleep.'

'The cold,' she said.

Roaring with savage intensity, the orange flames were hot enough to make Miranda's eyes water even at this distance. But inside her heart she felt something else, a deep, shivering cold like the water at the bottom of the sea.

'It's bad magic,' she said. 'What did Benjamin call it? Dark reanimate?'

Wilhelm nodded. 'A whole pit of it, right in the middle of this old park.'

Miranda leaned forward. 'There are more of them. Look. Down there. Two, three, four—'

'Nine,' Wilhelm said. 'Nine little wizards. What do you think they're up to?'

A creak came from behind them. Miranda jumped, almost falling over the edge of the viewing gallery before Wilhelm grabbed her arm. Together, they squeezed behind a stone parapet and watched with horror as the piles of junk between the trees began to move.

Blackened heaps of rubbish stood up, shifted into human or animal shapes, and walked down the steps to the lower circle, an orange glow emanating out of cracks in their bodies from some deep, dark core.

More were coming too, reanimated creatures that were recognisable from their form—sofas and chairs and windows, swing frames, car parts, metal lintels, tiny kitchen utensils marching in lines like toy soldiers, in their midst huge, twisted printing presses, threshing machines, pneumatic drills, mining machinery. The lines of reanimates bobbed and bounced down the steps with a metallic cacophony so loud both Miranda and Wilhelm clamped hands over their ears.

At last, the unworldly procession stopped. One of the robed figures lifted his arms, and the flames in the pit died down. The rustling of the reanimates meant there was no real silence, but when the figure spoke,

Miranda was able to catch his words over the crackle of the fire.

'The night has come, and the awakening is upon us. Step forward if you wish to be awakened.'

An enormous rustle began again as hundreds of the creatures shifted. Miranda glanced at Wilhelm, the boy's face an expression of horror as one by one, the reanimates jumped into the pit while the charred and blackened creatures applauded with the hollow beat of machines working a factory floor.

'Awaken!' screamed all nine robed figures together, like the screech of an angry flock of crows. 'Awaken and embrace the darkness!'

'Noooooo—'

The scream came from the lower circle to Miranda's left. She peered over the edge, looking for what had made the sound. In the shadows of a corridor leading into the earth, several of the burned creatures were struggling, something colourful in their midst.

The scream came again, then the struggling group shifted forward. Dragged by the burned creatures, a reanimated car, wheels twisted into arms and legs, struggled to break free.

Wilhelm's hand fell on her shoulder. 'Oh, God. I know him. That's Roy. He's from Underfloor. A reanimated Rover Mini. What's he doing down there?'

The burned creatures, their bodies pulsing with orange light like a fire's glowing embers in demonic form, dragged Roy down an aisle between stone benches. The nearest of the robed figures raised his hands.

'An infidel. An unbeliever. You must be purged in the fires of the Dark Man, and embrace your destiny. Awaken!'

Roy gave one last howl of anguish, then a dozen charred metallic arms shoved him into the flames.

Miranda glanced at Wilhelm again. The boy had tears in his eyes.

'What's going on down there?' he said, voice cracking up. 'Who are those people?'

'We call them the Dark Mages,' came a gravelly voice from out of the dark behind them. 'They were once pupils of Endinfinium High, just like you.'

Wilhelm let out a strangled scream as a black-clad figure rose behind him and clamped a hand over his mouth. Miranda turned, but there was someone behind her too. A hand that smelled of ash covered her mouth before she could cry out, and pulled her back into the darkness.

19

ESCAPE

It didn't make sense. The Grand Lord would never allow his imprisonment, and neither would Edgar Caspian. The Grand Lord was a confidant, and Benjamin considered Edgar a friend.

Benjamin's long standing belief that Professor Eaves was in league with the Dark Man was second in intensity only to Wilhelm's; his friend's attempts to stalk the shady professor had so far come up with nothing solid, but suspicion hung around old Dusty like a cloud of flies.

Of the other teachers, though, Benjamin couldn't believe any of them were on the side of the Dark Man. They had tried to suppress knowledge of reanimation magic, but only out of a sense of protecting the pupils from themselves.

So why the imprisonment? Why the taking of Godfrey's words over his own, when the boy was known to side with the Dark Man?

Benjamin sat on the floor of his room. He stood up.

He leaned against the walls. He peered up at the skylight, and he thumped his fists again the floor.

Nothing made any sense, unless the lies and rumours about his own connection with the Dark Man had begun to circulate and pollute rational thinking.

Except the evidence was there. He had seen the Dark Man's face, which bore an uncanny resemblance to his own. Godfrey claimed the same thing, and Godfrey had spent time in the Dark Man's shifting castle, far away in the High Mountains. The book on dark reanimate held Benjamin's name.

Then there was Sara. His recklessness had killed her.

And now Miranda and Wilhelm were missing.

He needed to escape and figure out what was going on, but trapped inside the room, he could do nothing.

The lock was sealed with a ward of magic stronger than his own. Attempting to destroy it with his own magic might kill him.

The skylight, too, was protected. Even if he could reach it—and Edgar had proven that with mastery of the magic it was possible to levitate, even if Benjamin couldn't do it himself—it was fixed shut.

And the rest of the room was solid rock.

Benjamin sat up. Of course.

It was a long shot, but….

The walls and floor were cold flagstones, fitted tightly, secured with ancient mortar. With a chisel he might be able to break his way through, in, perhaps, a thousand years. Stone was the safest substance in Endinfinium, because of its propensity to remain stone and not reanimate over time like everything else did, but that didn't mean it wasn't susceptible.

If you concentrated hard enough, you could wake up anything.

Push and pull. Draw from the substances around you, not from yourself.

Grand Lord Bastian's words were a mantra in his ears. Benjamin had scars from where he had drawn the magic unknowingly from his own body, a process that had only one eventual end: death.

However, no other way existed to keep your use of the magic secret from anyone who might be feeling for it.

Benjamin squatted down and placed his hands on the flagstones near the wall. He closed his eyes and concentrated, doing what at first had felt like the tensing of some invisible internal muscle, then later what first Edgar Caspian and then Grand Lord Bastien had taught him, to see, listen, and feel, not with the mind, but with the heart. And if you did it right, you would feel a connection with the world around you as though you were joined by a million strings, like a puppet master with an infinitely complex marionette.

And then all you had to do was choose which strings to pull.

The flagstone beneath Benjamin's hands trembled. He gritted his teeth, lifting his hands, feeling the mortar crack and break away. The flagstone slid free like something glued to the underside of Benjamin's palms.

When it was far enough out of the space to discard, he pushed it sideways, dropping it on the floor. Released, the magic drained from his body in an instant, leaving him feeling weak and lethargic. As he propped himself into a sitting position, he noticed a trickle of blood running down his exposed ankle. He pulled up his trouser leg to reveal a thin cut two inches long just below his knee.

If that was all there was, he was lucky. With a tired shrug, he wiped away the blood and pulled his trouser leg back down.

The hole was barely two feet square, but it was just big enough to squeeze inside. The wall wasn't doubled as he had hoped, but he had happened upon a thin shaft, perhaps an ancient, long-disused chimney, which he was able to shuffle down by using the ledges and corners of the stones as hand and footholds.

Once his whole body was inside, he closed his eyes again and concentrated on the air around the heavy flagstone, pushing it back across the opening. While someone looking would find it easily, to a casual observer, it would appear he had disappeared into thin air.

When it dropped into place, enclosing him in a pitch-black, stone tomb, at first all he wanted to do was panic. He gritted his teeth to stop himself from crying out, and held tightly to the rocks around him until the feeling had passed. Then, he began to descend.

The shaft seemed to go on forever. Hand after foot, remembering the basic climbing principles Captain Roche had instilled into them in climbing class—always have three points of contact—he moved down the shaft, the cold stone and the thick cobwebs his only companions. Perhaps he would come to a dead end, and have no choice but to either try to blast his way out, or climb back up to his prison. His body was tired and aching from the use of his magic, so it was entirely possible he would die here, lost, alone, and forgotten.

Then he touched something soft that crunched underfoot.

Reaching down, Benjamin found ancient embers scattered around him, cold, burned remains of logs sitting in a grate. Extending his arms, he found stone walls on three sides, and there, on the fourth, a wooden panel.

An old, sealed fireplace.

He pressed his ear against it, but heard nothing from the other side.

Leaning a shoulder against the wooden boards, he tested their strength, but they were fixed solid, jammed into the space, perhaps long ago expanding enough to get stuck tight.

His magic would shift them, but it was another risk. Instead, he sat down in the embers, braced himself against the back wall of the fireplace, then kicked out as hard as he could.

The board broke apart. Dim light pressed in as someone screamed.

Afraid of recapture, Benjamin scrambled out through the hole. He found himself in a quaint study furnished only by a desk, a tall bookshelf against the opposite wall, and a bureau standing by the door.

As Benjamin stood up, the bureau shifted and screamed again, one drawer opening and closing in a gesture of surprise. Twin inkwells in its centre revolved like startled eyes.

'I'm sorry to have scared you,' Benjamin said, lifting his hands. 'I'm afraid I got stuck in there.'

The bureau, standing up on its back edge, lowered back to the floor. It bumped up and down a couple of times, letting papers and other stationery settle back into place. Its front shelf opened and closed, creaking on old hinges, before finally it stayed lowered, and a twist of small stationery shelves inclined as though it were an owl cocking its head.

'And exactly who might you be?' came a voice Benjamin identified as the rapid rustling of paper from inside the bureau's front drawer.

'Benjamin Forrest. Formerly a pupil of Endinfinium High. Now, possibly, a fugitive.'

A front drawer opened and closed in a manner that suggested a nod. 'Well, it's a name with which I am familiar at least,' the reanimated bureau said. 'One synonymous with trouble, by all accounts. My name is Laurel. I am the official keeper of the history of Underfloor, which is where you now find yourself. Now, would you mind staying back by that accursed fireplace? You're getting cobwebs all over my carpet. We don't have the luxury of cleaners down here, you know. We have to do it all ourselves.'

20
REFUGE

The wispy beard made Timothy Long hard to identify. Emmie Bromwich at least looked the same as Wilhelm remembered, even if her clothes had become rags, and her hair a fuzzy mess that birds might nest in.

'I didn't mean to scare you,' Timothy said, his haunted eyes darting from one face to the other, then down to the nightmarish scene below and back again. 'But if they catch you….'

Miranda stifled a gasp with the palm of her hand. Emmie nodded.

'In you go.'

'It's barbaric,' Miranda whispered.

'It's a ghoul factory,' Timothy said. 'Everything that goes in there comes back out as a ghoul, but charred and cooked. They're more dangerous that way, more impervious to magic. During the day they rest, but at night they hunt for reanimates pulled in by the island.'

'How long have you been here?' Wilhelm asked.

'A year, give or take. It's been six months since Sara tried to escape.'

'A year? Six months?' Wilhelm shook his head. 'That's impossible. Your triangulation was only a few weeks ago. You can't have been here a year.'

Timothy shrugged. 'We kept a tally for the first few months. Now we go by the seasons.'

Wilhelm shook his head. 'That's impossible.'

'You keep saying that, but look. We're right here.' Timothy pulled up a threadbare grey shirt that Wilhelm recognised with dismay as the faded remnants of a school uniform. Timothy pointed to a welt below his armpit. 'See that? Got stabbed the first week here. We were still wandering around like idiots, looking at the scenery. Almost died. Sara used her magic to heal it.'

'Sara? She knew magic?'

Timothy rolled his eyes. 'Don't sound so surprised. She wasn't the only one quietly learning on the sly while the teachers buried their heads in the sand.'

Miranda nodded. 'She got away?'

'About six months ago. She stole a boat, reckoned she could use her magic to get free. She was planning to warn the school about the island.'

'We found her,' Miranda said. 'In the Haunted Forest.'

Both Timothy and Emmie gasped. Wilhelm glanced at Miranda, wondering how she would tell it.

'We, um, took her back to the school.'

'She's all right?'

Miranda looked pained. 'Um, yeah. A bit tired, maybe. She, um, doesn't say much.'

Timothy punched a fist into his palm. 'We didn't believe her. At least she's safe now.'

'Yeah, at least there's that,' Wilhelm said, stealing a guilty glance at Miranda, who responded with a grimace.

'What did the teachers say?' Timothy asked.

Wilhelm shrugged. 'No idea. We ended up here not long after we found her.'

Down in the amphitheatre, lines of burned reanimates moved forward. Howling with excitement, they dropped over the edge of the fire pit, sending up clouds of sparks and puffs of orange-grey smoke.

'What are they doing now?' Miranda asked.

'As far as we can tell, they're bathing,' Emmie said. 'They do it every few nights.'

'Why?'

'Whatever is in that pit is constantly causing them to reanimate,' Timothy said. 'Each time they emerge, they're even more twisted, but stronger, faster, bigger.'

'And those people? What did you call them?'

'Dark Mages.' Timothy shrugged. 'It's as good a name as any.'

'Who are they?'

'Former pupils who've turned to the side of the Dark Man and dark reanimate.'

'What?'

'You'll see them walking around during the day, but never, ever approach them. One of them is Paul Lewis, who was captain of the rugby club two years ahead of me.'

Emmie nodded. 'Don't be suckered in. At first we

couldn't believe it when we met some other people. Sara was always suspicious, but we were taken in.'

Wilhelm glanced at Miranda. 'But they know you're still here, right?'

Timothy nodded. 'By day we hide. By night we hunt for other survivors like yourselves.'

'But they must be able to find you. The island can't be that big.'

Timothy shrugged. 'We're both Weavers. We're no threat to them. Sara, she was a Channeller. If she used magic, they could sense it and find her. She was dangerous to them, so they tried to make her join their group. She escaped and fled the island. You're not Channellers or Summoners, are you? If you are, you're in great danger.'

Wilhelm opened his mouth to speak, but Miranda blurted, 'No, of course not. We're both Weavers.'

'Yeah,' Wilhelm agreed, swallowing. 'Both Weavers. The rubbish ones, completely useless.'

Timothy nodded. 'That's good. You should be able to hide. Come on, we need to go.'

'Where?'

'Our safe-house.'

'Where's that?'

Emmie smiled. 'Follow us. Quietly, now. Ghouls are everywhere, so stay close and don't get lost.'

Timothy and Emmie hurried back up the path to the amphitheatre's ticket gate. They paused underneath it, then, when neither Wilhelm nor Miranda made any move to follow, they waved frantically.

'What do you think?' Wilhelm asked. 'Do we trust them?'

Miranda stared at the ticket entrance. 'Timothy once taught me how to cross-stitch,' she said. 'It was before you arrived. The seventh-years were doing a community help day. I remember he was really patient, even when it was clear I had no idea what I was doing. He was kind to me then, so I believe we can trust them.'

Wilhelm shrugged. 'Okay, let's go.' They started up the hill. Halfway up, Wilhelm added, 'Taught you to cross-stitch, eh? I wonder why he doesn't fix up his clothes.'

'Is that supposed to be funny?'

'Funny and sunshiney,' Wilhelm said. 'Just like this park. Welcome to Sunshine Land indeed.'

From the shadows beneath the ticket entrance, Emmie flapped a hand. 'Come on, hurry. When they're done bathing they go on patrol. If they find any trace of us they'll turn this place upside down.'

Timothy took the lead, with Emmie at his shoulder. Wilhelm and Miranda came after, running side by side as Timothy led them down a meandering boulevard heading east away from their first hiding place. Dark buildings rose on either side, occasionally broken up by the entrance to some ancient ride. Once, Wilhelm glimpsed a wide lake through the houses, and in the distance hills rose, topped by the snaking metal frames of long-unused rollercoasters.

They turned a corner and found themselves in a small plaza. Wilhelm grabbed Miranda's arm as they came to a stop.

'What's that?'

A glowing neon sign announced TERROR TOWER—ENTER IF YOU DARE.

'Why is the sign lit up?' Benjamin asked Timothy.

'It's started to reanimate. Things do here from time to time. Anything that's capable of moving gets thrown into the pit. A group will probably come past tomorrow to pull down that sign, so we'd better take cover.'

'This way,' Emmie said. 'Around the back. This was the safest place we could find.'

'Although if we're discovered here, we're stuffed,' Timothy added.

Wilhelm peered up at the tower looming above them. Like a very thin, almost overbalancing tower block, it rose high into the twilit sky.

'The inside is hollow,' Emmie said. 'There's only the ride car which has rusted solid at the top. It used to drop down the shaft and terrify people on board. Come on.'

'You've got to be having a laugh,' Wilhelm said.

Timothy led them through an old ticket gate and around the back, bypassing the main doors into the waiting area. He stopped at a fallen metal billboard for the others to catch up. Then, holding up a corner, he waved them underneath.

'Quick, inside.'

'Where does this go?' Wilhelm asked.

'Maintenance access.'

Wilhelm could think of nothing polite to say. He gulped, felt Miranda's fingers thread through his and squeeze tight, then Emmie was leading them into a small shaft with a single rusty ladder heading up.

'You two go up first,' Emmie said. 'We'll check there are no ghouls around. Don't worry, it's easy. There are a couple of broken rungs about halfway up but the rest is safe. You don't need to worry about how high you are because it's too dark to see anyway.'

'Ladies first,' Wilhelm said, offering Miranda a flourishing bow.

'Oh no you don't,' she said, her fist snapping out to strike his upper arm, making him wince. 'You and your whole 'I climbed up the teachers' tower to spy through their windows' business, and you think I'm going up there first? No chance.'

'I had a harness,' Wilhelm protested. 'Anyway, I thought you liked climbing. You're always buttering up to Captain Roche in climbing class. Benjamin reckoned you fancied him.'

Miranda glowered. 'Did he really say that? I'll kill him.'

Wilhelm opened his mouth to say something else, but a great howl rose from back in the direction they had come, echoing through the empty streets. It sounded like thousands of sorrowful people crying out in pain.

'Will you two hurry up?' Timothy snapped. 'That's the order for the hunt. We have to get off the ground now.'

'I'll go first,' Miranda blurted, pushing Wilhelm away from the bottom of the ladder. 'I love climbing.'

'Told you,' Wilhelm said.

Fear got them to the top. By the time Wilhelm followed Miranda on to a platform surrounded by a wire cage with a door in one side, his heart had been pounding for so long he was certain he was having a heart attack. His shoulders and thighs screamed from the constant pull and push, and the palms of his hands were chapped from the roughness of the metal rungs.

'Through the door,' Emmie said, coming up behind them. 'That's our safe-house.'

The door in the cage opened inward. There was a perilous six inches of clear space underfoot before another door opened that led into the old Terror Tower ride car.

The interior of the car stank of human sweat and a thousand layers of food tastes gone stale. There appeared to be no windows, and the light through the open door was only enough to provide an outline of a poor living space: bundles of blankets in one corner, ragged boxes that might have contained food in another, a jumble of metal pipes and other crude weapons lying near the door.

Miranda and Wilhelm went inside. Emmie and Timothy followed them in, with Timothy closing the door and pulling across a safety bar.

'Okay, we can use the light now,' Emmie said from out of the pitch blackness.

Wilhelm heard Timothy moving over to the wall with the sureness of someone who had done this hundreds of time before. There was a rustle and then the room filled with pale green light. The glow illuminated Timothy standing with a piece of plywood in his hands. The light was fitted into the wall at the back of the room. It was vibrating slightly, making Wilhelm's vision go funny.

Emmie reached up and slid a piece of yellow plastic in front of it, changing the colour to a far more agreeable one.

'It's the emergency light,' she said. 'It reanimated. It's the best we can do. None of the others have yet.'

Fittings on the floor showed where seats had been bolted in, some of which had been stacked against the back wall, and Timothy urged them to sit down and rest. Emmie pulled out a plastic container of water out of a cubbyhole and offered them a drink. From another box she pulled a couple of round, green apples.

'There was an orchard by the south entrance,' she said. 'The fruit tastes a bit strange, but it's kept us alive these last months.'

Wilhelm turned one of the fruits over in his hands, glanced at Miranda and shrugged. Before she could shake her head, he bit into it, and chewed a piece down.

'Yuck. It's not sweet at all.'

Emmie shrugged. 'There's not much else. We find stuff washed up on the beaches from time to time, or sometimes old souvenir boxes have reanimated and reproduced, but the ghouls eat them if they find them. They don't seem to like fruit, though.'

'This place is crazy,' Wilhelm said.

Timothy sighed. 'You don't know the half of it. You'll find out in time.'

A drumming from outside caught Timothy's attention before he could say anything else. He exchanged a glance with Emmie, who nodded.

'They're hunting,' she said. 'Do you want to see? I think it might help you realise how much danger there is here.'

'The light,' Timothy said. 'Can't let them see it.'

Emmie went to stand by the door while Timothy covered the light. As soon as the room was pitch black, Emmie opened the door and let them back out into the cage at the top of the maintenance ladder.

'From here you can see them,' she said.

The sound was louder now, the thundering of hundreds of feet. At first Wilhelm could see nothing as he peered out of the cage's mesh walls at the ground below. Then Miranda's fingers closed over his arm, squeezing tight.

'Oh, I can see them. Wow.'

'Where?'

Miranda's voice trembled as she said, 'Everywhere.'

The ground below appeared to be moving as hundreds of black shapes rushed in all directions like ants hunting for food.

'They're searching for reanimates captured by the island,' Timothy said.

Wilhelm stared, hypnotised. The black shapes scuttled and ran, slithered and flapped. Their movements appeared to be random, but then a sudden cry rose from a couple of streets away.

'They've caught one,' Emmie said.

At the sound of the cry, the scuttling creatures stopped. They stood up on their hind legs and turned toward the sound. What had been a black, almost invisible army now exposed their pulsing dark orange undersides like hundreds of giant fireflies.

Then, in a sudden rush, they raced as one in the direction the cry had come from.

'I hope the reanimate can fly,' Emmie said, her voice hopeless. 'Otherwise he'll be a ghoul this time tomorrow.'

Wilhelm glanced at Miranda. The girl returned his look, and again her hand slipped into his, squeezing with an uncomfortable tightness that betrayed the fear she felt. He wondered as he watched the swarming mass of burned ghouls if she was thinking what he was thinking: that Lawrence was out there, trapped under the water, while other captured reanimates, who had managed to get up on to the island, were being dragged off one by one, to be thrown into the pit and turned into ghouls.

21

PLANS

'BENJAMIN, YOU PUT US IN AN UNCOMFORTABLE situation,' Moto said, his face-wheel revolving through a variety of emotions. 'I'm happy to see you, of course, but you can't ask us to take your side against the school authorities. The reanimates of Underfloor try to remain neutral in all situations, you know that.'

'I'm not asking you to take sides,' Benjamin protested. 'I'm just asking you not to hand me over. They'll imprison me again and I didn't do anything.'

'By harbouring you, we risk damaging our relationship with them,' Moto said. 'And it's tenuous already. There are those among the teaching staff who resent our sharing of the school. They would take any excuse to have us cast out.'

'I don't want to have anyone cast out,' Benjamin said. 'Can't you just tell no one?'

'It will be written in the annuals,' Moto said. 'Especially since you made your entrance through

Laurel's room. He's quite forgetful, but that will have left an impression. And there are those who work in the school too. You can hardly expect them to lie for you.'

Benjamin clenched his fists. He felt his magic down there, a growing knot in his stomach, wanting to be released. He would be imprisoned no longer. If they came for him again—whoever 'they' were—he would fight.

'This is complete injustice.'

'Haven't you always craved a return to your former life? Is it any better there?'

'No, but—'

'Then take what time you have to find out what's going on. We will do what we can to help.'

Benjamin lifted his eyes. 'But you said—'

Moto's face-wheel spun to an expression of happiness. 'I said we wouldn't harbour you. I didn't say we wouldn't assist you, providing what you ask concerns simple matters of research.'

Benjamin was about to reply when the door burst open and a familiar yet bizarre creature marched in. It looked like a racehorse which had died and been reincarnated as a disco dancer. A lucid purple satin shirt hung over a ribcage visible through decayed flesh.

'There you are. I heard you'd shown up here.' Gubbledon, housemaster of the pupils' dormitory, glared at Benjamin out of dead, milky eyes, one of which was covered by a monocle. 'Do you mind telling me what you're playing at? You're in duh … deep trouble, young man.'

At the best of times, Benjamin found it hard to look

directly at Gubbledon Longface, and now, being scolded by the housemaster whose stutter always worsened when he was angry, he found it impossible. He stared instead at two front hooves awkwardly forced into a water-damaged pair of neon pink Nike trainers.

'I was imprisoned for something I didn't do,' Benjamin said, aware of the petulance in his voice but unable to help it. 'I know I didn't hurt Cleat or leave the archive doors open, but I got blamed for it and locked in that tower room. I decided to let myself out.'

Gubbledon turned to glare at Moto, as though the reanimated motorbike was responsible too.

'What you're doing is the very reason the teachers forbid the use of reanimation magic,' Gubbledon snapped, his teeth clicking together as he talked. 'Don't you understand? If you don't pull back into line you could get cuh ... cast out.'

'I don't care,' Benjamin said.

Gubbledon shook his long head. 'Oh, I think you do. Your friends, Jacobs and Butterworth, cuh ... could you just walk away from them? Come on, Benjamin, see sense. Come back into the school, confess to escaping, and apologise. It's worked for Godfrey, and he was in league with the Dark Man.'

Benjamin looked up. 'Wait, wait. What worked for Godfrey?'

'Grand Lord Bastien has pardoned him for continued goodwill and for bravery in the face of danger. He's now the head prefect for all first-, second-, and third-year pupils.'

'Tell me this is a bad dream.'

'I'll tell you what, if you promise to return of your own accord and take measures to im … improve your behaviour while curbing your wanton use of forbidden muh … magic, I'll put in a good word for you. If you're lucky, the teachers' circle will agree to keep you busy in the locker room instead of ex … ex … expelling you.'

Benjamin scowled. He felt a tightening in his stomach again, the surge of power. It felt destructive, untamed. It would be easy to lash out, but he forced himself to take a long, slow breath.

'No,' he said. 'I will not be punished for something that I didn't do. I am seeking refuge in Underfloor.'

Gubbledon sighed and shook his big, horsey head. He looked at Moto. 'Well, I guess this makes it your problem. If you'll excuse me, I have to get the pupils ready for dinner.' He headed for the door, then paused as he reached it, looking back at Benjamin. 'If you change your mind, have someone find me. I like to think the pupils in my charge can trust me, so for that I'll say nothing about you being here.'

'I appreciate it.'

Gubbledon gave an awkward, lopsided shrug. 'For three days. That's long enough for you to come to your senses. After that, the requirement of my job that I concern myself with the welfare of the pupils in my charge means it would only be appropriate to inform the teachers of your whereabouts.'

Benjamin rolled his eyes and nodded. 'Fine.'

'Good luck, Buh … Buh … Benjamin.'

Moto found him a room he could use with a dusty old bed, while in Underfloor, unlike the rest of the school, there was plenty of good food. An old, reanimated gas stove going by the name of Arnold Kitchens cooked him up a delicious pumpkin pie using ingredients left over from the canteen and sent to the incinerator. While none of the reanimates actually required food for sustenance, some had the ability to enjoy it, so, like most pleasurable things, they had developed a system for its production. Benjamin, who was unsure when he had last eaten, tucked in with a welcome level of enthusiasm, particularly as the sweet but boring custard dumped over everything in the pupils' dining hall was nowhere to be found.

When he was done eating and had taken a nap on a bed far more comfortable than the one in his former cell room, he acquired a pen and paper and tried to arrange his muddled thoughts into a plan. Finding Miranda and Wilhelm became his priority. He had come to think of them as the other arms of his protective circle; together they were unbreakable, but alone he was no stronger than a piece of cracked glass.

Protesting his innocence could wait. No one would believe him anyway, which led him to the problem of Godfrey. The snakelike, green-eyed boy needed bringing down a peg or two. He had lied about Benjamin and stolen the book on dark reanimate. He had likely coshed Cleat over the head, too.

Benjamin needed allies. While Moto and the other reanimates would help him with day-to-day things, they would avoid anything that appeared they were picking sides. Getting other pupils involved just became complicated, so that left the teachers. On a sheet of paper stained with seawater circles, he drew three columns:

Likes me hates me doesn't care either way

The second column was easy to fill. He added Professor Eaves and Captain Roche, then to the third column he added Professor Loane, Ms. Ito, Mistress Xemian, Grand Lord Bastien, and a few other teachers who mostly taught the upper grades and whom he had only spoken to once or twice.

The first column was a bit more difficult. It took him a minute to think of anyone, then finally he wrote a single name: Edgar Caspian.

Edgar had only returned to the school a little under a year ago, after decades of exile for his refusal to hide the existence of reanimation magic from the pupils. Even now he was mistrusted by the other teachers, many of whom had never forgiven him for taking pupils displaying magical abilities—known as Miscreants—under his wing against the express wishes of the school. He now taught reanimation science to the lower years and basic manipulation logistics to elective groups containing only Channellers. He was also tasked with identifying which of the three basic principles of reanimation magic each pupil displayed.

Most kids at the school were Weavers. They had no magic of their own, but when in the presence of a Channeller—the second largest group—they provided a huge boost of power. Channellers could use small amounts of magic on their own, or larger amounts with the help of a Weaver. Those in the third group, Summoners, were capable of wielding vast amounts of power at a time.

Of the current pupils, there were only two known Summoners.

Benjamin, now a second-year, was one.

Godfrey, a year above, was the other.

It was becoming increasingly clear that within the walls of Endinfinium High, there wasn't room enough for both of them.

22

RISING DARKNESS

In the dim glow of the single candle on the table in the centre of the room, the assembled faces appeared to float in the air, disembodied. Godfrey, his hands behind his back, looked from one to the other, wishing he could see inside their souls to test their loyalty, but taking comfort in the fear he could sense like a thick, overbearing smell.

'Thank you for coming,' he said, clapping his hands together sharply enough to cause a collective intake of breath. 'I am pleased to see that all members of the Dark Reanimation Society are present. Our numbers continue to grow. Soon, we will be the largest society in the school, and our claim to legitimacy will be impossible to deny. First, a word from our patron.'

Professor Eaves stepped out of the shadows into the candlelight. The hunchbacked old man glanced around with his squinty, ratty eyes, nodding slowly as a smile spread across his face.

The Lost City of the Ghouls

'How many of you remember your first day here in Endinfinium?'

A few hands lifted. Godfrey nodded. A couple of kids from the higher years—disillusioned by years of secrecy into joining his fledgling society—shook their heads, but most nodded.

'And your impression was likely the same as mine, more years ago than I care to remember—that you had awoken in a hostile, unforgiving place, alone and helpless.'

A couple more nods.

'A terrifying experience, I'm sure. Yet many of you soon discovered that hiding within you was something you had never known before, a feeling of power, a way to manipulate the world around you. Am I correct?'

More nods.

'And you realised that in this place where the rules were different, you too were different, that you had a tool you could use to equalize the imbalance, to make yourselves safe?'

Mutters of agreement.

'So, how did you then feel when you were told that the use of this one tool to defend yourself was prohibited, upon pain of imprisonment or expulsion?'

A couple of pupils muttered angrily under their breath. Some, still unfamiliar with the use of reanimation magic, stayed quiet, while the rest nodded obediently like dogs on the first day of a behavioural training course.

Professor Eaves held up two hairy hands. 'I will tell you no lies. I admit to you now that I was one of those involved in prohibiting your use of your power. I agreed with the other senior figures of the school, and together we made that decision. You see, we too were afraid. It was a situation for which we had no logical solution, so we did what mankind has done since time immemorial: we attempted to suppress it.'

A couple of bolder kids muttered forceful agreement. Godfrey stepped forward. 'Tell them why you decided to turn against the teachers' circle, Professor.'

Professor Eaves grinned. 'You see, I have a different perspective to the rest of the teachers.' He stretched suddenly, and shook off his jacket. 'As you can see, unlike the others, I'm not all human.'

Great billowing wings plumed from Professor Eaves' shoulders and beat at the air. Several younger boys began to cry. Only a moment of forethought from Godfrey to grab a magical hold on the candle's flame prevented the room from plunging into darkness.

'I am, at least in part, a reanimate. And I consider the suppression of the magic that gave me life to be nothing less than an insult to my existence. Any questions?'

There was a hush around the room, the only sound one boy whimpering in the corner. Then, from back in the dark, one of the fifth-years muttered, 'Can you fly?'

'Of course I can fly!' Professor Eaves flapped his wings, creating a great draft that again threatened the candlelight, but otherwise succeeded only in knocking a box of spare candles to the floor. 'When there's enough available space,' the professor added.

'We are lucky,' Godfrey said, stepping forward while Professor Eaves awkwardly attempted to fold up his wings. 'The professor here is on our side. He gives legitimacy to our claims. It will soon be time to step out of the shadows and announce ourselves to the rest of the school. But now, it is time to swear allegiance to the good of the society. And in order to have your full trust, it is necessary to give you a demonstration of the power of dark reanimate.'

More whispers from back in the dark. Professor Eaves had succeeded in refolding his wings and now stood a little back from the light, his arms folded, his face set in an expression of satisfaction.

'Derek, bring the box.'

The tall third-year stepped forward, carrying a shoebox in his hands. He set it down on the table and removed the lid. Godfrey reached inside and withdrew the tiny body of a hamster lying on a bed of straw.

'This is my friend Snout's hamster,' Godfrey said, trying to keep the bitterness out of his voice that Snout had refused to come. 'It is a rarity to find non-reanimated animals other than humans here in Endinfinium. Other than some birds and fish, few survive the journey, yet this little guy did. Until, that is … I murdered him.'

Godfrey paused for dramatic effect, looking around the assembled faces, meeting the eyes of those that dared to meet his until they looked away. Good—they believed every word, and like fish caught on a hook, they were ready to be landed.

'Behold.'

He pulled a box from his pocket. He put it down on the table beside the hamster, his fingers tingling at the deep chill that emanated out. He lifted the lid, turned it upside down, and let a little black rock drop out.

'Dark reanimate. The giver of all life. Bow your heads, quickly now. Do not show disrespect to what gave this world life.'

All eyes dropped, even those of Professor Eaves. Godfrey smiled. They didn't even question it; he was a preacher, a magician, enchanting them, controlling them with his words, the most powerful magic of all.

'And now, with the blessing of the Dark Man, I will restore life to this pathetic beast.'

Godfrey gave the hamster a little tap, releasing the magic he had used to hold it still. It sat up, looked around, then scurried to the piece of valueless coal and took a tentative nibble.

'You see?' Godfrey shouted, raising his arms. 'While we play our games with magic, dark reanimate is the only thing that can truly give or take life.'

He considered beating the hamster to death with the piece of coal, but that might have spoiled the effect. Instead, he picked it up in his hands and gave it a little stroke.

'I'm sure that Snout will be delighted to hear of the return of his best—and only—friend,' Godfrey said. 'I will return Moffy personally.'

More murmurs. 'Moffy?' someone chuckled at the back.

'And with that, our meeting tonight is concluded,' Godfrey said. 'Go in peace, but remember what I said.

Dark reanimate can take life as easily as give it. Remember with your eyes, but say nothing with your mouths.'

The boys filed out, until only Godfrey and Professor Eaves remained. As soon as the door was closed, Professor Eaves knocked the piece of coal away across the floor and rounded on Godfrey.

'You play a dangerous game, boy,' he said. 'You really expect those kids to stay quiet about this? I told you, it should have been kept between us.'

Godfrey narrowed his eyes. 'Every one of them is a Weaver, Professor,' he said. 'We will need their strength if it comes to a battle.'

'A battle we have no chance of winning without this dark reanimate you speak of.'

'It's coming, Professor. Can't you feel it? Close your eyes. That cold in your heart. There it is. A few more days at most and we'll be able to exact our takeover, and prepare for the return of the Dark Man. And then we can all have what we want most of all.'

Professor Eaves gazed off into the distance and smiled. 'It would be nice to get a few more miles on the old clock, that's for sure.'

'The Dark Man will restore you to your youth, Professor.'

'His shadow has hung over the school for as long as I've known,' Professor Eaves said. 'How can you possibly know what he plans to do?'

'Because he has promised me. He tells me in my dreams every night. And it is time for us to carry out his greatest request, Professor. The usurper, Benjamin

Forrest—he is all that stands between us and the Dark Man's coming.'

Professor Eaves chuckled. 'I won't be sad to see the back of that boy,' he said. 'And I'm sure I won't be alone. This should be easy. He's under guard in a tower room.'

'We must be careful not to be found out,' Godfrey said. 'I will make a plan for Benjamin Forrest once I've been past the incinerator room to get rid of this useless rat—'

Godfrey yelped as Moffy, until then sitting quietly on Godfrey's palm, bit into his hand and leapt for freedom. Godfrey kicked out, trying to strike the hamster, but in the dark he couldn't see it.

'Useless thing.' He felt for his power, and sent a blast into the wall, making dust shower down, and the rocks tremble and break free from the ancient mortar.

'You, boy, have an impetuous streak,' Professor Eaves said. 'You would do as well to keep a calm head.'

'That stupid animal bit me.'

Professor Eaves frowned. 'Do you think it was a spy? I've seen stranger things….'

Godfrey scowled. His cheeks burned from his stupidity, and it felt like all his carefully considered plans were about to blow up in his face. The Dark Man wouldn't be pleased. Godfrey remembered the screams from the Shifting Castle, far, far to the west.

'We must make haste,' he said. 'Benjamin Forrest must be made to disappear. Tonight.'

23

PECULIARITIES

EDGAR CASPIAN WAS LEANING OVER THE DESK IN HIS study, his head in his hands, his pointed white beard bent into a little wave over the scarred wooden surface. A book lay open but turned face down near his right elbow. Near his left, a hand-painted ceramic mug with a chip in the lip steamed with something that smelled like coffee.

'Don't haunt me. I know you're there. I've been waiting for you to come.'

Peering through a crack in the wall, Benjamin hesitated. Did Edgar sense him? He had used no magic at all because Edgar would feel it, but perhaps his breathing was creating an echo. He opened his mouth to announce himself, when Edgar slammed a fist down on the table.

'I don't want you in my head,' he snapped. 'It hurts having you in there. If you are coming, then come. Stop tormenting me.'

Someone rapped on the door, then opened it before being bid enter. Ms. Ito stood there, her white hair frizzing over the straight black like smoke rising from a burned field. Spectacles balanced on her birdlike nose, and, as always, the over-long plaster cast led her into the room.

'There's news, Caspian,' she said with her familiar bluntness, as though each word was a knife-edge looking for something to chop. 'The boy has got out. Inevitable, I guess, with a runaway power like his.'

'The cold is seeping in,' Edgar said, running a hand through his thinning hair. 'Can't you feel it?'

'My word, you're starting to sound like Loane. What's got into you people?'

Edgar shook his head. 'I feel like my head is full of cold water. I can't think straight.'

'You're a man. It's an evolutionary failing. Are you surprised?'

Edgar grumbled something unintelligible and shook his head again.

'Did you not hear me? The boy has got out. He broke through the ward without even knowing he was doing it. He contains a power never known before and he has no control of it. Roche told me what happened in the forest.'

'An accident.'

'You really think so? Are you as stupid as you are mad?'

'I'm not mad. Just … tired.'

'He could be anywhere. All the pupils have been instructed to notify a teacher if they see him. And not to approach. We could see real deaths if he starts throwing his power about. Real deaths.'

Edgar groaned and clenched his fists in front of his face, then leaned over as though to touch his nose to the desk.

'This is my fault.'

'What is?'

'Benjamin ... the disappearance of Miranda and Wilhelm ... everything.'

Ms. Ito arched an eyebrow. 'I'd blame myself too, were I you. But to think you have so much influence is a little presumptuous, don't you think?' She snorted. 'I'd expect that kind of dung to come from Eaves's mouth, but I expect better from you.'

'I pushed for reanimation to be taught.'

Ms. Ito groaned. 'Bastien has wanted it for years. No one ever paid attention, did they?'

'But—'

'Snap out of it, Caspian. It's the boy that's caused this. You know it as well as I. There's been no contact with the Shifting Castle since I was running around these corridors in a frilly frock and ballet shoes. Then Bastien has a dream about a boy showing up on the beach and he's off on his magic carpet to negotiate. Next thing we know, there's a new boy causing trouble around the school and we have an army of ghouls bearing down on us. You want to tell me that's a coincidence?'

'No, but—'

'I'm telling you, it's that boy. Forrest. He's upset the balance, and it was on a precipice as it was. He's dangerous, and now he's out there somewhere, who knows what could happen?'

'What about the others? Miranda and Wilhelm?'

'What about them?'

Edgar shifted in his chair to look up at her. 'They've been missing over a week. Lawrence has also gone.'

'Are you expecting me to show normal human emotion for a pair of troublemakers and your reanimated pet?' Ms. Ito lifted her cast to give the floorboards a hard crack. 'How long do you have to wait, Caspian?'

'Does it not concern you at all?'

'Butterworth is a weak Channeller and Jacobs a mere Weaver. If I allowed myself to feel sorrow for every kid who walked out of this place, I'd be drinking the stuff, would I not? We have far greater issues to deal with.'

'The Grand Lord freed Godfrey.'

Ms. Ito smiled. 'A commendable decision. A fine young man.'

Benjamin, his face pressed against the cold stone, frowned. Had he misheard?

'You think Benjamin's dangerous? Godfrey's turned against us at every possible opportunity. He's the dangerous one, not Benjamin.'

Ms. Ito shook his head. 'He's done everything since his return to prove that he's learned his lesson. A pity others couldn't follow his example. If there were more boys like Godfrey in Endinfinium High we likely wouldn't have so many problems.'

Edgar looked about to protest, then sighed. 'Maybe you're right,' he said. 'Right now I'm too tired to care.'

Ms. Ito stumped back to the door. 'Get yourself to the nurse if you're not feeling well,' she grunted. 'You sound like a race car with a flat tire.'

Edgar smiled. 'I feel like one.'

Ms. Ito didn't smile back. She scowled at him, then went out, the door slamming behind her as her cast clumped off down the corridor.

As soon as the door was closed, Edgar leaned over the table, his head on his hands, and began to shake as though caught in a strong wind.

'So cold,' he muttered again, then at last pushed himself to his feet, stumbled to a cot bed fitted into an alcove, and lay down.

'Sleep,' he murmured, lifting a hand to point at the gas lamp flickering in the corner. Benjamin felt a sudden flush as Edgar's magic extinguished the flame, then the room plunged into darkness.

After a few moments, Edgar's quiet snoring became the only sound. Benjamin watched through his peephole, his eyes slowly widening as Edgar first appeared in profile outline, then his features became clearer, and finally Benjamin could make out the creases in the old professor's clothes.

A chill made his skin crawl. The source of the light, a dark, almost sunset orange, was emanating from Edgar himself.

24

FOG

SIMON PATTERSON, THE BOY EVERYONE LIKED TO CALL Snout, took his regular seat in the third row of Professor Loane's Earth History class. Twenty pupils would usually be present, a mixture of electives from the first, second and third years. Snout, officially a third-year, even though he had arrived near the end of the third term and as a result had always struggled to fit in, was one of four others from his year. To his right sat Cherise White, a snarly third-year girl who was nevertheless too beautiful to look directly at for fear of being caught looking, and directly in front of him Tommy Cale, a diminutive second-year who spent most of each lesson doodling cartoon characters Snout could no long remember in his notebook. Behind him, unfortunately, was Derek Bates, Godfrey's current best friend, who usually spent the first twenty minutes of the lesson poking Snout in the back with whatever stationery he had to hand, before getting bored and falling asleep.

The Lost City of the Ghouls

Professor Loane, always a good sport, only ever woke up the pupils likely to benefit from his teaching. Derek was left to sleep.

Today's topic was the third in a series on the Spanish Armada, something that Snout found of great interest, particularly after part of a Spanish galleon had washed up on the beach below the school just last month. Professor Loane had led an expedition, and the pupils had even managed to find a few old coins among the wreckage. Unfortunately, after a week of sitting idle, the wreck had reanimated one night and disappeared back into the sea. Snout had mourned its passing, but the opportunity to see something authentic that connected to their current class topic had brought a far greater realism than any textbook or blackboard diagram.

'Where's Speckles?' muttered Cherise, using the currently accepted nickname for the suddenly greying professor. 'It's five past.'

Snout, who knew by default that the question wasn't for him, stayed silent and stared at the score lines in his desk. Once, in another world, someone had hacked *Bazza luvs Gina '84* in the surface, while someone else had added a rude word in front of Gina's name that Snout had spent a couple of lessons picking off with the tip of a compass. It wasn't nice to disrespect the possibly dead.

The seconds ticked by. By quarter past, with still no sign of the usually punctual professor, the classroom had descended into chaos. Three first-years had gamely tried to do some work in their notebooks, only for Derek to throw one book onto the top of a glass cabinet filled with rusty war medals. At the back of the room, Cherise was snogging a third-year from the rugby team called Pete Thompson, while Tommy Cale was trying to get his pen out from where Derek had kicked it under the teacher's desk.

The door flew open.

The pupils froze where they sat or stood. One of the first-years was half on top of a cabinet with Derek's arms wrapped around his leg, the older boy's face frozen in a smile. Cherise and Peter had snapped apart like a broken egg, and now stood comically back to back. Snout, playing with a spider he had found in his desk, was the only pupil actually sitting down.

Mistress Xemian, as dark as Ms. Ito was pale and as tall and slender as Captain Roche was squat and wide, glided into the room, the flowering dark green skirt that hung down to her ankles revealing nothing of legs that reached to most of the pupil's chests. So tall that only certain classrooms—particularly those in the maths block where she was usually found—were comfortable for her, Mistress Xemian had a smooth, ageless face that was a magnet for pupils' eyes, a smile that attracted adoration, and a deep, calming voice that relaxed rather than anaesthetised.

'I gather you found yourselves with a little time on your hands. It would be appropriate for you to find your seats once more.'

With a shuffling of feet, everyone found their way back to their desks. Even Derek sat upright, and the first-years, none of whom would have yet been taught by

Mistress Xemian, stared at her as though she had appeared in a cloud of smoke.

'Professor Loane is suffering a malady. As are, incidentally, most of the other teachers. I must admit to feeling a little queasy myself, although it appears to have struck the male teachers worst of all. It has been decided that you will return to your dormitory and be placed under a temporary quarantine. If there is an infection going around, it would be best to contain and then eradicate it before it causes further harm, wouldn't you think? Are there any questions?'

Fat Adam stuck up a hand.

'Your name, boy.'

'Adam Kimber, Miss.'

'And what is your question?'

'I wondered about dinner, Miss. Will we still go to the dining hall?'

'You'll be given information soon. The kitchen staff are, for obvious reasons, immune to any such infectious outbreak.'

'It's a plague,' Derek whispered, poking Snout in the back with a ruler.

'All classes are suspended until further notice,' Mistress Xemian said. 'Your housemaster, Gubbledon, is arranging extracurricular entertainment, and we are in consultation with some of the reanimates to arrange additional lectures and seminars on a variety of topics of interest. Schooling will continue, albeit in a different form. However, if you begin to feel unwell, be sure to notify Gubbledon at once in order that you may be placed under observation in the nurse's room.'

Tommy Cale stuck up a hand.

'Yes … Tommy, isn't it?'

'That's right, Miss. Is that where Butterworth, Jacobs, and Forrest are? Did they get sick?'

Mistress Xemian's assured demeanour faltered momentarily before she regained her composure. 'I'm afraid that Miss Butterworth and Masters Forrest and Jacobs are currently missing.'

'Did they get taken by scatlocks?'

Mistress Xemian's face hardened. 'Master Bates, I would prefer you to raise your hand if you wish to ask a question. Basic politeness is a foundation upon which civilization is built, is it not?'

Derek squirmed in his seat. 'Just worried about my friends,' he said.

At the obvious lie, there were murmurs of protest from the back, but Mistress Xemian ignored them.

'As we all are,' she said. 'And the best for everyone right now is to stay calm, wouldn't you think?'

A couple of other hands went up.

'Yes, Cherise?'

'Is Professor Loane going to die?'

Mistress Xemian laughed. It was the coldest thing about her, but it still filled the room like the fluttering of a dove's wings.

'Don't worry. I've seen the professor survive a lot worse than this. He's got a little chest infection, that's all. I'm sure he'll be back to impart the delights of Earth History upon you within a few days. One more question … hmm. Adam again?'

'If we're quarantined, will we still have sausages for dinner this week? Godfrey said—'

'I don't care what Godfrey said.' Mistress Xemian's palm had paused a centimetre above the desktop, but her face was as hard as if she had struck it. Snout had never seen her so angry. 'We will not worry about trivial things at this time. Now, everyone, pack up your books, and let's get you over to the dormitories.'

Snout fell into line with the others as they filed out. Derek had caught hold of his arm and was jabbing him in the back with a finger, but his attention was elsewhere. Adam was muttering about dinner. Tommy was rabbiting to Cherise about card games, while she was glaring at Pete Thompson, who was in conversation with Amy Simkins at the front of the queue.

They passed no one as they made their way back to the clifftop precipice that led to the rickety wooden dormitory. Mistress Xemian waited as they donned scatlock capes and one by one made their way across. Snout was second to last in front of Tommy Cale. Mistress Xemian helped the little boy put on his cape, then gave them both a wave.

'Take care over there,' she said, in a hollow voice that made Snout fearful something truly bad was about to happen.

He went out onto the precipice and waited for Tommy to follow, feeling protective of the little boy. Mistress Xemian closed the door, and for a moment Snout saw her watching them through the glass, then she bowed her head, turned and walked away, disappearing into the shadows of the school.

'Right, over we go,' Snout said, reaching out to take Tommy's hand.

'Foggy today, isn't it?' Tommy said, as they started out.

Snout, who usually kept his eyes firmly on the narrow path at their feet, looked out toward the sea.

Tommy was right. The fog had really closed in, leaving them not so much as a view of the beach below, let alone the edge of the world a couple of miles out from shore.

Snout frowned. It was the first time he could ever remember fog so thick.

'It's chilly too,' Tommy said.

'We'd better get over then,' Snout said, leading Tommy across, throwing one last glance over his shoulder as they went inside at the white veil that entirely obscured the sea, thinking that to have such a sudden fogbank roll in was really quite strange indeed.

25

DISCOVERIES

WILHELM OPENED HIS EYES AND ROLLED OVER TO look at Miranda, who was snoring, her mouth wide open to release great tremulous groans that made the plywood fitted over the reanimated light shudder in its makeshift fittings.

'They've gone out again, by the look of it,' he said, shaking her awake.

Glimmers of light peeked in through cracks in the ancient ride car and from around the door. The piles of blankets where Timothy and Emmie always lay were empty, pulled back, and their shoes were gone, too.

'Okay, that's it,' Wilhelm said, pulling back his own blankets and going to the door. He pulled it open, flooding the room with grey light. Outside, the vague outline of the yellow sun peered through the haze, announcing what Endinfinium called dawn. The red sun, usually visible near the western horizon at this time of day, was entirely hidden by the fog rising off the sea around the island.

'What's going on?' Miranda replied, sitting up and rubbing her eyes. 'I feel like I haven't slept at all.'

'We're sleeping too much is the problem,' Wilhelm said. 'I don't care what Timothy and Emmie say. I'm going outside today. I'm sick of being cooped up in here.'

'Have they gone out again?'

Wilhelm picked a flake of rust off the metal wall and tossed it out of the doorway. 'Of course they have. Every day. Foraging, scouting, whatever they want to call it. What a waste of time.'

'I thought they were trying to find a way off the island?'

'Yeah, and if they do, do you really think they'll come back and get us?'

Miranda smoothed her hair with her hands. 'So what do you suggest? We haven't even got a map, and you saw how many of those burned ghouls there were. Say we don't make it back before dark? What then?'

Wilhelm waved her to the doorway. He pointed to the left. 'See it? That rollercoaster?'

'The big one?'

Wilhelm nodded. 'It's way higher than where we are now. If we climb up to the top, we'll be able to see the whole island. We'll be able to get our bearings and come up with a plan.'

'I thought you didn't like heights?'

Wilhelm stepped out on to the mesh platform above the maintenance ladder that was their only way down.

'I don't. But I'm getting used to them.'

He gave the wire mesh a little press with his foot, but something cracked so he stepped back into the doorway, almost knocking Miranda over.

'Yeah, not a good idea.'

She gave him a weak punch on the arm, then hugged him from behind.

'Let's do it,' she said. 'I've finished reading all their books.'

Getting down the ladder took a lot longer than getting up had because of the constant fear of falling and the relentless need to check their own footing, but after what felt like fifty years of hanging over an ominous drop, Wilhelm's feet finally touched solid ground.

'We'd better watch out for ghouls,' Miranda gasped, when they both stood at the bottom, their breathing harsh and ragged.

'Timothy said the ghouls slept during the day, but I don't believe that for a second.'

They headed what they felt was north, in the direction of the towering rollercoaster. Having spent three days holed up in Timothy and Emmie's bolt hole while their hosts went foraging during the day, both were eager to explore, and despite the obvious danger, found themselves peering around doors, through windows, and over balconies as they passed through sections of the park built to resemble different ancient civilizations.

Wilhelm soon realised that the park came from his future, but for Miranda, who scoffed at how archaic some of the futurisms were, it had come from some time in the past. An area labeled Moonbase World, for example, contained a number of structures Wilhelm had never seen in picture books, but Miranda shrugged them off as out-of-date.

'Yeah, they started off building them like this,' she said. 'Those round ones didn't work in the solar wind. I remember watching a documentary about it in history class. I think they went with triangle shapes in the end, but for whatever reason I don't remember. I was probably dozing off by that point.'

And while he remembered rollercoasters from a rare orphanage day out a year or so before he woke up under a tree in the Haunted Forest, none were as spectacular as this rusting, twisted ruin had once been: towering peaks and cascading spirals, near-vertical rises dropping into rolls of loops like the stretched remains of giant bed springs.

He was still marveling at it when Miranda grabbed his shoulder.

'Ghouls,' she said.

She pulled Wilhelm back behind a pillar, and together they peered out at an open plaza littered with the charred remains of hundreds of random shapes, the objects they had once been distorted into mere remnants of their original forms.

'Can you feel it?' she said.

'The cold?'

'Yes.'

Wilhelm nodded. Despite the fog, the air was warm,

but in his heart he felt a damp chill as though he had swallowed an ice cube that refused to melt.

'It's coming from them,' Miranda said.

Without warning, she stepped out from behind the pillar and walked straight out across the plaza. Wilhelm hissed at her to come back, but when she ignored him he reluctantly ran out after her, catching up as she came to a stop just a few paces from the closest burned remains.

'They only come out at night,' she whispered. 'Why do you think that is?'

Wilhelm shrugged. 'Conserving energy?'

Miranda cocked her head. 'Could be.'

'Perhaps they just get tired like everything else.'

Miranda shook her head. She stepped forward and nudged the nearest blackened lump of metal with her foot.

The creature, a mixture of a speaker cabinet for a torso with two guitar fretboards for arms, jerked up, knocking its nearest companions aside. Human eyes blinked from out of a skull shape set into a moulded plastic upper frame, looked from Wilhelm to Miranda, then closed again. The ghoul slumped back down among the others.

'Creepy,' Wilhelm muttered, then looked at his feet as though they had acted without instruction to take him ten or twenty paces back from where Miranda stood. As the ghoul went still again, Miranda slowly retraced her steps to Wilhelm's new position.

'Might be best not to disturb them,' she said.

'Come on,' Wilhelm said. 'Let's go find our hosts.'

Timothy and Emmie had often talked about the orchard where they collected most of their food. They claimed it was outside the south entrance, on the opposite side of the park to where Wilhelm and Miranda had arrived, growing on a makeshift beach that had once been the edge of a boating lake long ago broken off the island like a calving glacier.

With the park proving far larger than either had expected, and few information signs having escaped the island's speedy progression of age, they headed for the ticket gates for the largest of the rollercoasters. It was enormous, towering over the surrounding area, as high as a block of flats, and made up of two connected tracks that interwove with each other. A rare surviving sign announced it as "Double Helix: The World's Most Terrifying Coaster".

'This should be easy,' Wilhelm said, pointing to a maintenance platform protruding from the highest peak which towered over their secret home in the Terror Tower. 'It's on a slope.'

The rollercoaster's starting straight was a steep incline up to its highest point, where the maintenance platform stood. Wilhelm could imagine crowds of terrified kids screaming in their ride cars as they trundled to the top, stood for a few dramatic seconds then plunged over the edge into a sheer drop that accelerated them through the next series of loops and curves. Alongside the incline was a maintenance staircase, but it had taken a far greater battering than the enclosed ladder on the Terror Tower, with whole sections rusted through and fallen away. Several times they had to climb across onto the old tracks and shimmy up old metal frames that threatened to break away beneath their hands.

When they finally made it, both were caked in rust and ancient grease, soaked in sweat, and gasping for breath.

'Well, at least we can see where we are,' Wilhelm said. 'Which way's south?'

The abandoned theme park lay spread out around them. Tourist streets lined with abandoned shops and restaurants twisted among the remains of rollercoasters, boating lakes, fake jungle canopies, and dirty, rubbish-strewn plazas. The amphitheatre and its glowing pit were visible not far to the north, its surface covered during daylight hours by a sheet of metal. A little to the northwest rose the tower, its height insignificant compared to the platform on which they now stood.

'That's not an orchard,' Miranda said.

Wilhelm turned. To the south the fog had lifted somewhat, revealing a plaza surrounded by ticketing gates, but whereas to the north the land fell quickly away to the water's edge, to the south houses bunched close to it, streets led away, and even an old train station was visible.

'It's part of a city,' Miranda said. 'They must be foraging in there for food.'

'And that's where most of the rubbish must be coming from,' Wilhelm added. 'I wondered how a theme park could have so many fridges and televisions.'

'If everything in there is slowly turning into ghouls,

it won't be long before they'll have a huge army,' Miranda said.

Wilhelm said nothing. He turned to look north again, beyond where a fog bank obscured the sea and with it the section of the island's edge where Lawrence was trapped underwater. Something had caught his attention, a dark protrusion poking out of the cloud.

'See that?' Wilhelm said, pointing. 'Do you know what that is? Oh dear. That's not good at all.'

Miranda frowned. 'It's not part of the island, is it?'

Wilhelm shook his head. 'We're moving,' he said. 'Drifting slowly north. I know what that is because I used to climb it.' He gave a long sigh. 'It's the teachers' tower at Endinfinium High.'

26

CLASSMATES

It was the same wherever he looked. The burned orange light emanated from everywhere, as though a creeping mould was taking over the school. Benjamin, sneaking through the hidden corridors of Underfloor like a mouse in the school's walls, spied on everyone he could find, and it was the same. The male teachers had all taken to their beds, afflicted by an indefinable sickness, while the female teachers were also slowly succumbing. He had found three of them, Ms. Ito, Mistress Xemian, and Ms. Castillo—the language teacher for the fourth- and fifth-years—deep in conversation, but behind the flickering of the candles the orange wash rose up the walls, and Benjamin knew it was only a matter of time before they too succumbed.

The pupils, though, were another matter. He had seen one group being led by a faltering Captain Roche back to the dorms, and while the captain himself was clearly struggling with whatever afflicted him, the kids in his charge were entirely unaffected. He had closed his eyes and concentrated, but while the chill of dark reanimate had emanated from Captain Roche, the kids were normal. Seemingly unconcerned, they had been looking forward to enjoying a few days free from classes.

Eventually, certain that the school was almost deserted, Benjamin left Underfloor and headed back into the corridors of the school proper.

It felt good to not be squeezing through dusty, cobwebbed spaces between walls, for while the central area of Underfloor was open and spacious, most of the secret passages that led all over the school were narrow, low-ceilinged and difficult to navigate. There was also no way across to the pupils' dormitory.

With no one around to challenge him, he headed straight for the kitchens. Hunger had gnawed at him for several hours, but he had another reason to visit. As he tucked into a bowl of vegetables left over from today's lunch, he looked around for the remains of Sara Liselle, but didn't see her. Other cleaners ambled back and forth, paying him no attention, but of the girl there was no sign.

After eating his fill, he headed down to the nurse's bay. Nurse Meiling was nowhere to be seen, but old Cleat lay on a cot against one wall. He had bandages wrapped around his head and his eyes were closed. Benjamin sat down next to him and reached out for the old man's hand.

'Cleat,' he whispered. 'Can you hear me?'

The hand jerked, and the old man groaned. Benjamin concentrated, reaching out to Cleat with his magic. He remembered what Edgar had taught him about using it: 'Try to visualise what you want to achieve. Use it to build, not destroy.'

He opened his eyes. Cleat was staring up at him.

'You,' Cleat muttered. 'There you are.'

'Who hit you, Cleat?' Benjamin asked. 'Was it Godfrey? I know it was.'

Cleat gave a barely perceptible shake of the head. 'No. Not Godfrey.' His eyes drifted from Benjamin's, and his breath came out in a long sigh. 'We were classmates, you and I. What became of you, old friend? I often … wondered.'

Benjamin frowned. Cleat's eyes closed, and his breathing went shallow. Instinctively Benjamin knew he had done something wrong, that he had taken a great risk in trying to pull Cleat out of his slumber. To try further might harm the old man irreversibly. Instead, he adjusted Cleat's head on the pillow to make him more comfortable then tidied the blanket over him, and resolved to return to check on the old man again as soon as he could.

Then he left the nurse's room and headed back upstairs to the entrance. Mrs. Martin, the school secretary, and the twin sister of the secretary of Benjamin's school back in England, wasn't behind her desk. Benjamin used a little magic to pick the lock, and went inside.

Everything hummed with reanimation. The teachers' collective sickness meant things weren't getting done, and in a place with a high concentration of salvaged modern appliances like the school office, it wouldn't be long before the reanimation was out of control. Benjamin squeezed between a rocking photocopier and a fridge that was shuffling back and forth to get to a tall chest of drawers at the back of the office.

It was a long shot, but he guessed if there were records of former pupils anywhere, they would be here.

He began going through each drawer. Most of them were filled with nothing: stationery, paper stocks, lists of salvaged items, class lists, drafts of timetables, lunch menus so similar that their pointlessness indicated too much free time for whoever was making them, enrollment forms as equally unnecessary, dormitory sleeping layout plans, even a list of school uniforms and how many needed to be made before the next entrance ceremony.

Finally, near the bottom he found a drawer labeled "Triangulation". Inside were several plastic files of varying degrees of newness. In the topmost, the first sheet of typed paper was a record of the most recent triangulation, with the names of Sara Liselle, Timothy Long and Emmie Bromwich under the option for leaving the school. Benjamin began to thumb through the pages, seeing lists of names he didn't recognise.

With the humming all around him growing in intensity, he thumbed his way back until he found an age-worn sheet with "Terrance Cleat" written under the option for school service. Then, with a shaking finger, he searched down through the rest of the list.

He was anticipating the name of Professor Eaves, but when he found the single name he recognised he felt

The Lost City of the Ghouls

a shiver go down the back of his neck. He dropped the folder to the floor and backed away shaking his head, muttering, 'No, no, no,' under his breath as he pushed between the bumping appliances and stumbled out of the office door, leaving it swinging loose behind him as he dashed for the school's main entrance.

Pushing through the glass doors, he ignored the wisps of fog that drifted past his face and the scatlocks diving and wheeling in the air around him as he stumbled to the stone wall that bordered the outer courtyard from the tumbling cliffs below. There, he vomited up what he had just eaten, then stood up, realising that the sea was gone, replaced by a tumultuous shifting cloud with a single twist of metal appearing out of its upper reaches, but unable to fully comprehend what he was seeing because of the white elephant crushing down on his chest and the memory of the name he had found written on the old piece of triangulation paper.

Instead of the name he had been expecting, he had found another name, one he recognised.

His own.

PART II
LANDFALL

27

REDUCED

Edgar woke to a bed soaked with sweat. He groaned through a headache far worse than any he could remember and reached out with his magic to tug a little oil and flame into the gas lamp, using a sharp twist of the air around it to make the gas ignite.

Light filled the room, a dark, burnt orange. Edgar frowned, trying to recall a dream. The clawed fingers of a hand protruding from a robe, the glowing orange eyes of a face hidden in shadow beneath a hood, words that sounded underwater, calling his name.

Come. Come.

Edgar sat up, the room spinning around him. His stomach constricted, but whatever he had eaten yesterday stayed down. With a sharp thrust, he found his feet and staggered across the room to his desk.

A pen and a sheet of paper lay on the desktop, and Edgar stared at the words written there until they came into focus, wondering if he could possibly have written such a terrible thing.

Reduce Benjamin Forrest.

He had repeated the word "reduce" more than fifteen times. Some versions were tidy and neat, others were scrawled across the page, and one had torn right through the paper to leave a pen line on the wood surface beneath.

He had no recollection of writing them, but the very nature of the world 'reduce' brought a frown to his face. What could that mean? Not kill, or destroy, or even expel … but reduce.

Reduce into what?

Something creaked behind him. Edgar turned, but it was only the door, standing slightly ajar, creaking in a breeze from somewhere further up the corridor. His study was on the same level as the water systems outlet from the upper floor shower blocks, and sometimes the system was flushed. Rust was particularly susceptible to reanimation, and several hundred little rust mites running around in the pipes could cause a blockage. It usually came with a creaking groan loud enough to wake him, but he had slept right through.

And he always locked the door before he slept, placing a little ward on it to ensure he wouldn't be disturbed.

He staggered across the room, absently wishing his legs would wake up, but the lock had his full attention.

The ward was still there, a tiny circle of warmth only someone looking for it would notice, but it was broken.

Someone had come in while he slept.

He went back to the desk. The scrawl, although erratic, was in his own handwriting, and as he stared at it, more meaning came.

Forrest … the boy was a troublemaker. The Dark Man's eyes had turned to Endinfinium High after years of calm, and Benjamin Forrest had been the trigger. The boy had riled the Dark Man enough to raise an army to destroy the school. Many people had nearly died. The rule concerning the Dark Man had always been the same: don't poke the hornet's nest.

While the Dark Man kept his distance, they were safe.

Benjamin Forrest had endangered everything by forcing them to confront the existence of reanimation magic. The boy was an abomination.

He had to be reduced, for the good of everyone.

But what did that mean?

And hadn't Edgar himself gone into exile because he disagreed with the denial of the reanimation magic upon which the whole of Endinfinium was built?

He gave a vehement shake of the head, then swiped up the only thing in reach—a ceramic cup in which stood a number of pens and pencils he had found along the shoreline. Many of them had intricate designs, floral patterns, twisting snakes made of metal, and the cup itself was in some world an ancient thing, ornately carved into a latticework pattern, its surface lined by the cracks of great age.

With a howl, he flung it to the floor. The cup shattered on the flagstones and the stationery scattered.

Then, gathering his magic, he dragged the pieces of the cup back together and moulded them into a monstrous version of what they once had been, then once more slammed the object into the flagstones.

He had nothing of the power Benjamin could harness if he only understood how. The boy was ignorant, lacking the ability to see inward. The teachers had known it immediately, and if ever there had been a boy for which an Oath such as that of Endinfinium High had been created, it was Benjamin Forrest.

Ms. Ito was right. He could not be allowed to run free. He had to be stopped before he caused more damage.

Edgar slumped down on his chair. The pain that savaged him now ran right down his back, as far as his hips. It was Benjamin Forrest's fault. Everything was Benjamin's fault. The figure in the dream said so.

As Edgar began to scream, a desperate wail that was anger and suffering intertwined with one another, a vision of himself and Benjamin as friends attempted to claw through the veil covering his sanity, but with one swift bloom of his magic, he blew it apart, and only one solution remained.

Benjamin Forrest had to be stopped.

He had to be *reduced*.

28

CROSSING

'Look closely. You can see them moving.'

Miranda brushed a matted lock of hair out of her eyes and squinted. She resisted the urge to use a little magic to sharpen her gaze, a trick Edgar had taught her. Thin out a tunnel of air between you and the target area, and watch everything become clearer.

No, she wasn't to use magic. She understood the dangers, but nevertheless, the urge was overwhelming.

Three days of sneaking out after Tim and Emmie had left in the early morning and they were yet to find their supposed friends, but each day had revealed greater levels of peril that threatened Endinfinium High and everyone who lived within it.

Not all the ghouls slept during the day. In fact, vast numbers of them were employed in stripping down the houses of the adjacent city and dragging whatever they could find to the edges of the pit, ready for the evening's ritualistic burning ceremony.

The mystery of the city and the theme park nagged at Miranda. The theme park felt far older, as though it had already been abandoned when the city was built alongside it, even though that made no sense at all. Perhaps the park contained something of value? Street signs were visible, albeit in a language neither knew. The houses, squat and low, built with stocky walls, suggested its original location was somewhere cold.

'It looks like a polar research station,' Wilhelm said. 'I saw one in a book once. And it did say "the most northerly theme park" on the entrance sign. Perhaps it got abandoned but there was loads of stuff here for the people to use.'

'Yeah, but isn't it a bit big for something like that? It's like a whole town.'

'Perhaps they had a lot of research to do.'

'Maybe.'

'There's only one way to find out. Let's go in and have a look around.'

'Just as long as I can use my magic if we get in trouble.'

'You'll have to, otherwise we'll be stuck. Let's hope we can avoid it, though.'

They climbed down from the roof of an old children's theatre from where they had been observing the city's nearest streets, traversing a rickety fire-escape on the rear wall. Less than a football pitch's length from the park's exit and the city's entrance, it had allowed them to spot teams of twisted ghouls emptying out the houses one by one, piling the trash into the street and then hauling it back to the park, where they dumped it into great heaps in the southern entrance plaza.

'Lots of things here,' Wilhelm said. 'One thing I don't see, however, is an orchard.'

Miranda shook her head. Neither wanted to believe Tim and Emmie were lying, but the baskets of fruit they returned with each evening had to be coming from somewhere.

'Perhaps they meant on the other side of the city?'

'Let's find out.'

It wasn't easy to get to the city without being seen. Comically holding up the doors of two old fridges they had found like big plastic shields, they skirted the southern plaza until they found themselves at the remains of a perimeter fence. Mostly rusted down to jagged fingers of wire, there were ample holes to climb through, and soon they found themselves on a thin strip of rubbish-strewn beach.

'I bet this used to be a frozen river,' Wilhelm said. 'When it ended up here, it melted. Do we really have to swim across?'

What had likely once been a single strip of land separated by a frozen river was now two distinct islands with narrow triangles of sea on either side of a single bridge. Ghouls moved back and forth across from the city to the park, carrying rubbish then going back for more.

'It's the best way,' Miranda said, glaring at Wilhelm, remembering an argument they'd had the day before. 'Strip down, put your clothes in the bag.'

She pulled out a plastic bag they had pinched from

Timothy and Emmie's hideout and held it open. It was quiet, but in one corner showed signs of a previous attempt to reanimate. Wilhelm, blushing with self-consciousness, stripped down and piled his clothes inside. When he was done, he stood awkward and naked on the beach, like a reluctant winter swimmer.

'Now, hold it out and close your eyes. Do not open them or I will gouge them out.'

'Sure, sure, just hurry up. There's far too much breeze.'

Miranda stripped down, glaring at Wilhelm the whole time for any hint of his opening his eyes. To be fair, he heeded her warning well, keeping them tightly shut. She was only thirteen, but she had been reading a lot of stories in the common room at the dormitory, and liked the idea of being treated like a princess. And every princess needed to maintain her dignity.

'Keep them shut. I'll get into the water first. Once I'm in, I'll tell you. Keep your eyes on your feet, though. Okay?'

'Sure, whatever. Just hurry up.'

Miranda tied the bag as best she could and then ran over to the water's edge. It was as cold and unpleasant as she remembered it, and the current bumped her about as it splashed and sloshed between the two islands. Holding the bag over her head, she waded out, until the freezing water was up to her neck.

'Okay. Come on.'

Wilhelm, holding his hands in front of him to protest his modesty, ran to the water's edge and dipped a toe into the water.

'It's so cold.'

'Yes. As you can see, I'm already aware of that. Get a move on.'

'Can't I go round and meet you on the other side?'

She was about to spit an angry reply when she spotted the small crease of a smile. Instead she just gritted her teeth and snapped, 'Hurry. Up.'

Wilhelm climbed into the water, holding one hand over his mouth to suppress yelps of shock. Miranda held the bag still and waited as he waded over.

'Right, there's a bit of a gap we have to swim across, but it's only a few feet. Are you ready?'

Wilhelm nodded. 'Let's go.'

The edge of the city island was no more than a swimming pool's length away. Their intended landing spot was behind a large outhouse built right on the very edge, which would give them plenty of cover from the stream of ghouls moving back and forth across the bridge.

'Here goes.'

Miranda pushed off, kicking hard with her legs to propel herself forward, holding the bag over one shoulder and using her free arm to balance herself. Behind her, Wilhelm, who'd always hated swimming class at the school, floundered as though weights were tied to his feet. By the time they were halfway across, Miranda was five or six metres in front.

'Come on, hurry up. If I have to wait for you on the far side, you have to swim the remainder with your eyes shut. You know that, don't you?'

Wilhelm grimaced. 'I saw something down there.'

'Where?'

'Under my feet. It was moving.'

Miranda gulped. She remembered Lawrence, stuck to the northern side of the island, and wondered what else might be down there. Things were supposed to stick, weren't they?

'Help!'

Wilhelm's arms flailed, and his head went under. Miranda turned, kicking back toward him. She was almost over his spot when something hard and metal closed around her ankle, pulling her under.

Water filled her mouth, stifling a cry. Wilhelm was flailing nearby, legs and arms kicking out. Something had a hold of him too, so Miranda reached out with her magic and gave it a little shove, breaking its grip on both of them.

She bobbed back to the surface as something blocky and metal flashed past her. She took a desperate breath of air and looked around for Wilhelm. He was a short distance behind her, treading water, watching a grey shape as it emerged from the water and hauled itself up on to the shore.

It looked like a rowing boat with arms.

'It was trying to get out,' Wilhelm said. 'Miranda, quickly. They're coming.'

Further along the shore, a team of ghouls had stopped their hauling and were heading along the beach in the direction of the reanimated rowing boat, which was still climbing out.

'We have to get out of the water,' Miranda said. 'If they see us, we're trapped.'

They kicked for the city-side shore, making it just as the ghouls reached the struggling reanimate. It let out a wail that made tears spring to Miranda's eyes, the ghouls taking hold of it and dragging it up the shore. There were more than two dozen of them in the group, leaving the poor reanimate no chance of escape even as it struggled and fought.

Miranda wrapped her arms protectively around Wilhelm's dripping shoulders. 'That could have been us,' she whispered.

'We'll free them all,' he said through gritted teeth. 'Somehow we'll find a way. Quick, let's get dressed and get out of here.'

Miranda felt her cheeks flush. She let go of Wilhelm and looked down at her empty hands.

'I dropped it,' she whispered. 'When the reanimate grabbed me … I dropped the bag.'

They both turned. Wilhelm pointed as he spotted it first, far away down the widening channel between the two islands, drifting into the fog and the open sea. Part of it had ripped open, and as Miranda watched, it turned in a slow circle, disgorging its contents.

'I guess we're stuck,' Wilhelm said.

'We can go after it—'

He shook his head. 'No. They've spotted us.'

Miranda looked up at the opposite shore. The reanimated rowing boat had been dragged off, but a group of ghouls still remained, standing on the shoreline, hideous twists of metal that shared only one common feature—the skulls with their deep orange eyes, that now stared, each and every one, at where Miranda and Wilhelm stood.

As one, they began moving in the direction of the bridge.

'We'd better run,' Wilhelm said.

29

FOREST

He ran.

Through the corridors of the school, out of the doors on to the grassy cliffs, along lanes heading among fields filled with chamomile flowers and vegetables, along bustling streams and past rocky gorges gouged out by flood waters. He ran until his lungs ached, then he drew on his magic and used it to propel him until the world around him was just a blur, faster and faster until he felt trapped in his own oil painting, the composite of a human face caught forever in torment.

And when the anger and the frustration died down, he let go, and his body let go, and he tumbled, over and over, until he came to rest, bloody and bruised, enveloped with a sense of helplessness unlike any he had felt before.

When he sat up, it could have been his first day all over again, except that now, instead of finding a beach below him, he felt the crunch of fallen pine needles, soft and springy like the memory of his own bed, far away on a quiet street in a town called Basingstoke, with parents who had jobs and birthdays and a telephone number he could no longer remember, and a very special brother whose name was (*David, David, David—his name is David*), a brother who had the unlikely ability to open a door from one world into another.

A bird called from a branch above him. A little blob of poo landed on the brush just a couple of feet to his left, and Benjamin, like a prisoner released from a life sentence, found himself laughing at the pure absurdity of it all.

He was alive.

That was a start.

A line of ants had taken a path that led them across his ankle. Benjamin stared at them for a few minutes, mesmerised by their regimentation, calmed by the sense of order. Ants, here. Foraging for food. It could be a normal forest. It could be the same forest he had played in on the outskirts of Basingstoke, the last forest he had known in England before he had woken up here, in Endinfinium. The forest where he had seen orange lights among the trees and heard his brother's crying.

He closed his eyes, remembering his brother, a truck, a tearing sound as David drew back a rent in the earth, and a rushing, roaring river of colour which was the last thing he remembered.

'I miss you, Davey,' he murmured, as the last ant climbed down off his ankle and followed the others on its way. The act terrified him, because now the world belonged again to him, Benjamin Forrest, thirteen-year-old schoolboy from Basingstoke, England, and he had to choose his path before it once more chose him.

Something creaked in the undergrowth. Benjamin jumped to his feet and slipped behind the nearest tree.

Blood was trickling from a long cut on his forehead. It might have been from a fall during his madness, or as a result of his magic use. He still struggled to control it. Perhaps he was the liability they all said he was. Perhaps—

A man stepped out from behind a tree and beckoned him forward. Benjamin started. It wasn't really a man, but a human-shape made from twigs woven together. It had no eyes to see or a mouth to form words, but an arm with five intricately detailed fingers beckoned him again. Then, without waiting to see if he followed, it turned and headed off into the trees.

It set a surprising pace that Benjamin had to hurry to follow. It didn't help that he had cuts on his legs that stung when he moved, and that his bad hand felt so cold he could barely use it to push branches out of the way.

The land rose and fell. Smoky wisps of mist began to appear through the trees, and Benjamin realised the woody creature was leading him back to the coast. When he emerged onto a headland he found the mist so thick he could barely see the grass at his feet. The wooden man slowed so he could keep up, and together they followed a path where the grass had been broken and half ploughed by a large, dragged object.

It stood on the very clifftop, with mist swirling

around it, and the crash and roll of breakers beating the shore drifting up from the beach below.

Benjamin smiled. A tear rolled from his eye as he came to stand beside the huge tree stump.

'Fallenwood. I should have realised.'

'Your flight took you into my woods,' the stump said, the whistle of wind pushed through holes in his porous body forming words. 'My Fallenwoodsmen felt your presence immediately and alerted me. Alas that I can't welcome you into my home, but as you'll have noticed, I'm in the middle of an excursion.'

Benjamin hugged the stump until knots and protrusions began to bruise him. 'Please tell me you're not after me, too.'

'Does it look like it?'

'No.'

'There's your answer. Not that I could catch you anyway, is it? You have some troubles, yes? I have neither voice nor ear within the school these days, yet I still hear rumours, and there are many.'

The tears Benjamin had held in for days began to soak his cheeks. He tried to control his sobbing, but once started he had no choice but to let it run its course.

'I see that such weather brings out the worse in you too,' Fallenwood said. 'I'll be a mouldy wreck for weeks after this.'

'They all hate me,' Benjamin said. 'They think I attacked Cleat and let out the archives monsters. They think I've made the Dark Man attack the school. That girl—Sara—I turned her into a cleaner. Miranda and

Wilhelm have disappeared, and everyone hates me, and everything....'

A creaking cluster of wooden fingers encircled his shoulders and pulled him close to Fallenwood. The Fallenwoodsmen, weaving into arms, began to pat him on the back and head.

'A polluted river can only become fresh again by emptying out what ails it,' Fallenwood said as Benjamin cried. 'Empty out your pollutant, young Forrest. Ah, what a delightful name, it so enchants me. How are you going? Has the tide begun to turn?'

'Not yet,' Benjamin sobbed.

'Time, time,' Fallenwood said. 'One of the great mysteries of this place of many. Take your time. I've heard that you humans always benefit from the bleeding of a little emotional blood. Bleed, young man, bleed.'

Benjamin looked up and wiped his eyes. 'I can see why Wilhelm likes coming to see you,' he said.

'We both know it's because he feels sorry for this old stump,' Fallenwood said. 'There. You're looking much improved. The weight of the world is a great thing, is it not?'

'Which world are we talking about?'

'All of them.'

'I can imagine you smiling as you say that.'

'I can imagine it too. Now, what to do. That is the question, is it not?'

'Everything I have tried has failed.'

'Everything?'

'Well, I managed to escape.'

'So you lied. You haven't failed at all. You have

attained a new position from which to seek success. So, tell me, Benjamin—what needs to be done?'

Benjamin took a deep breath. 'Something is going on at the school. The teachers are sick. Something is attacking their minds.'

Fallenwood nodded. 'And I think we both know what it is, don't you?'

Benjamin nodded. 'What is it?'

'Why don't you take a look?'

'If I use my magic, the teachers … they'll find me.'

'And you think they don't already know you're here? You used your magic to get here. I'm afraid that your running is not yet done, young Benjamin.'

'Then I have nothing to lose.'

Fallenwood rocked from side to side. 'Not as I envisage it, no.'

Benjamin let his breathing slow. He took a step in front of Fallenwood and lifted his arms. He felt a momentary flush of warmth, as though rubbing his hands together to ward off the cold. Then, concentrating on the air in front of him, he began to push the fog aside, creating a wedge in the haze, revealing first the headland, then the cliff edge, then the sea below, and finally the vastness of an island, one upon which an abandoned, crumbling theme park stood, adjacent to a city of square houses laid out in a grid.

In its centre rose a flat-topped pyramid.

He let go. The mists rolled back in, obscuring the island once more.

'What is it?' he asked, turning to Fallenwood.

The stump had adopted the face that made

The Lost City of the Ghouls

Benjamin and his friends feel a sense of familiarity. A mouth Benjamin knew had nothing to do with how Fallenwood spoke began to move.

'It's the lost city of the ghouls,' Fallenwood said. 'A mythical place from Endinfinium's far south, hidden in a place a greater distance than any have been and returned. But it looks like it's no longer lost.'

30

FRENZY

It took the overturning chair to bring a hush to a common room filled with kids enjoying unexpected free time. When Godfrey climbed up onto a table and screamed—yes, he really screamed—for silence, it spread out from those nearest to him, until even the older kids near the back, who viewed him as little more than a petulant brat from one of the lower years, had fallen into an uneasy quiet.

'I have something to say and you'd better listen.'

'Hurry up, then,' someone shouted. In response, one of the light-fittings exploded, showering a group of kids near the window.

'I gather you were warned about Benjamin Forrest,' Godfrey said. 'You were told to look out for him and report his presence to a teacher. Well, he found out, and now he's on the run.'

A few gasps of surprise came from the younger kids, but several older kids shrugged and shook their heads.

'The teachers are sick,' Godfrey said. 'All of them. I hear some of you are, too.'

A handful of kids were feeling unwell and had gone upstairs to sleep early. No one had thought it any more than a cold being passed around.

'Their condition is worsening. And Benjamin Forrest is responsible.'

'How?' someone shouted. 'You can't just stand there and accuse him without letting him defend himself.'

'He had the chance but he chose to run instead. He attacked a librarian. He sabotaged the archives floor. And ... he killed a girl.'

A few gasps came from the younger kids again.

'Yes, yes, it's true,' Godfrey said. 'In the Haunted Forest. Benjamin Forrest ran off with his friends to practice his secret magic.'

At the mention of magic, several kids tensed. Older kids, instilled with years of denial, were still mostly skeptical. Younger kids were staring at Godfrey with awe.

'And there, he encountered a girl some of you know. Sara Liselle.'

Gasps came from the back now. Godfrey gave a slight nod, his pinched face never so much as threatening a smile.

'Yes. Sara Liselle. Having changed her mind after her triangulation, she was coming back to the school, but encountered Forrest and his ... cronies. Afraid of being discovered, he killed her.'

'Rubbish,' someone near the back said. 'How could he do that?'

'He stole her life energy, and took it for himself.'

'You're an idiot,' someone else shouted. 'All that hocus pocus talk.'

Godfrey leaned forward, his neck craning out over the crowd. 'Is it?' he said quietly. 'Is it really? Look carefully at the cleaners next time you go to lunch. One of them rather closely resembles Sara Liselle.'

Pandemonium erupted among the older kids, many of whom had grown up with Sara.

'You're a liar!'

'Wait!'

A boy from the fifth year, Nathan Handscomb, stood up. He looked around at the others. 'I thought I saw her,' he said. 'She was serving on the drinks counter last night. She's one of the new ones.'

A couple of other boys also shouted to back up Nathan's words. Slowly, the looks of disbelief among the older kids turned to nods, grimaces, and clenched fists.

'So, you know the truth about Sara Liselle,' Godfrey said. 'What about Wilhelm Jacobs and Miranda Butterworth? No one has seen them for days. They were with Forrest that day. Did they threaten to talk? Did he murder them too? He must be hunted down before he can kill again. Who's with me?'

'Yeah! Let's hunt him!'

Derek Bates jumped up, a fist clenched in front of him. A couple of other known consorts of Godfrey were quick to join their voices in support, but others were standing up too, a few impressionable first-years, one or two fourth- and fifth-years who had always held a suspicion, and—possibly—a level of jealousy for the esteem many of the teachers had for Benjamin. The stories that followed him, of thwarting the Dark Man's armies, of saving his friends from dragons at the very edge of the world, for many anonymous kids they had only caused resentment, a slow, creeping distrust which required only a catalyst to become outright dislike.

Soon, of the group he had been playing trumps with, Snout was the only one still sitting down.

As Godfrey's hateful gaze scanned the crowd, Snout stood up too, wondering where Gubbledon had gone, wishing the reanimated horse was here to restore order. When fists began to pump the air and hands drummed on the tables, Snout fell into line, joining in with the 'Hunt Benjamin Forrest!' chant that was slowly taking over the room, not because he believed in it, but because the look in Godfrey's eyes made him too afraid to do anything else.

∽

As he looked out over the room, Godfrey smiled. Sheep, each and every one of them. They had given themselves over to his whims with pathetic ease, leaving much of his planned speech unsaid. Placing his Dark Reanimate Society friends in strategic locations had worked like a charm. Godfrey had wanted to slap Derek for standing up so soon, expecting ridicule for such over-the-top theatrics, but the crowd had already succumbed.

Now it was a case of organising them into easily manageable groups. The Channellers in the Dark Reanimate Society would each lead a group of unsuspecting Weavers, who would be none the wiser when their power was drawn upon. There were a couple of problem kids who had more of an inkling of their power than others, and they would have to be carefully managed. Godfrey had noticed, for example, how slow Snout had been to get to his feet. The boy's unique ability to draw ghouls out of the earth would come in useful, but his loyalty might prove a problem.

As he headed back across the causeway to the school, leaving his society friends to organise the kids into hunting parties, he wondered if Snout might benefit from the same treatment as old uglyface Gubbledon.

He looked down as he crossed, but the mist completely obscured the rocky shore far below, where he hoped the reanimated racehorse was enjoying a swim.

31

FLIGHT

'Run!'

'Have they seen us?'

'If we stop to check they probably will if they haven't yet. Your red hair is a dead giveaway among all this grey.'

'Well, I'm so sorry to be an inconvenience. Next time I won't bother saving you. I'll let you drown in that murky old water.'

'Look—'

'Shut up.'

'You shut up.'

'Hurry up! Quick, there's one.'

Wilhelm grabbed Miranda and dragged her into a doorway as a ghoul lumbered past, a reanimated forklift truck, a madly grinning skull leering out of a yellow and black exterior, metal forks clacking together like giant scissors.

'Did it see us?'

'I don't think so.'

'That was close.'

Wilhelm let go of her. Her skin was clammy with sweat from their flight. Her hair was matted around her shoulders, but he turned away before allowing himself to look too closely, prior warnings still ringing in his ears.

'We have to keep moving,' Wilhelm said. 'They'll be searching all over.'

Miranda shivered. 'It's getting cold.'

Wilhelm peered out of the doorway, checking each way for ghouls. Above them, the mist had lifted briefly, but as he looked around, it closed back in, drifting in great shifting clouds through the streets. From far up ahead, the eyes of two searching ghouls appeared like car headlights.

'Others are coming.'

They dashed across the street, into an alley on the far side. Hurrying around piles of junk, they broke out on to another street, bolted across, and dived into another alley. Here there was little to tell the houses apart: they were squat and uniformly square, many with shuttered windows and heavy, locked doors.

'I can't keep running,' Miranda gasped. 'We need to hide out somewhere, wait them out. It's getting gloomy. What time is it?'

'Hang on, I'll just check my watch.'

'Are you being sarcastic?'

Wilhelm gasped for breath as he tried to laugh. He shook his head. 'Would I? I think it's lunchtime. I'm pretty hungry.'

'No sign of an orchard yet, is there?'

Wilhelm met Miranda's gaze with a knowing look. 'Not yet.'

'Do you think they lied to us?'

Orange lights flashed across the entrance to the alleyway where they crouched. 'To be honest, I think we have worse to worry about. Come on.'

Wilhelm took the lead as they ran down the next alley and out onto the street. The haze was thick here, hiding them more easily, while the lights of the ghouls' eyes were visible from a greater distance. Wilhelm was shivering, the cold starting to take its effect. Miranda now hugged him close, uncaring about her own nakedness as they sought warmth against each other.

'Cold, Wilhelm,' she said, her teeth chattering as she spoke. 'I can make a fire if we can find somewhere safe.'

Wilhelm shook his head. 'No. They'll feel us. We'll be captured. Do you want to end up in that pit?'

'No, but what choice do we have? Freeze to death?'

'Are you giving up?'

'No, but … cold.'

Wilhelm jerked around. Miranda was shivering. 'Miranda, it's not that cold. What are you feeling? It's not the air, is it?'

She looked up at him and slowly shook her head. Without a word, she reached out and took his hand, leading him up the street.

At the corner she paused, ducking back into the shadows beneath an overhanging roof. A plaza opened out up ahead, and across from them stood a squat, grey pyramid, blending in with the mist all around. On its facing side, steps led up to a wide entrance.

'In there,' she said. 'The cold, it's coming from in there.'

Wilhelm remembered the robed figures they had seen on their first night. The Dark Mages, Timothy had called them.

'Do you think they're inside?' he said. 'Those people we saw?'

Miranda nodded. 'I can feel them. Not just one. Many.'

Wilhelm closed his eyes. His perception of the dark magic wasn't as good as hers, but he could still feel them, like little tickles of cold caressing his stomach, the tentacles of some deadly, insidious beast.

'What are they doing?' he said.

Miranda frowned. Her bottom lip trembled. 'I think they're feeding,' she said.

'On what?'

Miranda shrugged. 'I can't be sure unless we go in and take a closer look.'

'Yeah, well, I think we have other things to worry about first.'

He pushed her behind him. Out across the plaza, a ghoul had turned in their direction. A skull with orange eyes shone out of a blocky metallic body, like an oversized filing cabinet. Its jaw clacked. On its upper surface, a spiky assortment of aerials, satellite dishes and antennae whirred to face in their direction.

'Oh my, it heard us,' Miranda said.

'Move.'

A whirring came from inside the ghoul's blocky chest compartment, and it sped across the plaza in their direction, racing on small wheels. Wilhelm pushed Miranda in front of him, and together they ran through the collapsed entrance of one of the few buildings that had more than one floor, a three-storey structure that lay set back from the road behind a dusty courtyard strewn with weeds.

The whirring confirmed the ghoul had followed them.

'I can destroy it,' Miranda said, turning as they reached a flight of stairs leading to the upper floor.

'No magic,' Wilhelm reminded her. 'Let me try my idea.'

He kicked at a loose tile on the floor and broke it free. It was two thirds of a square, jagged on one side, thin enough on the other for a hand to comfortably grip.

'Do you think they have hive minds?' Wilhelm asked, pushing past Miranda to take up a position blocking the ghoul's path. 'Because I really hope not.'

The ghoul broke through the entranceway, heading straight for them. Wilhelm waited as it closed, picking his target. At about twenty feet away he flung the tile, watching it spin through the air to crash into the array of aerials and antennae on the ghoul's top. They smashed apart, and the ghoul spun around, emitting a grating moan.

'Quick, up the stairs,' Wilhelm said. 'While it's disorientated.'

He followed Miranda up the stairs and into a room, and together they slid across a heavy door, breaking through the rust caked along its rails. A simple hook locked the door and they both sat down hard, breathing heavily.

'Did that warm you up?' Wilhelm gasped.

'Where did you learn to throw like that?'

'We had a frisbee team in the orphanage,' Wilhelm said. 'I wasn't good enough to be captain, but I was like third best or something.'

Miranda patted his arm. 'You nailed it.'

Wilhelm grinned. 'I did, didn't I? Bull's-eye. The part of it that was still a TV or a giant radio or something got confused long enough to lose sight of us.'

They fell silent for a few minutes. From outside came the rumble of machinery, larger ghouls moving back and forth, clearing out rubbish and driving it into piles for their smaller counterparts to carry back across the bridge to the pit in the amphitheatre.

'You know something?' Wilhelm said at last. 'We're in some sort of a science research station. Kind of like one of those old-style ones. I said so, didn't I?'

'What do you mean?'

He pointed at the far wall, which at first glance appeared featureless. 'Those are cupboards.'

'Where?'

He climbed to his feet. Through the single window the room carried a level of gloom that required some eye adjustment, but when he walked to the other wall he found the hand grips he had thought he saw to be real.

'These are handles.'

'Wilhelm, I'm not sure you want to open that.'

He grinned. 'Could it possibly be worse than a

bunch of burned-up reanimated monsters or guys in cloaks with a chip on their shoulder?'

Miranda lifted her hands and peered through her fingers. 'Just in case there's something horrid in there. Go on then.'

Wilhelm jerked the door. At first it resisted, stuck tight with age-accumulated dust, then it broke open, concertinaing back, the momentum making Wilhelm let go. He fell to the floor with a heavy bump as Miranda screamed.

Rows of hanging people stared out at them.

'Suits!' Miranda gasped with one hand over her heart. 'Oh my, they're suits.'

Wilhelm couldn't speak until his own thundering heart had calmed. When he felt capable of thinking clearly, he went back over to the cupboard.

Full body suits. They had looked like people because they were enclosing right down to the gloves for the wearer's hands.

'They're a bit musty,' Miranda said. 'And some of them have got holes.' As she spoke, she pulled one down off the hanger and held it up for size. 'But it's close enough.'

They both quickly donned the suits. While not designed for warmth and with holes that let the air whistle through, the suits at least took away their uncomfortable nakedness and eased the air's chill. At the back were zips, and while Miranda's jammed halfway, they both decided to leave the face masks hanging loose anyway.

'Right,' Miranda said, giving Wilhelm a twirl. 'How do I look?'

He smiled. 'Hideous.'

Miranda laughed. 'You too. What on earth do you think they were doing here?'

Wilhelm shrugged. 'Research. I reckon that old theme park had something nasty buried under it. Like radiation or something.'

The upper floor was also empty, as though ghouls had come through and cleared out everything visible, but in another cupboard they found fold-out mats that were as soft as anything they had seen so far. Despite the hunger gnawing at them, both were exhausted. They lay down beside each other and looked up at the ceiling.

'Just five minutes,' Miranda said.

'Five minutes,' Wilhelm agreed.

But when he closed his eyes, Wilhelm felt weariness washing over him, and suddenly he was fast asleep, dreaming of dark people, and burned monsters, and boiling pits of fire.

When he awoke, night had fallen. The room was almost dark except for an orange glow that came through the single small window.

Miranda was snoring. Wilhelm gave her an extra five minutes, then nudged her awake. As she groggily came to, he pointed up at the window.

'I think we have a problem,' he said.

32

HUNTED

They were coming for Benjamin. He could feel their magic like fish hooks tugging at his clothes. As he crouched in the undergrowth not far from the cliff path, he saw a group of them approaching, driving in one of the vehicles out of the school garages, an old minibus, partly reanimated with metal tentacles that hung from its sides to lift it over rocks and other obstacles. Not yet reanimated enough to develop its own sentience, he could feel little sparks of magic as whoever controlled it commanded the tentacles to move.

As it came closer, he listened for voices that he recognised.

'Come on, faster! He's getting away!'

Derek Bates. If there was anyone who came close to Godfrey's level of sadism it was Derek. Benjamin frowned. He recognised other faces through the bus windows: a couple of new first-years, and one or two skeptical middle-years who had no interest in magic but who now wore rabid grins.

'He's over there!'

Benjamin frowned. How could they know? He wasn't using his magic. Then he felt it: a cold sensation in his hand that was rapidly expanding.

Whatever Derek was doing to follow his trail, it was picking up on the taint in his hand and homing in.

The bus bumped up and over an outcrop of rock, tentacles propelling it forward, and then only open grass separated them. Mists swirled around the cliff edge, but it wouldn't hide him if they had other ways of looking.

A short distance ahead, a path led down to the beach. Benjamin bolted for it, aware of running feet from behind. He remembered something that Edgar had said once: that reanimation magic flowed nowhere greater than in the water itself, and that if someone needed to hide, it would be where the magic was concentrated the most.

He reached the beach just as the bus, tentacles flailing, began to climb down the rock face. Several kids were already pursuing him on foot, but he had a good head start, and the mist was thicker here.

Behind the haze, an orange veil hung over the sky. Benjamin had never noticed it before, but now it was sinister, foreboding. He looked up at it one last time, then turned back to the beach—

Something caught his foot and sent him sprawling. A chrome-black creature churned the sand, and the boot of what had once been a car snapped down over his leg.

Benjamin howled with pain as the turtle-car hauled

him down. Using his magic would give him away, but he had no choice. Feeling for it, he concentrated on pushing the air around the creature's jaws, forcing them open.

With a grunt the turtle-car let go and shrank back. Benjamin scrabbled away, kicking at the sand.

'Grab him!'

Flashlights flickered through the haze, bringing with them shadowy running figures. Benjamin turned, prepared to fight them, but it was no use. Despite the orange miasma encircling them, they were just boys; some he had sat beside in science or maths class.

'Stay back!' he shouted, lifting his hands. 'I'll … I'll … blast you!'

'Go on, get him! He won't dare if he values his life!'

If only he could shut Derek up he might be able to convince the others. Benjamin saw him, cowardly standing at the back, egging on the boys he had worked up into a frenzy. What if … what if … what if…?

Moving an object, even a small one, was tough. It took more concentration than he could give right now. But water … water was already in motion.

Benjamin called his magic, plunging it into the sea, pushing it toward the shore. A wave broke over Derek's head, knocking him to the sand and dragging him back down the beach. The other boys, closing in with flashlights, sticks, and other crude weapons, paused. Benjamin created a second wave closer to them, water rushing up the beach to suck at their ankles. Some fell, others ran up the beach, but in the confusion, Benjamin made his escape.

At the base of the cliff, he spotted a tunnel entrance where a river ran down to the sea. He dashed inside, running as far in as he could, then turned and used his magic to push the accumulated sand up into a great wedge covering the entrance. The cave fell into darkness, the wind dying away. Benjamin had trapped himself, but with his magic he could find a way out. In time the river would pool behind the mound, find a way through it and begin washing it down to the sea, but before Derek and the others could find a way in, he would be long gone. All he had to do was follow the river up through the tunnels until he found where it entered them.

He took a deep breath and turned to follow the sound of trickling water, just as red eyes glowed out of the dark in front of him, and a metallic hand clamped hard over his mouth.

33

ANIMATTER

'Where are they going?' Miranda said, leaning over Wilhelm's shoulder as they peered out of the window at the procession of ghouls in the street below.

'Looks like they're heading for the pit,' Wilhelm said. 'Do you think they've forgotten us?'

Miranda shrugged. 'Maybe.'

'Well, if they've all gone, now's our chance to have a look inside that pyramid, see what they've got hidden in there.'

They crept downstairs. The street outside had fallen silent, so they opened the door and slipped outside. A chill wind gusted, and a light snow was dusting the streets.

Miranda scooped some up in her hands. 'Is this what I think it is?'

Wilhelm's eyes widened. 'You've never seen snow before? It's what happens when rain gets really cold.'

'First time,' she said, shaking her head. 'We were never allowed outside at the facility.'

'It's fun,' Wilhelm said. He scraped a handful into a little ball and tossed it at her.

'Hey!' she snapped as it struck the front of her uniform. She shook it off, then scooped some up and threw it back.

Wilhelm grinned as he jumped out of its path. 'You'll have to do better than that. Come on.'

He ran off down the street. Miranda laughed and ran after him, scooping up more snow as she ran. Wilhelm reached the corner and turned, but as he did so, he realised he had reached the plaza with the pyramid on its far side.

The excitement drained out of him. When Miranda's well-aimed snowball struck him on the side of the head, he could only shrug. She came up beside him, her laughter quickly cut off.

'It was nice to forget for a few minutes, wasn't it?' she said.

Wilhelm nodded. 'Yeah.'

The plaza had taken on an eerie orange glow. The yellow sun had long ago set, while the hidden red sun gave them just enough light to see.

'Well, we're here now,' Wilhelm said. 'We might as well go and take a look.'

The doors were made of stone. Wilhelm didn't want to think about the weight of such things, but they were open enough to allow access. The ground around the bottom was scratched and scored; the doors had been forced a long time ago and left where they now rested.

Wilhelm went first, holding the door for Miranda. They found themselves in a wide atrium with high, vaulted ceilings, a marble floor, and orange lights flickering in alcoves in the walls. Another pair of doors stood open at the far end.

Wilhelm's heart pounded as they crept closer, staying close to the wall. Adrenalin had soaked him in sweat, but his terror at what they might find was lessened only by his curiosity. Miranda too, despite taking his hand and squeezing so tightly he could no longer feel his fingers, had an intensity to her eyes that told him nothing would distract her from finding out what was going on.

'Here goes,' Wilhelm said. 'Ladies first?'

'On three,' Miranda said. 'One, two … three.'

They stepped inside together. The interior was lit by a flickering orange light that made Wilhelm feel immediately disorientated. He leaned on Miranda's shoulder, blinking until his eyes could adjust, and in the flickering light saw her do the same. She held one hand over her brow as though to ward it off, even though it was uncertain from where the light came.

'What is that?' Miranda breathed.

The single item in the vast room lay amid a sea of scattered ashes as though it burned anything that approached. It was silver and rectangular, like an overlarge fridge. Metal chains as thick as Wilhelm's arms secured it to moorings fitted into the floor as it bucked and jerked like a chained horse.

'Wilhelm, wait—'

He ignored her. Her fingers slipped out of his and

he ran toward the silver monolith. The flickering light, he saw now, was caused by thousands of tiny fireflies, reanimated pieces of ash that plumed up from the silver object's surface, sparkled briefly in the air, then fell to earth, where they began the process all over again.

'Wilhelm, I don't think you should touch it—'

He reached out. Like a calmed animal, it ceased its movements beneath his touch. The chains fell slack and it hummed quietly like a contented cat. Made of metal, it was warm to the touch. A line down the centre suggested a pair of fitting panels that opened outward. He ran his fingers over it, looking for some kind of groove or opening.

'Wilhelm, what are you doing? Your skin … you're glowing orange.'

'Don't worry,' he said, fingers searching. 'I think it's a kind of computer.' His finger caught on a groove and he traced the outline of embedded letters that were difficult to see in the light, while the machine hummed, and a strange sensation made its way slowly up his arm.

'Wilhelm, let go of it.'

He shook his head. 'You should try it … it feels weird, like I'm warming up. I feel … awake … more alive—ow!'

His fingers broke free from the surface as Miranda punched his arm.

'What were you doing? You looked like you were in a trance.'

Wilhelm shook his head. 'I was reading that word.'

'What word?'

'On the front.'

'Well, what did it say?'

He frowned, shrugging off the memory of the unusually pleasant feeling, remembering the letters he had felt.

'*Animatter*,' he said. 'A-N-I-M-A-T-T-E-R. What could that mean?'

Miranda shook her head. 'I don't know. Come on, Wilhelm. I don't like it in here. Let's go.'

Wilhelm shook his head. The strange sensation had come all the way up to his face, even though he had let go. His cheeks felt warm, his eyes a little dizzy, but it wasn't … it wasn't … unpleasant.

He put his hand back on the machine, fingers running over its surface. Behind him, he vaguely heard Miranda shouting, but it didn't matter. Nothing mattered any longer except the machine.

'There's an opening,' he said, fingers brushing over something. 'I think there's a switch.'

'Wilhelm, no! It's cold, it's too cold!'

Miranda was clawing at his shoulders, her fingernails stinging, drawing blood. Wilhelm shrugged her off. There was only the machine, the Animatter, and the endlessly living and dying fireflies. The world had turned a shade of orange as Wilhelm's fingers found a groove and he pulled open twin doors to reveal a window behind.

A window.

A window.

A window—

The sound was everywhere, an endless wail of tormented souls, and he saw them, their haunted faces rushing at him, pressing against the translucent surface, wanting only to find rest, freedom, release—

—Wilhelm—

—*Wilhelm*—

—*Wilhelm!*—

Something hard crashed into the side of his face, and then they were gone, the tormented, the souls of the lost, trapped in their cage for the rest of eternity. There was only the relentless orange rain of the fireflies and Miranda's face, and hands shaking him.

'We have to get out of here!' screamed a voice from a million miles away.

Wilhelm tried to answer, but his tongue was a dead thing in his mouth, and the only sound was the rustling of the ash, the buzz of the fireflies, and the cackle of laughter.

∽

'We have to get out of here!'

Too late, Wilhelm slumped at Miranda's feet. She tried to haul him up, but he was a dead weight curled on the ground at the foot of the machine, the ash pluming over him like a tiny volcanic eruption.

Miranda reached for his shoulders, but laughter from the shadows behind the machine made her pause. Timothy appeared out of the dark, dressed now in a hooded cloak.

Miranda stared, her mouth gone dry. Timothy's eyes twinkled with orange light.

'There's … there's no orchard, is there?' Miranda

said, her voice feeling detached from her body like a floating creature with a mind of its own.

Emmie stepped out from behind the machine to stand next to Timothy. She smiled. 'Oh, there is. You just found it.' She lifted a hand and a group of fireflies converged, settling on her palm. She closed her fingers, and when she opened them again, a perfect, rosy red apple sat there.

'Aren't you hungry?' she said. 'We are.' One hand reached out to stroke the side of machine, and as she did so, her hand glowed orange. 'So, so hungry.'

She lifted the apple to her lips and took a deep bite. As soon as the flesh broke away, the apple turned back into dancing, luminous pieces of ash, exploding out of her mouth like a swarm of bees as she threw back her head and laughed.

'Were you always planning to give us up?'

Emmie shrugged. 'We were just waiting to see what you would do. Most turn on their own, you know. Once the … remedy sets in—'

'Remedy, my foot! It's poison!'

Emmie shook her head. 'You gave yourselves up by coming here. There's no escape. Sara tried, but it was too late for her, too. She didn't know, but she had already turned.'

'What are you talking about?'

Timothy grinned, but his face seemed plastic, as though it wasn't really a face at all but merely a covering for something sinister beneath.

'Once you become a resident in the city of ghouls,' he said, 'you can never escape. We did our best to hide, but in the end, there is only the pit, the Animatter machine, and your destiny.'

Timothy's fingers closed over his cheeks and nose and pulled. For a moment he looked bizarre, like a blurred photograph, then his grimace lengthened and began to unstick from his face. His eyes stretched, his skin popped away from the bone beneath, and then it was peeling back, revealing only a charred, blackened skull with two glowing orange eyes.

'Welcome to the Lost City of the Ghouls,' the monster that had been Timothy laughed. 'I'm sure you'll both fit in, just as soon as you've been cleansed.'

Miranda was struck dumb. Unable to take her eyes off Timothy, she reached for Wilhelm, trying to pull him up.

Movement behind her caught her eye. A line of hooded figures approached, their feet kicking up clouds of ash as the fireflies buzzed around their heads.

'The machine drew them,' Timothy said, his voice taking on a nervous pitch despite his horrific visage. 'As it draws us all.'

'What's inside it?' Miranda asked.

'Life,' Timothy said. 'Life stripped from every single person who ever passed through the gates of Sunshine Land. In the shadow of the pit, there is no escape.'

Miranda didn't have time to figure out what he meant. The closest figure drew back its hood. Miranda was surprised to see a woman's face. Her eyes, despite the orange glow, were youthful. What Miranda thought were age lines scored her skin, but then, as she spoke and her face moved out of sync to her words, she realised it was just a cover for the bare skull beneath.

'Take them to the pit,' she said, her voice as gravelly as the ash that plumed around her feet. 'They will make a fitting offering to the Dark Man. So young, so fresh.'

The other figures spread out, seven in all. Miranda gritted her teeth and felt for her magic. No way would she go down without a fight. It was there, a knot in her stomach, but the cold was all around, coming from everything. What chance did she have?

Fingers squeezed her wrist. She glanced down at the shape lying in the ash at her feet. Wilhelm's eyes were half open, watching her.

'No,' he breathed. 'One chance.'

She understood. She let go of her magic and stood up, waiting for them to come. Instead, the ashes around her began to stir, and then shapes rose up, creatures made of the glowing embers. Hands hot and rough secured her arms and then they were marching her back across the room to the door.

'To the pit,' shouted a voice from behind her, one tinged with amusement. 'To the pit, to the Dark Man, and to your destiny.'

34

HUNTERS

Godfrey was fuming.

'You're an idiot,' he shouted at Derek, who was sitting on a rock, picking seaweed out of his hair. 'You let him escape.'

'We can clear the tunnel,' Derek said. 'It won't take long. It's only sand, after all.'

'You're not thinking straight, are you? While we stand around here doing that, he'll be getting away. The question we have to ask is where is he going?'

'Back to the school?' one of the younger boys asked.

'Of course back to the school!' Godfrey flapped a hand over his shoulder. 'Where else would he go? The teachers won't help him though, and he knows we're on his tail, so where will he go to hide?'

Blank faces stared back at him.

'Come on, where do you think?'

Shrugs.

'He's hanging out with those monsters, isn't he? The

ones that hide under the floors. I say we confront them and demand they had him over … or else.'

'Or else what?' said Vince Orson, a fifth-year. 'Come on, Godfrey, mate, they're not going to pay any attention to us.'

'Ever cut your finger, Vince?'

'What?'

'Know what happens if you leave it too long before you wash it?'

'Huh?'

'It goes bad. First it gets septic. Then it gets gangrenous. Then—' Godfrey ripped his hands apart and made a chainsaw noise. It would have been funny done by anyone else, but by Godfrey, sneer like a jagged knife wound beneath snake eyes and wrapped with black curls of packaging, it just looked creepy.

In a tiny voice that only the nearest pupils could hear, Godfrey finished, 'You have to cut it off.'

'I've never had a cut go gangrenous,' said Fat Adam. 'Although there was this one time I had to pop a blister.'

'What's "gangrenous"?' asked Tommy Cale.

Snout, who had been listening to the exchanges with faked interest, turned to him. 'It's when—'

Godfrey waved a hand and Snout's mouth snapped shut. Snout rubbed where he had bit his cheek, and noticed several others do the same.

'We're wasting time,' Godfrey said. 'We have to catch Benjamin Forrest, and the only way to do that is to anticipate his next move. We lie in wait and then we spring.' He clapped his hands together, surprising a couple of younger boys sat near the front, one of which fell off the rock he was sitting on.

Everyone climbed back onto the bus. Snout, who had been near the front of Derek's crew but lingering back near the cliffs, waited until near the end. He didn't really want to ride the bus at all, and not because it wasn't right that buses had tentacles and could scale cliffs, but because he disagreed with the hunt for Benjamin. He started to edge nearer to the cave entrance, wondering if he could perhaps accidentally miss the bus altogether.

'Oi, Pig Nose. Get over here; we're moving out.'

Derek was leaning out of the front window. Snout felt a strange knot in his stomach and knew that if he pulled on it, he could get something to climb up out of the sand and bite off Derek's head. The temptation grew even stronger as Derek pressed a thumb against the tip of his nose and pushed it upward in a mocking mimic of Snout's own slightly upturned honker.

Not now, but perhaps there would come a time. Staring at the ground so Derek wouldn't see the anger in his eyes, Snout headed back to the bus.

∼

They weren't much of an army, Godfrey thought as the pupils broke off into their groups to continue the hunt for Benjamin Forrest. They had no discipline, few tracking skills, and were forever on the verge of mutiny, but it didn't matter. They were easily manipulated, and with the teachers all falling ill, he met little resistance.

The Lost City of the Ghouls

And in any case, the real army was set to make landfall in just a few short days.

And then, preparations could be made for the Dark Man's return.

Godfrey smiled. He would surely be rewarded. Perhaps he would even be made the new Headmaster of Endinfinium High.

In any case, it didn't matter. He was in possession of the book, and it had already revealed to him secrets that could see Benjamin Forrest expelled forever.

35

FALLING

THE PAINTED FACES OF THE CREATURES SITTING around him, a car crash of garrulous clowns, laughing animals, sea creatures, and more fantastical monsters, made Benjamin tremble with fear. Even more disconcerting was the one currently painting on the face of another who had somehow lost it. Beneath the paint the face was a grey square, as bland and expressionless as a metal box, yet mumbles and groans and occasionally even laughter came from the blank surface.

'Are you going to kill me?' he whispered.

The only answer was the echo bouncing back from the tunnels leading out of the cavern.

None of them moved except to shift a little where they were sitting, as though to find a more comfortable position. Had it not been for the strong plastic hands that had dragged him out of the water, hauled him up a steep tunnel and dropped him down in the centre of the circular cavern in which he now sat, he might have dared to stand up and quietly walk away.

'Can you speak?' he said.

Mumbles came this time. Some nodded rapidly. Fixed Cheshire cat smiles bobbed up and down.

The one painting the other wore a smeared pastel mask of a grinning crocodile. The original artwork had been exquisite, shaded to give texture and depth, right down to the shadows around the crocodile's teeth. Drawn either by a hand of great skill or one long-practiced, it had now begun to fade, with one eye almost entirely worn away.

'What are you?' Benjamin whispered. 'Are you reanimates?'

They answered with both nods and shakes of their heads, leaving him with no more understanding of their nature than before he had asked the question.

The light in the centre of the cavern came from a bowl with a wax candle inside. Crocodile Face dipped a stick into the pool of cooling wax and then smeared it on to the faceless one. With a couple of deft strokes, it took on the shape of an eyebrow. Then, dipping the same stick into a bowl nestled in the shadows, the creature began to outline an eye in black ink while the others watched.

From somewhere far down one of the connecting tunnels, a rumble, perhaps of water crashing into the rocks at the rear of a cave, brought a gust of wind billowing through the cavern. The candle flickered. In an instant the light was weakened, making the face of the one being painted nearly invisible. Groans came from the others. Some shifted, perhaps searching for a way to improve the light.

Benjamin saw his chance to gain their trust. Reluctant to use his magic for fear of Godfrey's cronies finding him, he figured that a little bit might not be noticed. Reaching out for the air, he gave the flame on the candle a little boost, and the cavern filled with light as a flame the length of his hand blazed from the candle tip.

Oohs and aahs came from the assembled creatures. Benjamin smiled, and one or two nodded in his direction, as though acknowledging his interference. Able to see them clearly now, Benjamin recognised them for what they were: reanimated shop mannequins, with limbs of uniform grey, featureless faces and bodies devoid of either character or individuality.

He remembered something that Professor Loane had told him after a science class about reanimates. While all objects could reanimate in time, it took place at different speeds and levels of complexity. Those objects not fused with another would obtain a level of intelligence relative to their own complexity. So, while a pencil could certainly reanimate, it would never be able to do more than simply bounce around. A computer, on the other hand, could all but take over the world.

'Hello again,' he said, lifting a hand. The creatures nodded. 'My name is Benjamin Forrest. I think you rescued me.' He coughed. 'Or maybe it was a kidnapping, I don't know,' he added under his breath. 'But thanks. Unfortunately, I have another favour to ask.

I need to get back to Endinfinium High. More specifically, I need to get to Underfloor.'

For a few seconds they all just stared at him, heads cocked, like puppies seeing a cat for the first time. 'Underfloor?' he continued. 'Do you know where that is?'

More stares. Benjamin lifted his hands, and made some gestures. His upper hand was the school, shaky and rickety. The lower hand was the snaking tunnels that comprised Underfloor.

Some of the creatures looked at each other. Cocked heads became nods of understanding. One or two began to chatter in a language Benjamin didn't understand, like birds tittering to each other around a food bowl. They had some kind of plan, but as yet he wasn't privy to its details.

A couple stood up and waved the others forward. In an instant the whole group was moving, heading for a corridor that led further into the hill. Benjamin stood up to follow, but found hands around his arms and legs, lifting him off the ground. Soon he was on their shoulders, rushing through tunnels that rose and fell. Nothing fazed the painted people: not great chasms or low ceilings, or narrowing tunnels so thin they had to pass both sideways and single file. No matter the obstacle, Benjamin was shifted about accordingly, and passed through each hazard like a crown wrapped in cotton wool until the cavern brightened in front of them, and then they were running out onto grey sand.

It was twilight, but the sky had taken on an orange hue, the cliffs glittering with what Benjamin at first thought were fireflies, then he realised were thousands upon thousands of roosting scatlocks. He tried to tell the painted people not to let him down, but they were running hard, straight for the seashore.

'Um, you don't need to go in there. I'm sure I can walk from here,' he muttered, as those as the front splashed into the water. A couple turned back, flapping their hands up and down in a mimic of his gesture, and he realised they had misunderstood.

Instead of Underfloor, they were taking him under the sea.

'No, wait—'

Water filled his mouth. He flailed as he went under, then sucked down a desperate breath as they climbed over something embedded in the sand just offshore. Then he was back under.

I have to breathe! I have to breathe!

He had no choice but to reach for his magic. With little idea of how or what he was doing, he tried only to envisage air, a bubble, something to surround his face and keep him alive.

Water sloshed all around, but he breathed. His eyes filled with water, but he breathed. He tasted salt on his tongue, yet, somehow, he breathed.

All around, the water churned with the marching painted people, the lines of reanimated shop mannequins fanning out around him like a protective shield. The water was lit only by a dim orange glow, and occasionally dark shadows would approach, before turning and flitting away. Benjamin, trying to concentrate only on pulling air into his lungs, saw nothing clearly, but he sensed, in the way that ants would protect their nest from a predator, that the painted people were protecting him.

And then, with a sudden rush, they were marching up onto a shore. Benjamin didn't recognise it in the gloom for it resembled the rest of the beaches around the school, but there, on the headland above, he saw a rickety wooden building leaning precariously over the edge, so close to falling it appeared to vibrate with anticipation.

The painted people lowered him onto the sand and gathered around. To his dismay, Benjamin realised all of their faces had washed clean, leaving them indistinguishable. As he waited, one of them stepped forward. It lifted a hand and touched his shoulder, turning him so he looked at the base of the cliff.

There, a large wooden door, like the entrance to a dungeon, stood embedded into the rock.

Benjamin let out a whoop of excitement that he quickly tried to suppress. 'You did understand,' he said, trying not to shiver for fear it might appear rude. 'You just took me by the most direct route.'

The mannequin cocked its head, then gave a frantic nod and patted him on the shoulder. All around, the creatures ummed and ahhed as best as their mouthless faces would allow, then, as one, they turned and ran back into the sea.

Benjamin stood alone on the beach, trying to absorb what had just happened. His hand ached, but he felt no pain anywhere else, so he had managed to control the magic long enough to keep him alive.

Above him, the dormitory shuddered and shook. Further to the south, around a curve in the headland, some towers of the school were visible, as were the low walls of the outer courtyard, set into the rock. It was so near, yet still so far away.

The door, however, was closer. Whether it led straight into Underfloor or somewhere else, there was only one way to find out.

Benjamin squeezed water out of his clothes as best he could, then trudged up the beach. Tendrils of mist snaked around him, while the sea was hidden by a wall of mist. The lost city he had glimpsed was coming closer, bringing with it whatever dangers it contained.

He didn't have much time, but halfway to the cliff, a noise made him stop and turn.

A short distance away, hidden behind an outcrop of rocks, Gubbledon Longface lay on the shingle, his body a twisted mess.

'Gubbledon!'

Benjamin dropped to his knees. The housemaster had landed on his side, and one leg was bent back on itself. There was no blood, but a bone had snapped, and a white stump protruded out of decayed flesh.

'I had a little accident,' the reanimated racehorse said. 'I think I'll just lie here a while until I can get back up.'

'Did you fall?'

'Someone pushed me. I didn't see who, because I was facing the other way.'

'Does it hurt? Are you going to die?'

Gubbledon shook his head, but from the way he lay

slumped on the rocks like the remains of a shipwreck, it was hard to imagine anything else.

'We reanimates don't die in the same way that you humans die,' he said. 'You'd have to chew me all up. It might be a while before I'm functioning again, however.'

Benjamin felt a shaking rage taking over him. 'Who did this to you? And why?'

Gubbledon's shoulders momentarily lifted off the stones in an attempt at a shrug. 'There are the usual suspects, of course. I guess Jacobs will have to be ruled out, what with his absence and everything.'

'He would never hurt you!'

'No, but there are others. There have always been plenty of others.'

Gubbledon didn't look capable of moving anytime soon. Benjamin squatted down and did his best to reorganise the parts of Gubbledon that had broken in order that the housemaster would reanimate as correctly as possible.

'Thank you, Master Forrest. You're too kind. But can I ask a favour?'

'Anything.'

'Things have gone a little strange of late. I'm not sure if you've noticed. That old city has come back again. I don't suppose you'd know anything about it.'

'No, nothing,' Benjamin said, but he stared at Gubbledon, wondering why he'd never thought to ask the housemaster. After all, reanimates far outlived humans, and their memories didn't seem to fade like those of humans did.

'Has it come before?'

'Yes, yes. Caused a terrible sickness. It's a root of pure dark reanimate, you see. The substance that gives us life can also take it away. It all depends on how it's been nurtured.'

'What do you mean?'

'When you raise a flower, it can be raised to face either north or south, can it not? It just depends on which sun it is designed to face.'

Benjamin, who had no experience raising flowers, just shrugged.

'Everything faces one way or the other, doesn't it? Sometimes you can change which way you face, sometimes not.'

'What are you talking about?'

Gubbledon smiled. His eyes closed as though he planned to sleep, or perhaps die.

'That city showed up before, a long time ago. You took it away, and we found peace again.'

'I did?'

'Yes, you.'

Benjamin felt heat growing around his ears. 'How?'

'That, I don't remember. I had other duties. But you never came back.'

'I didn't?'

'Not that time you didn't. Who knows about this time? No cycle is ever the same, is it? The scenery changes ... and other things.' Gubbledon let out a long sigh, that, had it could from one of the kids, Benjamin would have expected to turn into tears. 'It was nice to see you again,' the housemaster continued, 'even though we had to pretend. After all, so much is at stake. The school, us, you. Of course you. And everything. Isn't that the truth?'

Benjamin sensed Gubbledon was rambling like a hospital patient on lots of medication. He patted the housemaster on the shoulder. 'Shall I ask in Underfloor for some reanimates to fetch you?'

'Oh, that would be ... nice.' Gubbledon shifted. 'Oh, and about that favour...?'

'Of course. Just tell me what I can do.'

'The presence of that city, it upsets things. It makes the humans sick, and it sets off reanimation like nobody's business. The dormitory ... I know it's nothing but a few boards nailed together, but the memories ... and it's been my home all these long years ... could you protect it from falling, please?'

Benjamin looked up. The dormitory still shuddered and shook. A few rocks from its foundations broke free and bounced down the cliff face.

'I don't know if I can.'

'Puh ... puh ... please.'

Benjamin looked down at Gubbledon, then up at the shuddering dormitory. What did he care about an old building?

(rainy nights when Miranda came to his and Wilhelm's room, and the three of them sat around playing trumps by candlelight)

(enjoying breakfast in the common room while Snout, Fat Adam and Tommy Cale argued over whether the custard was better at lunchtime or dinnertime)

(waking up early on purpose to catch Gubbledon in the middle of his bizarre morning exercises)

(telling Godfrey to get stuffed and hearing the whole room erupt in cheers)

(lying in his bed at night, thinking about the fading faces of his family, then hearing Wilhelm's snoring and realising that things weren't as bad as they seemed)

(Wilhelm's laugh)

(Miranda's smile)

(the sun through the windows at the end of the hall in the early morning)

Benjamin smiled. He had his memories too. He didn't love Endinfinium, and doubted he ever could, but there had been good times, too. And many of them had happened inside the building about to fall into the sea.

Push and pull.

It definitely looked like a push situation.

'I'll do what I can,' he said, even though part of him knew it was a mistake, that Godfrey's crew would find him.

'Just calm it down a little,' Gubbledon mumbled. 'That's all I ... ask.'

Gubbledon looked as pitiful as the reanimated body of a dead racehorse could, and Benjamin felt both a dark anger toward whoever had pushed the housemaster from the cliff and a deep sense of regret over the hundreds of times they had mocked Gubbledon to his back.

'Leave it to me,' Benjamin said. 'And if I ever find out who pushed you, I'll ... smash them.'

'A severe scolding and a couple of thousand cleans would suffice,' Gubbledon answered, then lowered his head back onto the sand, as though the effort of speaking had become too much.

Benjamin stared up at the dormitory, and tried to figure out what to do. Usually he would draw the reanimation power from the air, but in this case he needed to take it away. He narrowed his eyes, concentrating on the dormitory, trying to imagine it was a glass of juice and he was the straw, sucking out its contents.

It began to move. Benjamin frowned, worried he'd got it wrong yet again, and that it would tumble down the cliff despite his best efforts. Then, after one last shudder, it stood still.

Benjamin let out a slow breath. Sweat had broken out on his arms, something not entirely unpleasant due to his wet clothes. He nodded, then looked down at Gubbledon. 'Let me help you up.'

Gubbledon shook his long head. 'No, no, you've done plenty to help me already. Just tell Moto where I am. He'll send someone to help.'

'If you're sure.'

'I am. Thank you, Benjamin. I was ... wrong about you.'

Benjamin nodded. 'Thank you for saying that, Housemaster,' he said.

'You should hurry now. I never did ask what you're doing down here. You're not supposed to be on the beach by yourself. Too ... dangerous.'

Benjamin smiled. 'I was lost, but I think I'm okay now.'

He turned to the door in the cliff, only for Gubbledon to say behind him, 'Oh, isn't that pretty.'

Something about the innocence in Gubbledon's voice gave Benjamin a deep sense of dread. He looked up at the cliff to see a line of flickering lights stretching along the path from the dormitory to the school and around the balustrade outside the main entrance.

Godfrey's crew.

They had found him.

36

SACRIFICE

The Dark Mages jostled Miranda along ahead of them, while all around, ghouls marched, stumbled, and staggered across the bridge into Sunshine Land. On Miranda's right walked Timothy, his monstrous face hidden again behind its human mask. As she glanced at him, it was impossible to tell that he could strip it away to reveal a blackened skull with orange eyes, but, already afraid she would never sleep again, she hoped he felt no need for a second demonstration.

Wilhelm was behind her. She could only tell from the Dark Mages' grunts as they dragged his inert body. Soon, like herself, he would be thrown into the pit with the rest of the captured reanimates and items yet to gather life. What would return, she couldn't guess.

As they paused shortly before the bridge, caught in a bottleneck of ghouls crossing over, Emmie came up alongside her. The girl wore a cloak with a hood, but otherwise looked like the same Emmie Bromwich

Miranda remembered from school, when she had been the manager of the flower-pressing club, a dinner monitor, and briefly Miranda's partner on a school project. Having not seen what might be hiding behind Emmie's face, Miranda felt a fraction less terrified. Before the girl could move on ahead, she struck up the courage to speak.

'Why did you choose to be one of them?' she whispered.

'What do you mean, why? There was no choice to make.'

'I mean, you only left the school a couple of weeks ago.'

Emmie sighed, then smiled. 'Once you have been where I've been, you'll feel differently. I serve the Great Scientist, and until now I had never known true happiness.'

'Oh. I was just asking because, you know, I've also decided to serve him. I just wondered what was going on.'

'Really? You've become one of us so soon? For some it takes months. Sara never turned. The decision had to be made for her.'

'But I thought you said there was no decision.'

'Not for me, there wasn't. Once I let the heart into my heart—'

'What heart?'

'The heart of dark reanimate. It's what Sunshine Land is built over. After the Great Scientist discovered it and acquired the park for his studies, it began to work its magic over all who entered through the gates.'

'How?'

'He built the Animatter machine.'

'That firefly thing?'

'Yes, that.' Emmie gave a cold laugh. 'The heart draws them, and the Animatter machine collects a little piece of payment from all who enter. You only see the fireflies because it's so overloaded it's on the verge of collapse.'

'Isn't that a bad thing?'

Emmie shook her head. 'No, no, no. It provides us with food. Without it, we would cease to be.'

'You mean die?'

Emmie laughed again. 'Oh, no. You can't just die here in Endinfinium. The ghouls would become reanimates, and we would become cleaners.'

'But what kind of food is it? Like that fruit? That's no real fruit, is it?'

'It's soul fruit. Created of the souls of the thousands who gave a piece of theirs when they came to Sunshine Land. Now, we strip reanimates of their life in order to keep it full, and keep us fed.'

'So all of you, the former pupils and the ghouls, are ... cannibals?'

Emmie turned to Miranda and gave her a sadistic grin. 'All of us.'

Miranda forced herself to laugh along with Emmie. 'Oh, it's, um, great, isn't it? I mean, it's not real food, but it's so tasty.'

'Isn't it just? You know, if you use a little reanimation magic you can turn it into anything—meat pies, parfait, sausages ... it's great.'

'It's such a shame I'm just an, um, Weaver.'

'Yes, terrible shame. But once you've been cleansed, we'll help you. We all help each other. That's what friends are for.'

'Um, cleansed?'

'Yes. You need to have any stray thoughts removed. It was a mistake we made with Sara, not giving her enough alone-time with the heart. For yourself and Wilhelm, we won't make such a mistake. I mean, you say that you've made your decision, but until the last lingering doubt is cleansed from your heart, you can never be fully trusted.'

'Oh, that's good. I mean, that soon I'll be cleansed.'

Emmie fell quiet as they continued to the bridge, squeezing among rows of charred, stumbling ghouls, only their bleached skulls and orange eyes shining out of their burned bodies. Miranda, sensing Emmie's tongue could be loosened further, decided to change tack.

'That machine … it's pretty clever, isn't it?'

'The Animatter? Yes, it's a work of genius. Something we've come to expect from the Great Scientist.'

'So, it, um, collects bits of soul?'

'Yes.'

'And what does it do with all these bits?'

'It stores them.'

'Why?'

'How should I know?'

'And this heart … what kind of heart is it?'

'It is the one true substance,' she said. 'The heart is pure dark reanimate. Only the Great Scientist has the ability to find it, and he used it to save mankind from itself.'

'That's ... nice, but how?'

Emmie put a hand on Miranda's arm. 'No need for so many questions. Once you have been cleansed, you will feel all the answers you need in your heart.'

'So, that machine, the Animatter … it contains the souls of people?'

Emmie shook her head. 'It contains the souls of the dead, but only a small piece of the living.'

'And you use it to feed yourself?'

'Yes. We have no need for human food. Our human bodies are gone, replaced by our new bodies, created by the heart.'

'But, perhaps, if we opened the machine, we could have a really big feast.'

Emmie's eyes flared as though Miranda had said the ultimate faux pas. 'Opening the machine would release the souls,' she said.

'And that's a bad thing?'

'Of course it is. They would all return to their homes, and we would be left with ... nothing.'

'Oh, we, um, don't want that.'

'No, we really don't. There'd be nothing left of us.'

They laughed together, Miranda hoping she didn't sound as wild as she felt she did. They moved on for a few more steps, before the procession came to a gradual halt.

'Oh, that's interesting,' Emmie said.

'What?'

'They've found a big one.'

'A big what?'

'Reanimate.'

A sense of dread filled Miranda from the toes up. When a low, frightened baying came from behind her, she didn't want to turn around, but the Dark Mages that held her were pulling her back out of the way so a new group could pass.

Hundreds of charred, orange ghouls, their bleached skull faces gleaming, carried Lawrence like ants transporting a captured caterpillar. A cobweb of ropes and cables held him still as the ghouls marched in the direction of the amphitheatre and the glowing pit. Lawrence strained at his bonds, but there were too many.

Miranda's hands trembled. Despite the terror she felt, she forced a smile.

'What happens when he goes into the pit?'

Emmie gave a cold laugh. 'His life energy will be taken by the Animatter machine and then shared among all of us. Such a large creature, we will surely feast.'

'And what happens to the reanimate?'

'He deanimates, of course.'

'So, he … dies?'

'I guess if you want to call it that. But he doesn't really. I mean, they're not really alive, are they? It's only borrowed life. Take it away and they're just rubbish, thrown away by mankind like everything else in Endinfinium. Like even this wondrous place was in the end. Such a terrible shame to waste so much, isn't it? Luckily the Great Scientist found a way to make use of it.'

Miranda had no idea what to say. The ghouls had carried Lawrence past her now, and the procession fell into step behind.

'I want to see,' she said, her mouth dry.

'We'll have ringside seats,' Emmie said.

With Lawrence's guard moving ahead, the procession began again. They reached the amphitheatre where ghouls of all shapes and sizes filled the rows of wooden seats. They hummed and moaned like the crowd at a Halloween gladiator event. Emmie and the other Dark Mages led Miranda down to the stage in front of the pit. Lawrence, still held by the rows of ghouls, was away to one side, struggling against his bonds, his eyes blinking with fear and disbelief.

The Dark Mages brought Wilhelm to stand alongside Miranda. His eyes were glazed and he swayed from side to side as though drugged.

'Feel kind of lightheaded,' he muttered. 'Like I could fly.'

'What are we going to do?' Miranda hissed.

'I have no idea.'

Miranda opened her mouth to say something else but an elbow in her back left her gasping for breath.

'Shut your mouth,' Timothy said. 'Show some respect.'

As he glared at her, his face clearly a mask in the orange glow emanating up from the pit, Miranda was too scared to reply. She tried to meet his gaze but gave up, and instead took an interest in her own feet.

'Harness them.'

The order came from a Dark Mage near the front.

Miranda closed her eyes, secretly feeling for their magic, and realised only three were Channellers like herself. Most were Weavers like Wilhelm, and only one was a Summoner, the one who had spoken.

'He's the dangerous one,' she whispered to Wilhelm, who nodded, but didn't look as though he understood. Instead, he swayed from side to side, a faraway look on his face.

'When they touch you, the fireflies, you can hear them,' he whispered. 'The people. Wow, it's crazy. I can hear all of them. Hundreds and hundreds, year after year.'

Miranda opened her mouth to reply, but a Dark Mage grabbed her arms and looped ropes around them. The next thing she knew, she was rising up into the air, suspended in a harness that swung her out over the pit. Wilhelm swung up behind her, and like a pair of giant marionettes, they swung back and forth across the pit while thousands of orange eyes watched them.

From above, the pit was nothing more than a hole in the earth. It wasn't even filled with proper fire, more a reedy orange substance, like streamers of papier-mâché blowing in the wind. Whatever the heart was, it was too far down to be seen.

It was only when Miranda closed her eyes against the smoke and felt with her heart instead of her skin, did she understand. The heart of the fire, behind the heat of the flames, was ice cold, like a glacier set alight. She let her mind approach it, then abruptly drew back as a feeling of darkness so bleak it was like the extinguishing of every light in the world brushed against her like the spines of a deadly, waking beast.

The heart that Emmie talked about might have the ability to give life, but of itself it was the most lifeless thing that she could imagine. It was so lifeless it was beyond dead.

'It is time for tonight's sacrifices to begin,' shouted the leading Dark Mage, arms raised aloft like a pantomime villain. 'Bring forth the offerings.'

Ghouls pushed forward several captured reanimates. Miranda closed her eyes at the sound of their terrified screaming, wishing she could close her ears, too. Below her, the first few fell in, tumbling down a slope into the black maw, still screaming. Each time, the crowd gave a low ahh, and a strange feeling of light-headedness came over her, a sense of euphoria.

Wilhelm swung closer. 'Do you realise what they're doing?'

'I'm not sure.'

'They're sucking out their life energy, turning them back into simple machines.'

'How?'

'I don't know. I only know I can feel it. After looking in that machine, I feel ... different. What happens to them is their life energy spreads out around us. Part goes into the Animatter machine. Part into us. The machine, though, it's overloaded. It can't take much more.'

'What can we do about it?'

Wilhelm frowned, not looking at her. His brow shifted as though tormented by indecision. At last, still not able to meet her gaze, he said, 'I want you to use your magic to cut me loose. Let me fall in.'

'No!'

'It's the only way. I'm young, I'm strong. If the machine takes me, I'll break it.'

Miranda frantically shook her head. 'But you'll die.'

'Maybe, maybe not.' He reached a hand out of his harness as they swung near and squeezed her hand. 'I can feel them,' he said. 'So, so many, both here in Endinfinium and elsewhere in the world we came from. If we break the machine they'll be freed. Many won't even notice the change, but for others their whole lives will be restored. If that's not worth a sacrifice, what is?'

Miranda, tears in her eyes, shook her head. 'No!'

'Do it. You have the power. Cut me free!'

In the stands around the pit, the ghouls were shifting, cajoled into movement by a great event. Lawrence, still tied, was hauled to the edge of the pit. He whimpered, despite the ropes holding his jaw closed.

The ghouls shifted into lines, readying themselves for the big push.

Lawrence, his claws caught in the ropes, scrabbled vainly at the earth. Miranda watched him, and for an instant their eyes met.

'Into the pit!' screamed the leading Dark Mage.

Miranda gulped. She knew what she had to do. She had no other choice. Pushing through the ropes, she called out to Wilhelm, 'Take my hand!'

As he swung across, she wished there was something she could say to him, something that was more profound than a simple goodbye.

37

LANDFALL

The air filled with a humming sound. Benjamin dived for cover just as a huge rock rose up out of the sand and then slammed hard back down right where he had been standing.

All around, other huge, buried rocks were pushing out of the sand, hauled by funnels of magic that Benjamin could feel like great dark fingers. He had no doubt Godfrey's Dark Reanimation Society were all up there on the cliffs, the Channellers drawing their power from the lines of gaping, unsuspecting Weavers.

As a rock crashed down just an arm's length in front of him, showering him with sand, he felt the hate rising up inside. How dare they? He had done nothing wrong.

'Gubbledon!'

The reanimated racehorse lay not far to his right. Unable to walk, the housemaster was like a bright red balloon stuck to a dart board. It was only a matter of time before one of the rocks struck him.

Another rock was rising up nearby, sending waterfalls of sand rushing around his feet. Benjamin gritted his teeth, feeling for his magic as the rock rose over his head.

'Oh, no, you don't.'

He pushed, hard. The rock flew away, much further than he had intended, crashing into the cliff not far below the wall of the school's outer courtyard.

As parts of the balustrade wall crumbled and collapsed, pupils ran back out of range, screaming in terror.

Benjamin stared. So close. He had meant only to knock the rock away.

Cheeks smarting with how close he had come to hurting someone, he ran to Gubbledon and tried to lift the reanimated racehorse up to his feet.

'Leave me,' Gubbledon said. 'I'm mincemeat now. Fit only for the knackers' yard.'

'Get up,' Benjamin snapped. 'If this was the—' he searched his brain for the name of a famous horse race '—Gold Cup, would you just lie there? Get up.'

'The Melbourne Cup,' Gubbledon said, with a hint of pride. 'I won the Melbourne Cup.'

'Well, that's nice. Let's try and win it again, shall we? The finish line is right over there, by that door.'

A rustling sound now filled the air. Sand, this time, rose up from the beach, creating a grey-ginger veil that blocked their view of everything but the sand at their feet.

Benjamin reached out, pushing with his magic at the sand and shingle beneath Gubbledon. The racehorse bounced up to his feet. One leg was crooked, the thigh bone snapped, but the other three were in working order.

'Lean on me, if you can.'

Gubbledon put one hoof on Benjamin's shoulder. The weight was surprising, but Benjamin pushed with his magic to hold the housemaster up. Each time he used it now, he felt a flutter in his heart, as though he were getting to the end of his strength. He only hoped they could make it to the door before his power gave out.

Somewhere in front of them, the ground shuddered. Another rock, hidden by the sandscreen, had struck the beach. The deadly rocks were invisible now unless Benjamin used his magic, but at the same time, he was invisible to his attackers on the cliffs.

'This way, back toward the water.'

'Are you sure? I don't want to get my feet wet.'

'You won't. We're just skirting around where those rocks are falling. They've put that screen up to stop us seeing them, but it makes us invisible, too. If we go back along the shoreline and skirt around, they won't expect it.'

With painstaking slowness, they made their way back down the beach to where the water lapped at their feet. Gubbledon balked when one hoof got splashed by a little wave, but Benjamin hissed at him to stay quiet. Together, they stumbled along the shoreline until Benjamin was sure they were out of range of Godfrey's rocks, then turned back up the beach.

'The sandscreen is thinner here,' Benjamin said.

A few steps further along, it cleared completely, and they found themselves at the edge of the shore, looking out at a tall fogbank half a mile from the coast.

'Is that the city of ghouls?'

Gubbledon nodded. 'Yes, yes. Very dangerous. You have to get rid of it.'

'How?'

'Like you did last time.'

Benjamin wanted to scream. 'I don't know what I did last time. I wasn't here then, was I?'

'Yes, you were. You took the city away. You saved the school.'

'I don't know what to do. You were here, why don't you tell me?'

Gubbledon sighed. 'I'm just a racehorse. I don't know anything really. Perhaps you could ask the teachers what you did?'

'Which teacher? They've all gone mad.'

'Professor Melford. He always liked you.'

'Who?'

'Oh, perhaps he's gone now. What about Mistress Sleek?'

Benjamin shook his head. Gubbledon reeled off a few more names of long-dead-and-gone teachers before Benjamin put up a hand.

'Look, I might be "back", if you think it was really me before, but everyone else has changed. I don't know what I did because no one can remember.'

'You went away and you didn't come back.'

'I don't want to go away.'

'Oh, but I thought you did. That's what Master

Jacobs and Miss Butterworth always say. That you keep trying to find a way home. Perhaps the city of ghouls is your chance.'

Benjamin scowled. Gubbledon's voice was slurring, high-pitched, and his words made little sense.

'There must be someone. What about Cleat?'

'The old librarian? Oh, he was a scamp. Lovely boy, bit of a tearaway. Not so different to Master Jacobs really. He was heartbroken when you left, and he probably never got over it. Just retreated to that dusty old cellar to spend all his time among those books.'

'You mean the library?'

'Yes, that's the one. Hideous place. The dust gives me terrible allergies.'

'Anyone else?'

'Well, the Grand Lord was here. He's been here as long as I can remember.'

'Grand Lord Bastien?'

'Yes.'

'Wouldn't he have told me?'

Gubbledon shrugged. 'Well, human memories aren't as clear as those of us reanimates,' he said. 'Perhaps he forgot.'

'Come on. We have to get you to that door.'

They clambered back up the beach to the foot of the cliff. Gubbledon groaned with each step, even though Benjamin was sure reanimates felt no pain. They were nearly in the cliff's shadow when Gubbledon stopped.

'Can I just sit down for a while?'

'Keep going. We just need to backtrack to the door.'

Gubbledon sighed. 'I know I'm just a reanimated

racehorse, but when you spend all your time around humans, you start to act like them.'

'Well, I'm not giving up, am I? Can't you act like me?'

'Oh, I'll try.'

The ground shuddered below them, knocking Gubbledon back down before he'd risen halfway to his feet. A second shudder knocked Benjamin down, too, and he sat hard on the sand, a rock poking into the back of his leg.

'What happened?'

Gubbledon pointed to the shore. 'Oh, dear. I think the city just made landfall.'

The fog was clearing. Where the sea had been was now a towering, waterlogged cliff rising slowly out of the water, grinding as it forced its way up onto the shore. Dozens of reanimates of all sizes struggled as they clung to ledges and crevasses.

'Oh, dear.'

Benjamin turned. Gubbledon was sliding down the beach, his body digging up a ridge of sand and rocks.

'What's happening?'

'It's the island. It's pulling me.'

The reanimates hanging from the rock were stuck to the cliff as though by glue, Benjamin realised, and soon Gubbledon would join them if he didn't hurry.

He closed his eyes, feeling outward. A cold wind met him, tendrils of dark magic encircling Gubbledon, pulling him in. With a surge of his own magic, Benjamin snapped them, sending them fleeing back to the island to regroup. Gubbledon pushed himself shakily back to his feet.

'To the door,' Benjamin said. 'Quickly, before it gets hold of you again.'

As the tendrils of dark magic came snapping back, Benjamin shooed them off again, then dragged Gubbledon up to the cliff. Further along the beach, the great veil of sand crashed back to earth, and several huge rocks hanging in the air did the same.

This close to the cliff, Benjamin and Gubbledon were hidden from the kids in the courtyard, but if he used his magic again they would find him. However, from the sounds coming from above, he knew that the island's appearance had distracted them.

As he stared at the island still driving itself up the beach, pushing a wave of junk, sand, and rocks ahead of it, with its trapped reanimates and the chill of its dark magic, the cheering from the cliffs over his head sent an arrow of horror piercing straight into his heart.

38

PIED PIPER

The door opened in front of them. Three reanimates Benjamin didn't recognise rushed out and carried Gubbledon out of his arms.

'Quickly, get back inside,' he snapped. 'That thing … whatever it is … it'll catch you.'

The three reanimates—two tables waving wooden legs like arms, and what had perhaps been a wheelbarrow but now was part made of soil—gave him barely a cursive glance before hurrying back inside. Benjamin started to follow, but found the door slammed shut in his face.

'Wait! I need to get inside.'

'You are no longer welcome in Underfloor,' came a muffled voice from behind. 'We are peaceful reanimates. We do not want to concern ourselves with the troubles of you humans.'

Exasperated, Benjamin thumped on the door, but it wouldn't budge. He thought about blowing it off with his magic, but that would gain him no friends, and he was hunted by enough people already. Instead, he turned to face the massive bulk of the island pushing up onto the shore, wondering quite how he had supposedly banished it once before, and wondering how he could do it this time.

If Grand Lord Bastien had the answers, Benjamin had to find him, and before Godfrey's crew found Benjamin.

If only Miranda and Wilhelm were here … they would know what to do.

Perhaps, if they were near, he could feel them—

He dropped to his knees on the shore and closed his eyes. Then, reaching out with his heart, he felt for Miranda's magic. If she was somewhere near, she might sense his in return.

Reanimation magic was most obvious as the presence of a preternatural heat, but if he concentrated, condensing it, Benjamin could visualise it as threads drifting in the dark space inside his mind, some even allowing him to identify their users. Some threads were ancient, the memories of long-vanished Channellers and Summoners who had left behind traces of their presence. Some were fresh but misguided, belonging to inexperienced Channellers who likely had no idea they were even using. Some belonged to the teachers, while others showed intent, like the black line of Godfrey's searching magic, hunting for Benjamin.

Nothing.

Miranda, wherever she was, was keeping her magic

hidden. In fact, there were no traces of her at all, as though she were doing her very best to hide her ability.

He was getting back to his feet when he felt the chilly touch of another user's magic.

Godfrey.

Benjamin ran to the cliff and began to climb. The rock rose sheer above him, abundant with ledges and handholds but angling out in a way that a single mistake would send him plummeting to the beach below. Without a climbing harness he felt helpless, so he gritted his teeth and concentrated on the basics: one hold at a time, rest, feel each hold for weight, shut your eyes, push up, and hope to everything that you don't make a mistake and go tumbling off.

Twenty minutes later he hauled himself up over the lip of the cliff and collapsed, exhausted, in the grass. Even in Captain Roche's climbing classes he usually cheated a little bit if he was worried about falling, but this time he had done the whole climb without using his magic.

He was sitting now on top of the cliff to the south of the school's main entrance. No way led down to the cliff on this side, so he was protected from view by a tall, crumbling wall of flagstones, occasionally interspersed with protruding metal girders and the odd lump of dusty plastic.

Dusting himself down, he climbed to his feet and turned so his back was to the wall, out of sight from above unless someone chose to brave the precarious overhang from the courtyard on this side.

The island, still partly fog-shrouded, shuddered as it pressed into the beach, still trying to move forward.

It felt like the island, like everyone else in Endinfinium, it seemed, was chasing him.

He stood, shaky on his tired legs. Whatever was about to happen, there wasn't much time.

The teachers' tower was around the back of the school, and Grand Lord Bastien's quarters were at the very top. It was a climb he had known only Wilhelm to do without the aid of magic. He had no chance. Instead, he headed for a set of stairs set into the wall a short distance back from the cliff. They ended at a metal gate, beyond which was an outside path leading around the main entrance to the school to a side door.

He took a deep breath, preparing to run again. Then, with a quick burst of his magic, he picked the old lock and slipped through.

A second to close his eyes and concentrate was all it took to see streamers of dark magic come snapping in his direction. Godfrey, Derek, some others, they were alert to him again.

He ran. Bolting past the main entrance, he reached the side door and found it locked. His magic opened it, but he had begun to panic, and he drew the magic wrong, a cut opening up on his shoulder as he drew from his own body instead of the air.

With a grimace he slipped through, slammed the door and created a quick barrier to hold the door shut, a wall of magic that would take a greater wall to break down. Then, he was running again.

Through the corridors, up and down stairs, past the

disinterested looks of a few cleaners he encountered as they went about their business unaware of any crisis, he ran, barely pausing to draw breath. Whenever he heard footsteps or shouting close by, he was more thankful than ever for Wilhelm, his friend having put a focus on knowing every route, every corridor, every secret door, every shortcut around the mazelike, ramshackle castle they called a school.

As angry shouts came from behind him, followed by a wave of heat that was one of the rookie Channellers trying to snare him with a magical net, Benjamin ducked into a science classroom, ran behind the back row of desks, through a door into a storeroom, and then out through a tiny door under a table, emerging on a low-ceilinged maintenance corridor with water pipes humming and shaking all around him. With the sound of slowly reanimating metal for company, he hurried to the end, opened a hatch and climbed out onto a major concourse leading to the teachers' apartments.

What seemed like years ago, he, Miranda and Wilhelm had got trapped by the teachers' own form of a gatekeeper—a quicksand-like area of wood outside the door which would set hard and trap any pupil without an appointment. Now, though, Benjamin followed the same passage but skirted along the edge, the solid floorboards memorised long ago on Wilhelm's suggestion, in case an emergency arose.

He still expected to knock to get inside; the door had always been protected by a powerful ward. Now, however, he found the door not only unprotected, but not even locked. It stood a few inches ajar, so Benjamin crept through then locked it from the inside.

The teachers' study, a miniature library filled with textbooks, was empty. Benjamin closed his eyes, searching for the threads of their magic. A few tendrils led up the spiral staircase to their living quarters, but none were active. Benjamin climbed quickly up to a living area complete with comfortable chairs and sofas, even a TV in one corner. Some chairs had begun to reanimate, rocking back and forth, one moving so much that it had knocked over a vase of chamomile flowers.

On the next level he found himself in a bathroom area far more modern than the rest of the school, and in fact far nicer than that which the pupils used in the dormitory. He ignored a wry bitterness and headed for the stairs in the corner.

The next level contained the first of the living apartments. The teachers' names hung on plaques over the doors: Professor Loane, Mistress Ito, Captain Roche, Professor Eaves, Professor Coach, Mistress Xemian, and many more, some he recognised, many he had never heard of. A couple of doors near the top had recently had their plaques removed, as though the teachers had gone on to pastures new. Where those pastures might be in Endinfinium, Benjamin couldn't imagine.

Finally, he reached the very highest door in the top of the tower, a tall, ornate wooden door complete with brass fittings, one of the few doors that seemed to naturally fit with such a place.

He lifted his hand to knock, but the door was slightly ajar.

'Grand Lord?' he whispered, slipping inside. 'Are you there? It's me. Benjamin Forrest.'

The room was dark, the furniture and shelves just outlines. Something felt strange, as though the room were a living thing. Benjamin went to the curtains and pulled them open on a grey evening. The yellow sun was just an hour from setting over the sea, while, out of sight, a crimson glow suggested the red sun hung low above the trees of the Haunted Forest to the west.

The fogbank hung over the sea, but was clearing in places. A few metal towers protruded out of its white mass, a few twists and turns of a long-abandoned rollercoaster. This close to the school, Benjamin could make out ancient cars rusted solid to the rails.

'Benjamin.'

He spun, looking for the owner of the voice. At first he couldn't see the Grand Lord standing in an archway that led to an inner chamber, because Bastien was without his robes for the first time that Benjamin had ever seen, and what remained was a thin, translucent being that glowed only slightly brighter than its surroundings.

"A disassociated soul" was the explanation Edgar had given Benjamin, but he preferred the one the kids used.

Ghost.

Grand Lord Bastien could be nothing else. The figure walked across the room, his footfalls silent, even dust motes caught in the last rays of the evening sun passing through him.

'It has returned,' the Grand Lord said. 'Soon, we

will find ourselves once more at battle—one that, this time, I don't believe we can win.'

'Where are the other teachers?'

'Sick in their beds, afflicted by a malady only such proximity to a heart of pure dark reanimate can cause.'

'What are you talking about?'

'That island, the Lost City of the Ghouls, it sits on a heart of dark reanimate discovered far away, in the other world, long before the city ever came here. Dark reanimate is the very substance that gives Endinfinium life. However, this much, it distorts you, pushes and pulls at the same time, breaks you. It is an evil, dangerous thing.'

'Is that why the other kids have gone crazy?'

The Grand Lord nodded. 'Yes. You have too, if only you could understand what crazy meant to you. You are more powerful than they; it has affected you differently.'

'I'm not crazy. I feel fine.'

'Are you sure?'

Benjamin felt a flare of anger. 'Yes!'

The Grand Lord nodded. 'And there it is. Do you not see what I'm trying to tell you?'

'My anger….'

'Not just your anger, but the linking of your anger to your magic as a destructive force. You are a Summoner, one of the most powerful. Few Summoners survive here in Endinfinium.' The Grand Lord's eyes drifted from Benjamin's face, and he frowned. 'When you keep a dangerous pet … eventually it eats you.'

'But what can I do?'

'You have to banish the Lost City of the Ghouls.'

'You mean like I did before?'

The Grand Lord looked down. 'Who told you that?'

'A … a friend.'

'A reanimate.' The Grand Lord nodded. 'It is true, that it appears you are part of a cycle, but it is more complicated than that. The Benjamin Forrest that lived in Endinfinium before, he wasn't *you*. You are your own person.'

'That makes no sense.'

'Yours is a life none of us can imagine,' the Grand Lord said, 'because you alone inhabit it. Endinfinium is a world which revolves around its own special sun. The sun created it, moulds it, brings life, and takes it away. And you, Benjamin, are that sun.'

Tears sprang to Benjamin's eyes. 'I didn't ask for any of this.'

'Life doesn't care for questions,' the Grand Lord said. 'But it doesn't mind a few answers.'

'So, tell me. How do I banish the Lost City of the Ghouls and save the school?'

'Are you familiar with the Pied Piper of Hamlin?'

The shelves shuddered as Benjamin clenched his fists. 'That's a stupid kid's story.'

The Grand Lord shook his head. 'The Lost City of the Ghouls is your village of children, Benjamin Forrest.'

'You've lost your mind.'

The Grand Lord nodded again. 'I'm not the man I used to be, that's for sure. I wish that I would be again, but alas, I believe it is too late for me.'

Benjamin ran across to the Grand Lord and reached

out for him, but his hands passed right through. 'I can't do this,' he said, looking up into the Grand Lord's eyes, yet at the same time seeing the shelves behind him, laden with trinkets recovered from the sea. 'I need your help.'

'I am the longest serving of the teachers,' the Grand Lord said. 'That alone makes me unique. I am a Summoner, it is true, but my power is nothing compared to yours. You must find a way. Sixty years ago, a boy named Benjamin Forrest saved the school from the Lost City of the Ghouls. Sixty years for us, but maybe no time at all for somewhere else. That boy took it away, but in doing so, he was lost to us. I hope that the same fate will not befall you too, Benjamin. You are too important to lose.'

'Says the man who knows nothing but a bunch of lies,' Benjamin snapped. 'I trusted you. I trusted you to help me.'

The Grand Lord gave a tired sigh. 'Don't you understand? The only person who can help you, Benjamin, is you.'

A commotion came from outside the door. 'Bastien?' came a strange, hollow voice. 'Are you all right?'

'The magic that you wielded in anger, Benjamin, it has awoken them, but the heart of dark reanimate has left them not in their right minds. They are a danger to you. Quickly, you have to go.'

'Bastien!'

Benjamin reached out with his magic, slamming the door shut. He imagined a wall holding it closed, but immediately felt a fat, heavy power crashing into it from the other side. All around, objects on the shelves shuddered, some falling to the floor where they shattered, pieces spreading out like the fallen leaves of flowers.

'The window,' Grand Lord Bastien said. 'Go, before they break through your ward. Remember what I said: you are the piper at the gate of the Lost City of the Ghouls. It is your village of children.'

The door shuddered, and Benjamin felt his magic breaking apart beneath a frenzied assault from outside. Should they break through, they would show him no mercy.

He ran to the window and pulled it open. A yawning chasm opened out below, the green of the clifftop obscured by wisps of fog drifting in off the sea.

'It's too high.'

The Grand Lord smiled. 'You control the best harness a man could have. Use it. Go, Benjamin. And heed my words. For what they are, for what they were, and for what they could be.'

Benjamin turned to look back. He wanted to say something to the Grand Lord, either 'thanks,' or 'sorry,' or 'why can't you help me?' but his throat was dry, his hands shaking with fear, and nothing, not even a muttered 'goodbye', would come. He gave the Grand Lord a nod, wondering if it was the last time they would ever see each other, then closed his eyes, and jumped.

39

ESCAPE

Making fire was one of the first tricks Edgar had taught Miranda. It was easy; push and pull at the air quick enough to create heat, then direct it at something that could easily burn. Once you had figured out how to move the air at the right speed, you could start a spark in moments, and as Miranda turned from one burning frond of the rope to the other, she wondered whether it wouldn't be easier to turn it on herself too, rather than risk what might happen when she fell into the pit.

Too late, she had time only to smile at Wilhelm before she was falling, the ropes burned away from her wrists and shoulders, the air rushing past as the pit's black-orange maw rushed up to meet her. The look of horror on Wilhelm's face was haunting, an understanding that as a simple Weaver, alone he was as helpless as the reanimates captured and dragged into the pit.

As she fell, she enacted the second part of her plan. She closed her eyes, and with her mind reached out for all the power she could channel: not from the air but from the Dark Mages, from the ghouls, from the reanimates, and even from Wilhelm. She took every last piece she could, and rather than use it, she drew it into herself, swallowing it down like a parched man dousing himself in water. Her eyes flew open as she was overwhelmed by a flood of sheer life, and all she saw around her was a brilliant, blinding, brightness.

And then there was nothing but an empty, soundless void, with the tail-lights of all existence disappearing into a distance that was infinitely large.

∽

'Miranda!'

Wilhelm grasped for her hand, but it was too late. Their fingers brushed for an instant, then she was gone. She had turned on him, denied him at the last, sacrificing herself in his place. As she fell, a brief smile came over her face before she was lost to the darkness, the pit swallowing her up.

'Miranda!' he screamed again. '*Miranda!*'

The air had stilled. The burned ghouls stood in rows, expectant. Thousands of glowing orange eyes stared at the pit.

Wilhelm twisted in the harness, trying to create a swing, looping himself up and over the lines of seats and the stage in front. The Dark Mages had run to the edge of the pit and were peering over, looking for Miranda.

On the far side of the stage, Lawrence lay still, encircled by ropes. If only Wilhelm could reach him—

'She's gone,' one of the Dark Mages shouted in a voice Wilhelm recognised as that of Emmie Bromwich. 'She has given herself to the heart in order that we may feast. Oh, what a glorious day.'

Wilhelm heard a loud buzzing that quickly became deafening. He stared as a dark orange swarm rose up over the amphitheatre, turned and rushed downward.

Fireflies. Millions and millions of them.

'That fool!' the nearest Dark Mage shouted. 'She has overloaded the machine. We must restore the balance.'

'Consume them!' shouted another, grabbing handfuls of fireflies out of the air and stuffing them into his mouth. 'The machine must not break!'

In the stands, hundreds of ghouls were doing the same, reaching up with claws and levers and buckets to scoop and grasp and pick the fireflies out of the air, stuffing them into the black maws of their skull faces.

'No!' Wilhelm screamed. 'You can't have her!'

Another mage pointed up at him. 'The boy. He must be used to address the balance. A sacrifice.'

Wilhelm struggled in his harness. Miranda had failed, but if he also threw himself in, surely that would be enough to overload the machine. With one eye on the Dark Mages below as they circled toward him, he pulled his arms free of the harness.

The pit flared below, like a dark orange eye. Tears streamed down Wilhelm's face as he pulled a leg free. As he leaned out of the harness, he understood how brave Miranda must have been to give up her life. He had offered, but had not been sure he could do it until she had gone in first.

'I'll never forget you,' he sobbed between gritted teeth, and pushed himself out.

For an instant he was plummeting into the pit. Then the world turned, spinning him in a circle as a magical force tugged on his legs, and his back came down hard on the amphitheatre's stone stage.

He was still gasping for breath when a figure came to stand over him.

'Not so fast. What, you think you're some kind of hero?' The figure pulled back his hood. Timothy grinned. 'You know what happens now, don't you?'

Wilhelm shook his head.

'We need to address the balance.'

'If you throw me in that pit, you'll break the machine.'

'Which is why we couldn't let you fall in.' Another Dark Mage came to stand beside Timothy. They looked at each other then laughed.

'He doesn't understand,' Timothy said.

'He's a fool,' the other Dark Mage said. 'They all are. He'll understand soon. Assuming ghouls have any understanding at all.'

An invisible force hauled Wilhelm up to his feet and held his arms at his sides. Magic, he realised, either Timothy's or that of the other.

'The heart is a simple thing,' Timothy said, grinning wildly. 'It takes life when it is offered, but it also gives life when it is absent. Look around you. Their eyes are everywhere.'

The air wasn't cold, but Wilhelm shivered anyway as he took in the hundreds of ghouls glowing orange through their charred bodies, the jawbones of their human skulls clacking together jubilantly as they chewed on handfuls of glittering fireflies.

'You cannot keep taking life without giving some back. To correct the imbalance your friend has caused, all we have to do is kill you before we throw you in.'

'No!'

Wilhelm jumped at the two Dark Mages, pushing his way between them. Timothy turned, and Wilhelm kicked him hard in the shin. Timothy just smiled, and then something invisible held him tight.

'Fool,' he said. 'You think we're still like you, don't you? We can't feel the pain that you can.'

'I don't care what you can feel.'

The second Dark Mage opened his mouth to reply, but a sudden jolt stole his words. All three of them looked around, before the second Dark Mage smiled.

'We just arrived,' he said.

'Where?'

'Where do you think? At Endinfinium High.'

Wilhelm looked from one Dark Mage to the other. Their faces were rapturous. He felt empty inside. Miranda was gone, and the island had reached the school. Soon, thousands of ghouls would rush up the beaches to engulf it.

'Do it then,' Wilhelm said. 'Kill me. I don't care.'

'With pleasure. Timothy, hold him.'

Timothy's arms encircled Wilhelm's shoulders. He

struggled, but it was no good; held partly by magic and partly by a stronger, older boy, he couldn't move.

The head Dark Mage smiled. He pulled a knife from inside his robes and held it up. A sensation like wet blankets on his skin encircled Wilhelm, crushing him. The Dark Mage was doing what Miranda said you could do with the air, pulling it, making it contract, but it didn't matter because he was trapped and the world was filled with a dazzling light—

The feeling vanished. The Dark Mage let out a cry and dropped the knife. He tumbled backward, arms covering his eyes. Timothy gave a surprised gasp and let go. Wilhelm elbowed him in the stomach, then dashed forward and shoved the Dark Mage hard, watching with satisfaction as the boy slipped back over the edge of the pit and tumbled down into its glowing orange depths.

'What have you done?' screamed Timothy, but he was lying on the ground, one arm covering his eyes. 'You'll spend forever dying for this!'

'We'll see,' Wilhelm said, lifting the knife. Further across the platform, other Dark Mages had turned in his direction, but most were shielding their eyes from the blinding light pointed right at them.

Wilhelm turned. Lawrence, trapped by the ropes, had switched on the huge, luminous headlights he used to navigate underwater, and had directed them right into the eyes of Timothy and the other Dark Mages. If Wilhelm's chest hadn't still felt part crushed, he might have laughed.

With the knife in one hand, he ran to the trapped

snake-train, shoved a couple of shrieking ghouls aside and hacked at Lawrence's bonds.

'To the school!' Timothy screamed behind him. 'Destroy them all! Destroy the unbelievers!'

One of Lawrence's huge feet broke free. The snake-train howled and knocked aside the nearest ghouls as they tried to restrain him. Then, struggling against his bonds, he broke his other front leg free.

'Stop them!' someone shouted.

'Inside,' Lawrence boomed, and a door on the side of his huge locomotive head flipped open. Wilhelm jumped in, and the door swung shut.

'Danger,' Lawrence said, using an internal speaker to relay his speech to Wilhelm. 'Hold on.'

Lawrence's insides were laid out like a regular express train, with two rows of seats either side of a central aisle. At the front, a large window showed what Lawrence was seeing. Wilhelm sat down in the front aisle row and clipped a seatbelt around him.

'She sacrificed herself,' he gasped. 'She tried to destroy the machine, but it wasn't enough and she's dead.'

Lawrence's locomotive head shook from side to side. 'Not dead,' he said. 'In Endinfinium, there is no dead. Just ... gone.'

'It makes no difference. What happens if she shows up as a cleaner in fifty years?'

Lawrence shook his head again. 'We have to go,' he said.

Through side windows, Wilhelm saw waves of ghouls rushing at Lawrence, their burned orange-black limbs flailing, their eyes glowing like the fireflies that still swarmed through the air. Lawrence shook them off and turned, clambering up through the amphitheatre to the main boulevard leading through Sunshine Land.

'The Animatter machine,' Wilhelm said. 'We have to destroy it. Can you go back to the city?'

Lawrence swung around. Hundreds of ghouls rushed for him, but he swatted them aside.

The boulevard led downhill to the bridge over to the city. Lawrence reached it in several large strides, bounding across like a dog let off the leash for the first time in too long. Wilhelm directed him through the city streets to the pyramid, but it wasn't necessary: the swarm of fireflies was like a string leading the way.

'There,' Wilhelm said. 'The machine is in there. We have to destroy it. It's the only way we can save the school and maybe Miranda.'

Lawrence nodded. 'How?'

'I don't know. Maybe throw it in the sea or something?'

Lawrence shook his head. 'Machine made of metal. Machine sink.'

'Well, I don't know, do I?'

'Talk to Edgar. Edgar always know answers.'

Wilhelm clapped his hands. 'That's it. That's our plan. Come on!'

Lawrence squeezed in through the pyramid's main doors, but the doors to the central chamber were too narrow. He tried to squeeze inside but it was too tight.

'Come on,' Wilhelm said 'Just a little more.'

'Door too small,' Lawrence said. 'Rope.'

'Rope?'

'Maintenance box. Rope.'

Set into the wall, Wilhelm found a cupboard containing flares, a medical kit, and a large coil of rope. It hummed with reanimation and practically jumped around Wilhelm's shoulder like an enthusiastic snake.

'Tie it,' Lawrence said. 'Then, we pull machine out.'

Lawrence opened a side door and Wilhelm climbed out, the coil of rope looped over his shoulder. He worried that it wouldn't be long enough, but as he tied one end to a steel strut between Lawrence's front feet, the rope stretched out as he unwound it then ducked under the stream of fireflies and headed into the Animatter chamber.

The machine was still where he remembered it, but now it was buried nearly halfway up its sides with ash. Wilhelm waded in, coughing as it plumed around him, filling his nose and mouth with an acridity that made him gag. As he moved forward, the ash got deeper, so that by the time he reached the machine he could barely keep his head above it, and the end of the rope, looped around his wrist, was entirely hidden.

And the ash here was shifting, moving to the machine like magnetised dust and then transforming into thousands of fireflies which buzzed off into the air, so that the top half of the machine was like a giant bee's nest. Wilhelm could see no sign of the metal casing at all.

'Okay, here goes,' he said, clamping one hand over his mouth and ducking down in the ash. As it shifted around him, he pushed forward, feeling on one side for the machine, and then doubling around the back. His fingers closed over a metal handle about halfway up and he looped the rope through it before tying it up. Then, he tried to stand up.

The ash had risen. His head no longer rose above it, and all he found was shifting, crawling fireflies engulfing him. He tried to scream, but his mouth filled with them and he swallowed a few dozen before he was able to get it shut. His fate was to drown in the things, he knew, but he thought of Miranda, her soul perhaps inside the machine, and he did the only thing he could think of which might save his life.

He pulled as hard as he could on the rope.

For a few seconds nothing happened. Then the rope went taut, and the ground slid away under his feet. A few desperate, suffocating seconds later, and he felt air around his face. He opened his eyes. The machine was sliding toward the door, Lawrence reeling in the rope.

Wilhelm glanced back as the door came up upon him. The fireflies still swarmed overhead, rising up off the top of the machine, but now the ash was following along behind like a gigantic trail of microfilaments, weaving back and forth as it clung to the machine.

'Wilhelm, get in.'

A door opened in Lawrence's head. Wilhelm let go of the rope and waded through the ash, climbing inside with a cry of relief. The door slammed shut, and through the windows Wilhelm saw Lawrence pull the machine through the door and then take it in his mouth, like a dog with a giant metal bone. The magnetic ash hung down below like a great beard, while the fireflies still rose from the machine like millions of symbiotic fish around a host.

'To the school,' Wilhelm said.

Lawrence, accelerating hard, burst out of the pyramid's main doors into the courtyard. The red sun hung nearly straight overhead, its light filtering through the remnants of fog. Wilhelm peered out of the windows, wondering which way was the school, while at the same time thinking it strange that the ground was reverberating, and the city around them appeared to be moving about.

'Problem,' Lawrence said, as something huge and blocky jumped into their way, and a great steel pole of an arm crashed down over Lawrence's front left paw, severing it clean off. Wilhelm knew Lawrence didn't feel pain like a human could, but the surprise made the snake-train gasp and draw back. The blocky creature turned, and a huge, gleaming skull appeared. A jaw widened in a smile, and glowing lights came on.

'Problem,' Lawrence repeated. 'The city ... the whole city ... woke up.'

40

DARK WAVE

FALLING, FALLING, FALLING.

Benjamin's vision spun as he tumbled over and over, the ground rushing up to meet him. At the last second, he put out his hands, trusted luck, and felt something cushion him from beneath, like a slowly deflating airbag.

Even so, he struck the ground hard enough to knock all the wind from his lungs, and for a couple of minutes he lay there gasping, the wet grass at the foot of the teachers' tower soaking his back.

He pushed himself up with what felt like the last of his strength, looked out to sea, and gasped.

The column of a rollercoaster rose above the edge of the cliff. The ground rumbled beneath his feet, and he knew that soon the city of ghouls would crush the ground the school stood upon, and with it, all the answers to this place.

And his friends.

He stood up and clenched his hands into fists, trying

to force himself to feel the fight that his body had given up.

The Pied Piper.

He felt like no such thing. How could he possibly save anyone?

Whatever had happened sixty years ago, he, or his namesake, had figured it out alone. No one had helped him. Perhaps the teachers then had similarly been affected with the madness brought on by the city being so close.

He walked to the edge of the cliff and looked down.

Hundreds of orange-black figures lined up along the edge of the island, a simple command away from storming the beaches below the school. Benjamin could tell from the glowing points of their eyes that these were ghouls, but of what kind, he couldn't tell. They came in all shapes and sizes, but they were charred and burned.

Benjamin sat down on the cliff edge to watch. Somewhere, the teachers and other pupils still hunted him, but even the fear of being caught was nothing compared to the threat posed by this army of ghouls. Nearly a year before, they had repelled one of the Dark Man's armies, but the school had no defence this time. The teachers and pupils had been turned to the Dark Man, and the reanimates refused to get involved.

He stood alone.

Where were Miranda and Wilhelm? He needed them like never before. He closed his eyes, feeling the great black wave of magic, and reached out for them.

Nothing.

'Where are you?' he whispered. 'I need you. I need you … my friends.'

Almost as though called, a single spark of light appeared, a finger of warmth touching his heart that he recognised.

Miranda.

'You're out there,' he whispered.

And then, with no warning, the ground began to tremble. Benjamin grabbed hold of two handfuls of couch grass as rocks crumbled beneath his feet. Out on the island the clouds swirled, becoming a spiral around a central vortex. A sudden chill filled Benjamin's heart, and he closed his eyes, hunting for Miranda, only to feel a massive bloom in her magic, like a single firework lighting up a dark, dark night, then it was gone.

And not just gone.

Vanished.

The cliff lurched. Cracks opened up around his feet and then he was falling once more, slipping down through a cascade of crumbling rock as the cliff fell out from beneath his feet.

Benjamin screamed, but the sound was lost in the roar. He reached out for his magic, trying to push himself through the tumbling rocks, back to the cliff edge and safety, but all he could find was a dark crack where he rolled, finding himself in a small tunnel opening, while a rain of rocks thundered past.

When it was still, he crawled, his body bloodied and battered, up to the end of the ledge, to look out once more at the island pressing in upon the beach. No longer did the lines of black-orange ghouls control his gaze, though. Now, from far across the island, a great column of flickering lights rose into the sky, burning up and falling back into the mists, only to be replaced by thousands more.

It was like the flickering of a million sparklers all at once.

And it had something to do with Miranda.

He rolled onto his back and lay facing up at the small cave's roof. His magic had knocked aside some of the falling rock, but not enough, and blood from a head-wound streamed down his face. He felt inside for his magic, but the well from which it came felt empty, dried up.

Weariness was like an unwanted companion lying beside him. He didn't even feel strong enough to test his body for injuries. Instead, he closed his eyes, letting his mind drift, to find the darkness with its streamers of light that were other users of magic.

Miranda's, which had bloomed so bright, was gone. Godfrey's no longer searched for his, while those of the teachers were a tangled mess, like the mat of threads at the bottom of his grandmother's sewing basket.

An army approached, and the school was defenceless. His friends were gone, possibly dead, and he lay battered and beaten in a cave halfway up a cliff face.

The Pied Piper.

What could it all mean?

Think, Benjamin, think.

He opened his eyes, saw only the dim grey of the cave, then closed them again.

Think!

The Dark Man was watching him. Godfrey had created the Dark Reanimation Society in order to bring the Dark Man to the school.

Darkness was everywhere.

In him.

He lifted his bad hand. He hadn't even noticed before, but as he stared at it, the cold he often felt grew stronger, and he realised it wasn't the cold from the air, but from the magic.

His hand was a block of ice.

The dark wave within which the tendrils of magic floated wasn't just background noise.

It was magic itself.

And it came from the island.

One giant thread of dark reanimation magic, and it surrounded him like a blanket made of oil.

He pushed himself up.

The Pied Piper.

Of course. The island had come to him, and it sought to get to him still. Why, he might never know, but it had come, and only he could draw it away.

'Miranda, Wilhelm … I'm coming,' he said, the pain from his head wound so great it brought tears to his eyes.

With a corner of his sleeve he wiped the blood out of his eyes, sniffed snot out of his nose, and crawled on down the tunnel.

41

CLIMBER

Pretty much everyone Wilhelm had spoken to had an opinion on the reanimates. Whether it was what constituted a true reanimate from something that was simply reanimating—Gubbledon Longface versus a jumping pencil, for example—to whether they could ever feel true human emotions and sensations no matter how long they reanimated for, everyone had something to say. The overall opinion, and one Wilhelm had often heard from reanimates themselves, was that they chose when to feel and when not to feel. Pain, for example, was something regrettable that only true animals had to suffer. Humour and elation, on the other hand, were really quite welcome.

But whether he really felt pain or fear, Lawrence was making a good show of it, howling in apparent terror as the blocky, reanimated houses came at him from everywhere. Even with one front paw severed, he was still able to use his back legs and long, snaking train-tail to manoeuvre himself through small spaces, and up over the top of them as they advanced. They were slow and cumbersome, but he was one reanimate against an entire city of ghouls.

'Master Wilhelm, hang on tight!' Lawrence shouted again, as though Wilhelm could do anything but, holding on for dear life as the locomotive head swung violently back and forth. Just keeping breath in his lungs was proving a chore with the belt across his chest regularly jerking so hard it winded him.

Through a side window Wilhelm saw one of the huge ghouls slam a fist the size of an outhouse down on Lawrence's rear carriage. Windows smashed and a rent opened up in the metal frame. Lawrence squealed but jerked out of range and dashed forward, running for a gap between two ghouls as they turned to face him.

He made it, just. The bouncing Animatter machine, still trailing along behind them, crashed into one of the ghouls, smashing part of its skull.

'The river!'

Lawrence raced for the bridge. Near the top of the slope on the other side stood the remaining Dark Mages, but now they were facing away from them. Wilhelm frowned, wondering what could possibly have caught their attention.

At the edge of the bridge, Lawrence paused.

'What is it?' Wilhelm said.

Lawrence lifted the metallic stump of his left paw. 'Can't swim,' he said. 'Sink.'

'Perhaps we can get back through the island to the beach?'

'Okay. Try.'

Lawrence limped across the bridge, the Animatter machine splashing through the river alongside, still disgorging its Strombolian spray of fireflies, and turning the river water grey with ash. Behind came the blocky house-ghouls, arms and legs made of stone, glowing orange eyes peering out of bleached skulls that had appeared in their windows and doors. A few smaller ghouls appeared in front of them, but Lawrence brushed them aside.

The road led up to a small rise not far from the amphitheatre. The machine gave Lawrence no place to hide, so he ran straight up its centre, snarling as he approached the group of Dark Mages, who scattered out of his way.

'Hurry, before they get their magic act together,' Wilhelm said.

They crested the rise a short distance to the Mages' right and Wilhelm saw what had held their attention.

The island had reached land, crashing into the beach below Endinfinium High. The island groaned as it continued to press forward, as though trying to fuse with the land.

'Escape,' Lawrence panted. Wilhelm, who hadn't known Lawrence could tire, figured it had to be the organic, creature part of him. Wilhelm leaned out of the window, looking for an alternative route, but their way was blocked by countless thousands of the charred foot-soldiers, all lined up in rows like an invasion force.

'Can't you smash them with the Animatter

machine?' Wilhelm said. 'Use it like a club or something?'

Lawrence growled something unintelligible and limped off to the right. Wilhelm craned his neck to see out, and found himself staring at the tangle of girders and struts belonging to the giant rollercoaster in the middle of the island.

'Um, not sure that's a good idea,' he said.

Lawrence paid no attention. Using his long snake tail as an extra limb, he began to climb. Wilhelm, so scared as they bumped and shook that he thought his heart would pop out of his mouth, hung on for dear life as the girders, part rusted through, creaked and groaned beneath them. The ground fell away, giving him a spectacular view of the hundreds of house-ghouls coming to surround them, their blocky hammer-arms smashing, ripping and tearing at the thick steel.

With every foothold, and each time Lawrence's lack of a front paw meant he had to hold on with his tail and jump upward for his right hand to get a grip, Wilhelm thought they were going to fall. Eventually, though, they reached the highest curve of the rollercoaster. Lawrence curled himself around the same maintenance platform Wilhelm had stood on with Miranda, and pulled up the hanging Animatter machine, dropped it into a curve in his body like a cat protecting a kitten. The fireflies still rose in an endless stream, climbing into the sky before burning up and raining down again as ash.

'What do we do now?' Wilhelm asked.

'Help,' Lawrence said.

'What kind of help?'

Lawrence's huge body shuddered with his own form of breathing. Wilhelm closed his eyes, feeling again for Miranda, and found the sparks of the Dark Mages' magic flickering below them.

'They're scared to attack us,' he said. 'They don't want to damage the machine. Perhaps if we drop it, it'll break?'

Lawrence shook his head. 'Don't break,' he said. 'Too strong.'

'How do you know?'

Lawrence shrugged. 'Don't know.'

Wilhelm nodded. He understood Lawrence's basic logic. How could they know if the machine would break? It might, but if it didn't, the Dark Mages would have it, and they would lose their bargaining tool.

The maintenance platform lurched. Magic or no magic, the house-ghouls would rip the rollercoaster down soon, and then rip them up. Not for the first time, Wilhelm felt completely useless.

'I have no magic,' he said. 'I can't protect us.'

'Help,' Lawrence said again.

'How?'

'School. Cover ears.'

'What?'

'Cover ears. Lawrence call school.'

'Huh?'

Lawrence's body creaked, as though contracting. Wilhelm understood just as Lawrence lifted his head, then jerked forward, letting out an astonishing bellow. Even with his hands clamped over his ears, Wilhelm felt like his brain was melting. The sound went on and on, the platform creaking below them as Lawrence's foghorn call filled the air.

When it stopped, all Wilhelm could hear was the ringing of a thousand church bells. 'What happens now?' he shouted, hearing only a whisper.

'Wait,' he thought Lawrence said.

42

OLD FRIEND

The secret door didn't want to open, but Benjamin had ways to make it. He swayed from side to side as he worked his magic on the walls, forcing the outline of the door to appear. Then, he stumbled forward into it, pushing through and leaning on it for support.

He found himself in an empty corridor. He staggered to the wall as the door behind him slammed shut then melted away out of view. Benjamin took a deep breath. A cut had opened up on his leg, adding to the others that the falling rocks had given him. He hurt in so many places he wondered if he had any blood left. It was a good thing he was only wearing his gym clothes, he thought, bizarrely. It would be a shame to spoil his nice school uniform.

Despite the pain that engulfed his body and the worry that encircled his mind, he found himself laughing. Gubbledon would be so angry when he saw all the rips and tears on his gym clothes. Miranda would scold him for not taking care of them, but Wilhelm would give him high-fives for the act of rebellion.

Oh, how he missed them. How he missed them all.

A door opened to his left, and a creature stepped out. It was a mass of metal and cloth, with a reptilian head. Green eyes blinked.

'Benjamin Forrest?'

Benjamin frowned, searching for the name of what he remembered was a reanimated clothes rail. 'George?'

'What are you doing here? You know Underfloor has been sealed against the invasion.'

Another figure appeared in the doorway, much larger, crowding George out into the corridor as it stumped out on huge tractor tires. The creature known only as Gatekeeper, due to his job guarding one of the entrances to the school, lifted a metal eyebrow over a chassis that had become a face.

'Well, well. People were wondering what had happened to you, Master Forrest.'

Benjamin shrugged. 'A few things. It'll take a while to explain, but perhaps if we have some tea and a sit-down....' He wiped dried blood off his cheek. 'I don't suppose you have a few plasters? Some that haven't reanimated would be best.'

'People are looking for you,' George said.

'I noticed.'

'And lots of bad things are being said.'

'Yes. Heard that, too. Doing my best to stay alive, uncaptured, and aware of what's going on, but to be honest ... I have no idea.'

'It's the island,' Gatekeeper said. 'The Lost City of the Ghouls.'

'It isn't very lost anymore,' George added.

Another door opened further up the corridor, and Moto stepped out. His motorcycle tyre revolved from an expression of surprise to one of anger.

'Benjamin. You know that you can't be here right now.'

'I need help.'

'You will bring them to us. You will destroy us all.'

Benjamin staggered toward him, George and Gatekeeper stepping aside to let him pass. 'I didn't do anything wrong, yet everyone is trying to get me.'

'Sometimes it's not what you're aware of doing that matters. Sometimes you're responsible for actions you had no idea you took.'

'Is this my fault?'

'You know the rules. We reanimates of Underfloor do not take sides with the humans. You do as you will, and we do the same. Many of us, such as Gatekeeper here, work among you. We help you out in your lives, and we ask in return only to be left to live ours in peace. This island, the Lost City of the Ghouls, it has come because of you. We cannot allow it to destroy Underfloor because we are harbouring you. You must be returned.'

'I thought you were a friend.'

'I am a reanimate. The safety of my own kind is my priority.'

'No—'

'Restrain him.'

George and Gatekeeper moved forward. Other reanimates appeared through other doors. Benjamin turned as metal fingers closed over one arm, and saw the sin keeper from the locker room standing by his side.

'I can destroy you all.'

Moto shook his head. 'No, you can't. Not all of us. There are too many.'

'I believed you. I helped you!'

'Your interests are not ours. I must protect those who trust me.'

'I need your help. It's the only way I can get the island to leave.'

Moto's head spun to a sad face. 'We have helped enough with humans. It is time to help ourselves.'

'No!'

Benjamin strained his neck as another creature came through a doorway. Gubbledon Longface limbed to stand beside Moto.

'Let go of him this uh ... uh ... instant,' he snapped, anger bringing on his stutter. 'You youngsters are forgetting yourselves. How many of you know who you have your hands on? Guh ... guh ... get back.'

'He is a threat to us,' Moto said.

'Oh, shuh ... shuh ... shut up. He helped me. He didn't huh ... huh ... have to. I'm his housemaster. I send him to the locker room, and I make him cuh ... cuh ... clean the dorm toilets for staying up too late. Yet he saved me. He didn't have to do that. And he's the only one who can save the school. Like he did last time.'

Moto let out a sigh. His face wheel spun to an

expression of frustration, then to one of confusion. 'How?'

'Benjamin?'

'I need help to draw the island away. I can send it over the edge of the world.'

'How?'

'I need someone who can fly.'

The reanimates turned to look at each other. 'No one here can fly.'

Benjamin shook his head. 'Basil can. Basil the Biplane. He once flew Jeremiah Flowers into the source of the Great Junk River.'

At the mention of the legendary man who had tried to escape Endinfinium through what most reanimates considered the giver of all life, there was a collective gasp.

'He can't fly anymore,' George said. 'No one's seen him in years.'

'He's tired of this old place, and I don't blame him,' said Gatekeeper. 'It can get a little wearing over time. It's only through some skewed sense of duty that I stay around. He's probably ready for the junk yard in the sky.'

Moto let out a low rumble, and his head spun to an expression of understanding. 'No, he's still around. He's down in the deep cellars. Benjamin and I went to see him once. He's grumpy, and he wants to deanimate, but he's still there.'

'Can you take me to him?'

'He'll tell you to get lost,' George said.

'No, he'll tell *you* to get lost,' Gubbledon said. 'He

might speak to Benjamin. Misery loves company, and look at the state of him.'

Benjamin rolled his eyes. 'Thanks. Coming from you, that's a compliment.'

'Don't backtalk me. I still have the authority to send you to the locker room, you naughty boy. Just wrecking your gym gear is worth five hundred.'

From behind them, the sin keeper sniggered. Benjamin risked a glance back at the reanimated suit of Samurai armour. He had never heard any hint of humour from him before, and it was a little unsettling.

'Sorry.'

'That's more like it. Come on. Let's go find that plane.'

With Moto taking the lead, the group headed down into the cellars of Underfloor. The gatekeeper transformed part of his tractor body into a platform for Benjamin to sit on, after Gubbledon pointed out that humans tended to weaken when hurt.

Soon, the walls closed in, and the corridors dimmed. It was difficult to see, but several reanimates had lights which flickered through doorways into cavernous store rooms filled with junk that had reanimated and deanimated so many times that it now just sat quietly humming away in the corners.

'Basil?' Moto shouted. 'Visitor. Where are you?'

They rounded a corner and something tall and wooden moved in the glow from the lights. Moto brought the group to a stop and slowly lifted his headlight beam.

A tall wooden box standing on end, with huge

wooden wings hung at its sides, lifted a red box of a head. Faded-paint eyes revolved and a white-washed wooden propeller spun in a circle.

'I was just on my way to find a ditch somewhere to lie in. Perhaps to finally rot away into nothing. What do you want?'

Benjamin stepped forward. 'Hello again, Basil.'

'Ah, the little boy who went looking for Jeremiah Flowers.'

'And found him, if you remember? I was wondering if you could help me. You promised me a flight sometime. I'd like to use it now, if I may.'

Basil sighed. 'Such nice manners. You must have a very attentive housemaster.'

Standing beside Benjamin, Gubbledon let out a pleasurable sigh. One of the reanimates sniggered, and there came the crunch of elbows poking into sides.

'I'm afraid that where I need to go might be a little dangerous. Jeremiah told me you were brave, and also wise.'

Basil scoffed. 'He would never have said that. He goaded me into his flight by telling me I was lazy and worthless.'

'I, um, don't remember the exact phrasing, but I'm sure the sentiment was the same.'

Basil swung his head in a lazy arc that might have been a shrug. A piece of wood broke off his shoulder and fell to the ground.

'I'm not in the best of shape. Aren't there any other planes you could ask?'

From time to time, Benjamin and the other students

had seen massive reanimated airliners soaring through the sky, their wings flapping like birds, but none ever came close to the school.

'None are as brave and intelligent as you.'

Basil scoffed. 'Well, since your housemaster has obviously taught you the art of sarcasm, I think it's only appropriate that I take you out and drop you in the sea in order to wash you clean of it.'

'Then you'll help me?'

Basil sighed and shrugged. 'I guess so. Hopefully we'll fly close enough to one of those ugly old suns for it to burn me up.'

Benjamin resisted the urge to jump up and down with excitement. His body wouldn't appreciate it, and he doubted Basil would care.

With Basil limping along, grumbling about everything that came to mind, the group headed back to the higher floors.

'I need somewhere safe where we can take off,' Benjamin said. 'The cliffs are too dangerous. Does the school have any flat sections of roof?'

Moto nodded. 'On top of the dining hall. There's a flat area that looks out over the school's main entrance and the cliffs. Even if you miss the take-off, you'll have a bit of time before you drop into the sea.'

'Probably just as well if we do,' Basil said. 'Get this over with. You're not expecting to succeed with this mission, are you? I know an optimistic fool when I see one. Jeremiah was much the same. What are you planning to do, anyway?'

Benjamin grinned. 'I'm the Pied Piper.'

'Oh, well good for you. And I'm Concorde.'

Benjamin patted the old biplane on the shoulder, wincing as a lump of crumbly wood broke off. 'I'd expect nothing less.'

'It's this way,' Moto said, stopping at the bottom of a set of stairs. 'We'll leave you here.'

Benjamin looked at the reanimated motorbike, feeling a sudden surge of betrayal. After everything, Moto and the reanimates were going to hide away in Underfloor while the school around them was devastated by ghouls. He opened his mouth to speak, but Moto's wheel-face spun to an expression of amusement.

'We have to secure the school,' he said. 'Make sure those things can't get inside. After all, you humans look after us, so we have to look after you.'

'War!' the sin keeper suddenly roared, waving his katana in the air and thumping a gauntlet against his breastplate.

'Good luck,' George said. 'We'll wait inside.'

'I'll come with you,' Gubbledon said. 'See you off.'

The three of them bade farewell to the other reanimates, who hurried off into the corridors. Benjamin went first, with Gubbledon behind and Basil grumbling along at the rear. At the top of three flights of stairs, a door opened onto a roof. Benjamin used a little magic to break open a rusted-shut lock, then stepped out into warm afternoon sunshine.

The roof was a rectangle with a raised glass window in the centre. Benjamin wasn't sure what it looked down onto, but thought there might be a gym on the floor above the dining hall. Looking from one end of the roof to the other, a distance of no more than a couple of hundred metres, he felt his confidence take a crushing blow. The roof was nowhere near long enough to be used for a runway, particularly not for a plane as old as Basil.

He would have to use his magic, if he had any left.

Behind him, Basil squeezed out of the low entrance, followed by Gubbledon. The ancient biplane stood blinking in the sunlight, a grimace on his painted face.

'So, that's what it looks like,' he said. 'No wonder I always avoided it. Daylight is so overrated. Come on, Master Benjamin, let's get moving. The sooner we get this job of yours done, the sooner I can hide away back in my cellar and hold a party for all the local woodworm.'

'Are you sure you'll be able to take off? It's not much of a runway, is it?'

Basil put a wooden hand on a crumbly wooden hip. 'You dragged me all the way up here just to doubt my ability?'

'No, but—'

The painted face broke into a rare smile. 'I guess you'll just have to find out.'

The tall reanimate squatted down, and with the creak and groan of tortured wood, he popped out his wings and lowered his chassis onto a pair of wheels that poked down out of holes in his undercarriage. Within a minute, a passable representation of an antique biplane stood on the roof, its propeller whirring.

'Get in then. I don't bite.' With a smirk he added, 'Unless I'm ticked off about something.'

'Don't you want a crash helmet of some kind?' Gubbledon asked.

Before Benjamin could respond, Basil snapped, 'Are you suggesting that I might endanger him?'

'Well, you might hit a crosswind.'

Basil's painted eyes narrowed, and his mouth opened to reply, but he was cut off by a shout from across the roof.

'Forrest! There you are!'

Derek Bates stepped out from behind the raised section of roof. He wore a black cape that was at least a size too big for him, its hem nearly tripping him as he walked forward. Seven other pupils fanned out behind him. Benjamin recognised Tommy Cale and Cherise White, both of whom wore glazed but sadistic expressions. The others were a mix of older kids he didn't know and a couple of new first-years he had never seen before.

Benjamin looked from one face to the next, then glared at Derek. 'This is none of your business.'

'You're a danger to this school. Godfrey said—'

'Godfrey is a little thuh ... thuh ... thug,' Gubbledon said, eyes narrowing as he stepped forward. 'And you are disobeying a direct instruction to remain in the dorms until the problem is suh ... suh ... sorted out. Get back there this instant. All of you.'

Derek blinked in surprise. Gubbledon waved behind his back at Benjamin to go. Aware he needed all his remaining magic for the coming flight, Benjamin didn't wait for another chance. He ran to Basil and jumped inside.

'Go on, you scamp,' Gubbledon shouted, limping toward Derek. 'How does a thou ... thou ... thousand cleans sound? How about two thousand?'

'I duh ... duh ... don't care,' Derek said, mocking the housemaster's stutter. 'You're an i .... i ... idiot.'

'And you're sleeping outside from nuh ... nuh ... now on. See how you like it.'

Basil started to trundle forward. 'I have an old tow rope,' he said. 'Any use for you?'

Benjamin glanced back at Derek as Basil gained speed. 'Um, I think so. Can you fire it around his legs?'

Basil sighed. 'I'll try. You might need to direct it a little, though. I'm not exactly GPS aligned, you know.'

'When I say, on three.'

'Got it.'

Derek had rounded on Gubbledon and was firing off insults like bullets. Gubbledon was attempting to hold his ground, but his stutter was getting worse. The rest of the pupils, with Derek's hold on them temporarily disrupted, stood around looking awkward, unsure what they should say or do.

Basil trundled past Gubbledon, barely moving above a light jogging speed. 'I'm pretty much maximum velocity,' he said. 'If you're firing, now's the only likely time.'

'Three!' Benjamin shouted.

The tow rope snaked out. It passed nowhere near Derek, missing Gubbledon by a couple of inches and heading for Tommy Cale's face before Benjamin reached out with his magic and gave the air a little push.

The rope jerked backward, wrapping around Derek's ankles. Derek screamed as it pulled him off his feet.

'Speed up!' Benjamin shouted.

'I told you, I can't!'

Benjamin pushed. The air seemed to contract behind them, then they were racing forward along the last section of roof, Derek shouting insults as he was dragged along behind.

'Um, no more roof,' Basil cried as the ground fell out below them and they plummeted toward the school's outer courtyard, the wind whistling around them.

'Up, up!' Benjamin shouted, and the air pushed Basil just enough to avoid the edge of the balustrade before they plummeted again, this time toward the beach. Dragged behind them, a deranged, screaming Derek brushed his shoes on the balustrade wall, burst through a flock of roosting scatlocks, then swung below them like Tarzan doing a cliff jump.

'Up more!'

Basil, propellers straining, began to rise. He arced around to the left, veering past the edge of the island where it had struck the beach, out across the open waters of the bay.

Derek, swinging below them, was shouting insults that Benjamin could barely hear. He smiled, then pushed the air just enough to unwrap the rope from Derek's foot. With a howl of terror, Derek plummeted into the sea. Benjamin saw a splash, then a moment later Derek resurfaced. He waved a tiny fist up at the plane, then turned and began swimming for the shore.

'That'll keep him quiet for a while,' Basil said. 'Quite the mouthy one, isn't he?'

'There's one that's worse,' Benjamin said. 'Hopefully we won't run into him.'

'Where next?'

'The edge of the world. Let's take that island on a trip.'

'If you say so.'

Basil arced back around in a northerly direction, then righted himself and turned toward the edge of the world a few miles distant. Benjamin closed his eyes, feeling for the great black thread he needed to draw in order to lead the island, but as he did so, a deafening boom shook the air behind them. It sounded like the roar of a metallic dinosaur crying for help.

'What on Endinfinium was that?' Basil asked.

'We have to turn back,' Benjamin said. 'That was an old friend. And it sounded like he was in trouble.'

43

KRAKEN

Lawrence was at the end of his strength, and Wilhelm's ears at the end of theirs. As Lawrence let out one last bellow for help, Wilhelm climbed out of his seat and slid open a side door.

The snake-train had curled around the highest curve of the rollercoaster. A small maintenance hatch stood beside it, so Wilhelm climbed out and looked down.

With the mist having burned off now the island had reached the coast, it was perhaps the best view one could find in Endinfinium short of the ability to fly. A mile to the west, Endinfinium High perched on the very edge of a headland, a convergence of architectural styles crossing multiple centuries which somehow created a unique kind of beauty.

In front of it, Sunshine Land laid itself out like a play map. Wilhelm saw where he and Miranda had first climbed onto the island, the boulevard where they had hidden the first night, and the Terror Tower Emmie and

Timothy had used as a secret base. In a basin below was the amphitheatre, while to the south were the empty grid lines of the town, the houses all gone now, only the pyramid still sitting in place.

The houses now were either marching through Sunshine Land on their way to the beach, or clustered around the base of the rollercoaster, ripping it to pieces one metal lintel at a time, in a gradual attempt to knock Lawrence off his perch and recover the Animatter machine.

Wilhelm started. The machine. Where had it gone?

He spun around, looking for the telltale fireflies, and found them pouring forth from a lower curve, Lawrence's tow rope having become tangled. The Animatter machine now hung precariously beneath the curve, dangling by a rope that had begun to fray.

'Lawrence! We have to get to it!'

The snake-train let out a defeated sigh. 'Tired,' he said. He lifted the stump of his left front leg, and Wilhelm stared. The metal was already starting to reform, slowly knitting outward like a Lego set that was building itself.

'Reanimating,' Lawrence said. 'Uses energy.'

Wilhelm nodded. 'I guess it's no different when we get sick, is it, really?'

Lawrence gave a tired nod. 'Sleepy,' he said.

Wilhelm peered over the edge of the platform at the maintenance ladder. It led down through the centre of the curve to another platform that connected with several other sections. In one or two places it had rusted through, but in others it was shaking back and forth.

He put a hand to the metal and felt warmth.

'What's happening, Lawrence?'

'Waking up. Machine feeding it.'

As the Animatter machine swung back and forth, the cloud of fireflies lifting from its surface swayed in turn, like smoke caught in the wind. On every northward sway, instead of fluttering up into the sky and dissolving, they flew straight into the metal of the rollercoaster's curve.

Wilhelm leaned over the platform edge. Far below, the colour of the rollercoaster was changing, from a dull, dusty grey to a vibrant green.

'Not long now,' Lawrence said.

'What can we....' Wilhelm trailed off. A couple of levels below, a figure climbed rapidly up the maintenance ladders, a knife in one hand. On the ground, a ghoul in the shape of a crane was lifting up a platform through the tangle of girders, while a couple of other Dark Mages waved their hands about, directing it.

The climbing figure reached a platform, ran along to another ladder, then looked up. Wilhelm got a look at his face.

Timothy.

'He's going to cut the machine loose.'

He looked up at Lawrence for a response, but the snake-train had lowered his head onto his remaining front paw and was snoring as softly as a reanimate of his size could.

Wilhelm took a deep breath. He already felt dizzy from the height, and he had no magic to protect him if he fell, but Miranda was gone, and for all he knew,

Benjamin was too. If he had any chance of doing something good, this was it.

He took a deep breath and hurried down the ladder, eyes closed the whole way, only opening them when his feet touched a platform.

It extended out over a spiralling curve of the track, but only halfway. He had no choice but to jump down onto the spiral and climb across. As he landed, one foot slipped, and for a moment he hung by one hand above the park far below, then he got a grip with the other and hauled himself up.

Above him, Lawrence already looked far away, wrapped around the steel girders at the top of the highest curve. Wilhelm frowned. A speck in the sky behind Lawrence was growing larger.

A plane.

'Huh?'

The rumble of an engine grew louder. As Wilhelm watched, it swooped over the top of the rollercoaster, bursting through the cloud of fireflies, then rose up and turned for another approach. A face Wilhelm hadn't seen in a long time leaned out of the cockpit.

'Benjamin!'

'Wilhelm!' came a faint response.

He looked up. Benjamin could take the machine away. Feeling a sudden sense of light-headedness, he danced across the rest of the spiral and leapt up onto the next maintenance platform. The Animatter machine swung in the air a couple of metres above his head.

Nearby, a piece of maintenance ladder had rusted through. Wilhelm leaned against it, bending it back, until the broken edges touched the machine. If he could climb on top and untangle the rope, perhaps Benjamin could catch it.

He had a foot on the bottom rung when ice-cold fingers closed over his ankle, dragging him back down.

'Not so fast.'

Wilhelm screamed and kicked out with his free foot. He caught Timothy flush on the nose, and the boy's face peeled away like a plastic mask to reveal a grinning skull, its eye sockets glowing orange. Wilhelm screamed again.

'You touch that machine and you're me,' the skull said. 'You think that was real food we were feeding you? You and Miranda are dead just like we are. You can't open up the Animatter machine. You condemn all of us, including yourself.'

'I'd rather be dead than live with a face like that,' Wilhelm shouted.

'Ah, diddums,' Timothy laughed. 'Don't worry, your mother will still love you. Oh, no she won't. She gave you up, didn't she?'

'Shut up!'

'That's what I heard, that you ended up in an orphanage because no one wanted you. Well, it's okay, because no one will want you now. You're dead, Wilhelm! Dead and gone. Go on, open it. I dare you!'

Wilhelm stared into the glowing orange eyes for a moment, then shook his head. 'Well, I guess you're right, aren't you? I don't have anything to live for, so I might as well just get it over with.'

He kicked out at Timothy again, knocking him off

the bottom rung. With a short head start, he clambered up the ladder and jumped onto the machine's top.

Fireflies swarmed past his face, into his ears, eyes, nose, mouth. He coughed, and his mouth filled with ash. He reached up, his fingers closing over the handle of the little window at the machine's front. He jerked on it, willing it to open, but nothing happened. It was stuck fast, immoveable.

'Open!' he screamed, slamming a fist against it. 'Come on, open!'

He was about to try one more time, when the whole rollercoaster lurched.

Wilhelm fell off the ladder. His hands scrabbled for purchase, and he found himself dangling, one arm hooked over a loop of Lawrence's tow rope, tangled in the girders. The Animatter machine was directly above him, creaking as it threatened to break loose and crash down upon his head.

Below him, Timothy cackled with laughter. The orange pinprick eyes narrowed even further, and above, the Animatter machine began to shake from side to side.

'Say goodnight, Wilhelm,' Timothy said. 'You always were a little runt. I don't think anyone will miss you.'

The rollercoaster lurched again, and a tangle of rope came loose. The Animatter machine swung down in a long arc like a giant pendulum. Wilhelm screamed, yanking on one end of rope, and managing to pull himself just far enough aside to avoid being flattened. As it swung back, he caught hold of a girder and held tight.

'Wilhelm!'

He looked up. The plane came swooping down, Benjamin leaning out of the cockpit. Wilhelm felt a momentary lightness, as though the air was pushing him up, then it was gone.

'The machine!' Wilhelm shouted. 'You have to destroy the machine!'

Benjamin frowned. Wilhelm waved his hands at the machine, making a crushing motion with his fists. Finally Benjamin nodded. The plane rose into the sky to make another pass.

Wilhelm untangled himself from the rope and tried to tie it into a loop that he could hook over the plane's landing gear. Then he climbed up a girder until he was out in the open air, with the rope looped around his waist.

'Benjamin! One more time!'

The plane started to come around. He glanced at Lawrence, only to see the snake-train dropping away below him. Lawrence opened his huge eyes and blinked, then glanced around in surprise.

'It awake,' he said.

The rollercoaster was moving. As the house-ghouls smashed away at it, great curves of track like the tentacles of a kraken slashed and cracked at them, flinging the ghouls away as though they were nothing more than large balls of sponge.

Wilhelm groaned as the curve of track on which he stood dropped away beneath his feet. He hung on like a barnacle as it smashed into a two-storey house-ghoul battering at a supporting girder with an uprooted tree. The ghoul howled as it bounced away, while above

Wilhelm's head, the Animatter machine battered back and forth between two metal frames.

'Benjamin,' he gasped, wondering how much longer he could hold on, as the rollercoaster-kraken rose again to make another strike.

44
ABYSS

Wilhelm had vanished into the churning mass of tentacles that the rollercoaster had become. Basil swung in as close as he could, but Wilhelm had vanished. Benjamin, initially ecstatic at seeing his friend, now scanned the thrashing green tentacles for some sign of him.

Lawrence had caught hold of a swinging track-tentacle then jumped free, landing on a wide boulevard and racing away between two lines of houses. One of Lawrence's front paws had looked damaged, the snake-train limping on one side, but the ghouls' attention was now fixed on the giant reanimated rollercoaster that was battering them to all parts of the island.

'There he is!'

Wilhelm had climbed the rope and now clung to one side of the blocky box from which the cascade of fireflies rose. Even without seeing Wilhelm's smashing gesture, Benjamin had sensed the box thing was the centre of everything. The glowing fireflies that rose off it shone even brighter when he closed his eyes and felt for the magic, like glitter spread over a carpet of darkness. The machine, whatever it was, contained great power.

'That reanimate is getting friskier,' Basil said. 'If you're going to get your friend, I think we have one last chance. I'm not quick enough to avoid those tentacles, and one hit will do us in.'

Benjamin grinned. 'Then let's go get him.'

They arced around again. The track-tentacles thrashed as hundreds of ghouls tried in vain to smash it apart. Benjamin glanced at the beach, where the lines of orange-black ghouls were disembarking the island, and knew they didn't have much time to get the island away. Soon the school would be engulfed, and nothing he did would save it.

'There he is. Are you ready, Basil?'

'No, I'm not. I've never been ready and I never will be. Unless you mean ready to die. In that case—'

'Now! Dive, dive, dive!'

Basil plummeted out of the sky. The sudden downdraft stalled his propellers, and his tail threatened to roll over his front. They were falling right into the middle of the beast, where a bright green disembarkation station had grown a wild, angry face. Track-tentacles slashed all around them, one clipping the end off Basil's left wing.

'Benjamin … hurry!'

'There!'

The track-tentacle in which the box was tangled, with Wilhelm clinging desperately to its side, rose to take another swipe at the house-ghouls. Benjamin waited until it was alongside them, then he reached out with his magic and pulled on the tangled rope. A loop of it hooked over one of Basil's landing wheels, catching tight.

'Up!' Benjamin screamed. 'Up, up, up!'

Basil's engine groaned as the little plane straightened. One propeller, then the other, coughed into life. Basil, growling like a mad army sergeant, powered forward, jerking the box and Wilhelm off the track-tentacle. Benjamin pushed with his magic, helping to break the ropes, then they were free, rising into the air, the box hanging beneath the plane, with Wilhelm still clinging to the side.

As they rose out of range, Benjamin leaned out of the cockpit. 'Wilhelm!' he shouted. 'Can you hear me? I'll climb down and pull you up.'

'Whatever that thing is,' Basil said, 'it would be a good idea to get rid of it soon. I can't see through all these fireflies. Although, I have to say, it does feel rather nice….'

Benjamin frowned. Basil's painted face was sharpening as the fireflies rushed up around him before extinguishing in the air and raining down on them as ash. A crack in the little windshield began to seal up. The wing tip that had broken off began to regrow itself with the crackle of shaping wood.

'You have to destroy it,' Wilhelm shouted. 'It's an Animatter machine. It steals the souls of everyone who comes close to it and gives them to ghouls.'

'We could drop it in the sea,' Basil said.

'No! We have to break it somehow. If it sinks to the bottom of the sea, all those people will be lost forever. You have to break it. Miranda tried, but it wasn't enough.'

'Miranda....'

'She jumped into the pit. She tried to overload the machine, hoping it would take her magic, but it wasn't quite enough.'

Benjamin could only guess at what Wilhelm was talking about, but there would be time for discussions later, once Wilhelm was safe. 'There's only one way to destroy it,' he said. 'It belongs to Endinfinium, right? We take it out of Endinfinium, and it does what most things do when you take them out of their natural place. It melts down.'

'But there is no way out of Endinfinium,' Wilhelm shouted. 'You've tried to find one.'

Benjamin shook his head. 'Oh, I don't know if there's another place, but there's certainly a way out. Basil, head for the edge of the world.'

Wilhelm flashed a grin. 'You're nuts, Benjamin. It's so good to see you again. I guess if we're going to die, we might as well die together.'

Benjamin shook his head. 'Basil and I go alone,' he said. 'I'm dropping you off on the way. I turned Sara Liselle into a cleaner. I'm not having something as bad —or worse—happening to you.'

He twisted to face the island. Among the trees on the eastern side, he saw Lawrence crouching, hiding from the ghouls. Benjamin cupped his hands together, then made a little spell that Miranda had taught him, creating a vacuum tunnel in the air to allow his voice to travel further. The condensed walls of air helped to bounce the sound along, but you had to make sure the line was straight, otherwise you could end up shouting back into your own face.

'Lawrence, can you follow us?'

Even though a couple of miles away, Lawrence's head snapped up. The snake-train looked up at the biplane, then nodded. Uncoiling, he bolted through the trees toward the nearest beach. In seconds he was gliding through the water, heading their way.

'Benjamin,' Wilhelm shouted. 'I can help you. Pull me up.'

Benjamin shook his head. 'I'm not going to let you get hurt.'

'And you think dropping me in the sea isn't going to be painful at all? Are you crazy?'

'I'll use my magic to cushion you.'

'Your magic? Miranda always said you were like a baby playing with a box of fireworks. You really think I can trust you?'

'She said that?'

'At least twenty times.'

'You're a liar.'

'Well, if I am, pull me up so you can punish me!'

'No.'

Benjamin sat back in the seat, ignoring Wilhelm's cries. He closed his eyes and let his mind drift, feeling for the great black wave of dark reanimate magic. His hand was a numb, cold lump at the end of his arm as it provided the link to the Lost City of the Ghouls, slowly turning in his direction. As it began to move, the island created a furrow of dispersed water, like a great ship moving out of port. The massive reanimated rollercoaster had broken free of the land and was moving across the island, batting dozens of house-ghouls as they sought to restrain it, while along the cliffs stood dozens of reanimates, ready to stand as the school's defence.

Would it make a difference, or was it too late? Was Wilhelm right about the Animatter machine? Was there a chance that somewhere, somehow, Miranda might still be alive?

The edge of the world was fast approaching, a grey line of rock over which the sea poured like an overflowing bath.

'You know,' Basil was saying, 'I told Jeremiah he should forget about the river. Over the edge, I said, that's the only way. Doesn't it make you feel alive, facing something so unknown? Isn't it wonderful?'

'I hope we come back from this,' Benjamin said. 'I'm sorry if we don't.'

Basil laughed. 'Oh, don't worry about me, little friend. I've been waiting for this my whole life. Not everyone likes prancing around like a human. I much preferred life as a simple plane in a museum. The quiet life and all that.'

They were flying a couple of hundred metres above the water, the heavy Animatter machine keeping a check on their altitude. While the fireflies still came, their flow was noticeably less, as though the machine was settling down. Basil now looked new, all smooth wood and sharply painted lines, powerful propellers and straight, unblemished wings. Benjamin had to admit he felt pretty good too, as though all the anger that had built up in him over the last weeks was draining away.

'We're nearly there,' he said. 'It's time to drop off Wilhelm, then see what's behind that wall of cloud.'

'Probably another wall of cloud,' Basil said, his newfound newness not completely negating his negativity. 'And then another, and another. For the rest of infinity. I mean, what else would there be? Everything ends, doesn't it?'

'I'm not sure,' Benjamin said. 'Let's find out.'

He leaned out of the cockpit. Wilhelm still hung from the machine's side and looked mightily angry about it. The water below thrashed and bucked, battered by winds off the edge of the world. Circling like an otter waiting for a bird to land, Lawrence was directly below them, looking up, waiting.

'Wilhelm,' Benjamin shouted out of the cockpit. 'I just wanted to say ... thanks. You're the best friend a person could have. I'll never forget you, as long as I ... live.'

'Oh, shut up, you fool. Pull me up.'

Benjamin wiped a tear from his eye. 'Say hello to everyone.'

He closed his eyes and pushed with his magic, aiming to loosen Wilhelm's fingers and let him drop into the sea. He would cushion his friend before he landed, and Lawrence would pick him up. It would all work out so well—

Something was encircling his head. He frowned, trying to knock it off, but it didn't move.

'Benjamin, he's here! Timothy!'

Benjamin's eyes snapped open. Something with a grinning skull face and shining orange eyes had climbed up from the underside of the Animatter machine, where its tilted angle had kept it hidden. A bleached jawbone opened and a chilling laugh filled the air.

'Oh, foolish kids. You think you can so easily thwart the Dark Man? This is his world. He is everywhere. He is everything.'

Basil rolled, dropping for the water's surface. Benjamin and Wilhelm both screamed as a great weight seemed to press down on them. Thrown from the cockpit, Benjamin managed to grab hold of the edge of a wing moments before he tumbled into the sea. He closed his eyes, pulling as hard as he could on his magic, trying to correct the attack.

Basil rolled again, then flew straight for the clouds at great speed, a twig caught in the winds of a cyclone.

The thing with the skull for a face that Wilhelm called Timothy was a Channeller. So close to Wilhelm, he had tapped Wilhelm's latent Weaver magic to increase his own. Benjamin had too little strength to overpower the magic, but if he used what little was left to break the rope and throw Timothy off, he would lost his hold on the island, and the Animatter machine would sink to the bottom of the sea.

There was only one thing he could do.

'I'm sorry, Wilhelm,' he whispered. 'Forgive me.'

Drawing on all the power he had left, taking it from

the nearest fireflies and his own remaining strength, he created a huge backdraft in the air which condensed and flung them forward over the edge of the world, into the churning mass of cloud that bordered all that existed in Endinfinium.

As they crashed into grey and white swirling cold, an unusual sound came from all around him, an ear-splitting whistle which sounded not unlike screaming, but not just from Wilhelm and Timothy, but from everyone, everywhere, all at once.

And then, and then, and then, there was a great cracking, and the whistling intensified until it was a blanket of sound, the world filled with fire and the howling of a million trapped souls finding release, and there was only orange, orange, orange.

Benjamin threw back his head and screamed, and the orange fire became everything. And as they plunged into the abyss, he wondered only whether somewhere, somehow, his family and friends would be all right.

'Goodnight,' he whispered, and then, like a single candle winking out in an otherwise dark room, everything turned from orange into black.

45

DEPARTURE

'Welcome!' Godfrey screamed, his arms aloft. 'Welcome to Endinfinium. Come in! Make yourselves at home.'

The army of burned ghouls marched past him in disorderly rows, bleached skulls glowing out of their orange-black bodies, gleaming eyes flickering. They marched past Godfrey on their way to the beach as though barely aware of his existence, parting slightly as though he was a tree to be stepped around.

Godfrey, for his part, was jubilant. The grin on his face matched the yellow sun's afternoon brightness, and everything about him suggested a prince welcoming its army home.

The burned-ghouls massed on the beach like an invasion force waiting for instructions. On the cliff's high above, reanimates stood in lines like children's toys come alive, a last wall of defence against the invaders. Of the teachers there was no sign, but some pupils, particularly the younger ones, had been seen following Gubbledon across the cliff path to the dormitory.

Further away, a great green thrashing thing was throwing houses with arms and legs and skulls for faces high into the air. The reanimated rollercoaster looked like a giant angry robot octopus, and only when a house-ghoul landed among the burned-ghouls, scattering them like bowling pins, did Godfrey really appreciate its power.

The speck that flew in low to the thrashing reanimate, circled through its arms and then flew out again, heading for the edge of the world, initially appeared to be a bird. Only when Godfrey screamed, 'Forrest!' was it clear that the bird was actually a plane, with a fugitive boy nestled in the cockpit.

Snout watched everything from a patch of undergrowth near the park's entrance. Too scared to move as the burned-ghouls marched past, he tried to keep Godfrey in his line of sight, not because Snout wanted to confront him, but because he felt safer knowing where the other boy was.

Something dangled from below Benjamin's aeroplane, a square thing that looked like a refrigerator. Snout guessed that to risk diving into the thrashing arms of the reanimated rollercoaster meant it must be important, but when Godfrey turned to face the departing plane, his face nearly purple with anger, Snout knew he had to do something.

Whenever he closed his eyes, he could feel creatures down in the ground, waiting to be called. He didn't know if they truly existed or not until he spoke to them, but he could feel a link between him and them, as though they were buried dogs and all he had to do was give the leash a good tug and up they would come. He had tried it in secret, but the kind of warped monstrosities that had appeared kept him awake at night, sometimes quite literally if he couldn't figure out how to get them to go back to sleep.

Godfrey had shown on several occasions that he possessed an unpleasantness Snout found disconcerting. He remembered with distaste how Godfrey, standing in the school's outer courtyard, had spotted Gubbledon walking back to the dorms and raised a strong gust of wind to knock the housemaster off, before turning to the group of pupils with him to boast that it didn't matter, because reanimates didn't feel pain. That wasn't the point as far as Snout was concerned; it was a cruel thing to do. Cruelty, though, was fast becoming Godfrey's new best friend.

Whatever Benjamin was doing, Snout trusted him more than he trusted Godfrey. And if he had to choose between helping one or the other, it was an easy choice to make.

As Godfrey lifted his arms in the direction of the little plane, Snout closed his eyes, and let his mind feel for one of the creatures underneath the ground. There was something down there, right below Godfrey's feet, a twisted thing made of metal and plastic that was waiting for an opportunity to experience sunlight for the first time. Snout concentrated, trying to call it.

Godfrey screamed. Snout opened his eyes.

Something grey had got hold of Godfrey's ankle as it broke out through the earth.

A length of electricity cable, snapping and twisting like a snake.

More followed, some as thick as pythons, others long and slender, grey water pipes and electric cables that had once powered the theme park, reanimating at Snout's will. Godfrey cried out as he brushed them off. Some exploded in showers of plastic as he used his magic, but they were swarming him like ants engulfing a grasshopper.

'No!'

Godfrey had sounded angry before, but now his voice took on a note of fear. Even though it was Godfrey, Snout didn't want to see him hurt. He just wanted Godfrey to leave Benjamin alone for once. But Godfrey didn't look in pain. He was reaching for something one of the pipes had pierced, a book, plucked out of Godfrey's back pocket, impaled by a length of wire and now swung around in the air just out of reach.

It wasn't like Godfrey to worry about returning library books. He often claimed to throw them in the laundry rather than take them back. He was grasping for this one, however, as though it was of great value.

Snout closed his eyes and concentrated. He tried to tell the reanimated pipes to go back into the ground. He had heard Benjamin and Miranda talk about threads of magic, but all he felt was something cold and heavy pressing against his forehead like a wet sponge. He gritted his teeth, compelling it to move out of the way.

In a rush, the pipes and wires snaked back into the

earth, burying themselves. Instead of releasing the book, though, the wire holding it cut through its pages as it withdrew, and the book exploded into a mass of scrap paper, fluttering away on the wind. Godfrey howled as he tried to gather the pieces in his hands, running back and forth as the sea breeze took hold of them.

Snout had never seen Godfrey look so distraught. He stood up from his hiding place, feeling guilty enough to confess, when the ground beneath his feet began to rumble.

He reached out for a nearby tree and held on as the shaking intensified. A glowing light coming from the edge of the world filled the sky, like a sunset but a hundred times brighter.

Godfrey had stopped trying to gather the book's scattered pages and was staring out to sea. The biplane had disappeared, but beyond the edge of the world, where grey cloud always swirled, a blanket of fire rose high into the sky, hot enough to warm Snout's face even at this distance. He stared in disbelief as it flared for nearly a minute before slowly fading away.

He was still staring when he heard a series of loud thuds that made him turn. The burned-ghouls were falling to the ground. As their orange glows faded they began to disintegrate, until all that was left were heaps of dark grey ash that the wind quickly picked up and blew away.

Over by the reanimated rollercoaster, the same thing was happening to the house-ghouls. One by one they sat down, their arms and legs shrivelling up, then the houses themselves breaking down into fine dust.

Snout was still watching, when arms grabbed him from behind, pulling him up.

'Come on, Simon,' Gubbledon said. 'The island's started moving away. You're not the best swimmer, are you?'

Snout followed the housemaster back through the theme park to the main entrance, and saw Gubbledon was right: the island was pulling away from the shore. Gubbledon helped him down a craggy slope to the water, and together they climbed in, floundering through the water with one hand on each other's shoulders. When they neared the beach, other pupils ran into the water to help them out.

'What's happening?' Tommy Cale said to Gubbledon, his eyes red as though he'd been crying. 'Where's that thing going?'

'Back where it came from,' Gubbledon said. 'And not before time.'

'We left Godfrey on the island,' Snout said.

Gubbledon scowled. 'He can find his own way. I'm sure he'll be fine.'

Snout sat down on the beach beside Tommy Cale. The great fire flare that had briefly appeared had gone, but the island was still slowly moving away, the channel of water between its edge and the beach, dotted with heaps of billowing ash, slowly widening.

'Right,' Gubbledon said, standing up, brushing ash and sand off his clothes. Snout noticed how one leg looked a little more bent than before. 'I'd better get you lot back to the dorms. You need to change for dinner.'

46

AWAKENINGS

Edgar felt like he'd just woken from a very long sleep. His head thudded as though he'd been butting the wall in his sleep, and when he got out of bed, he realised he hadn't cleaned or tidied his apartment for several days.

The first clue to what had happened was the scrawl on his desk, threatening to "reduce" Benjamin Forrest. He remembered chasing him through the teachers' tower with the rest, only for Benjamin to escape through Grand Lord Bastien's window. What had they all been thinking? That he'd tried to hurt a boy he thought of almost as a son gave him a deep sense of shame.

Outside, he found Ms. Ito and Captain Roche wandering aimlessly, looking equally confused. Only when they found the Grand Lord waiting in the lobby did they get any sort of explanation.

'He's gone,' the Grand Lord said. 'And he's taken the lost city with him.'

From the battlements above the school, Edgar watched the island's final moments. The yellow sun had fallen below the horizon, but the red sun was still high enough to give the island floating near the edge of the world in a clear silhouette, one which, as Edgar watched, dropped out of sight. For a moment the void where it had been felt overbearing, then Edgar blinked, and the last light of the setting sun seemed as natural as it always had.

He headed back into the school, not to look for answers, but to figure out where to start the questions.

~

Cleat tried not to say anything rude. The nurse was apologetic, promising that food would be coming soon.

'I can go and get it meself,' he said. 'I think I'm well enough now.'

'No, just you stay there,' the nurse said. 'You need a few more days of rest. Dinner will be here shortly. It's just that half the cleaners seem to have disappeared. I don't know what's going on. They were all there this morning.'

Cleat rolled his eyes. 'Well, it's a good thing I'm not hungry or anything.'

~

Miranda opened her eyes. Her whole body ached as though it had been broken apart and then put back together. Her mind, on the other hand, felt calmer and more relaxed than she could ever remember feeling, perhaps not since the day Benjamin had arrived. The world felt harmonious and kind, and she was an intricate part of it.

She rolled over and sat up, wondering where she was. She was lying on a downy mat of grass, not far from a gurgling stream—one that was clear, not full of junk like most others—not far from a hillside that rose up to a bald, rocky crest. Beyond it, mountain peaks rose high into the evening sky, jagged and unwelcoming.

Rolling onto her front, she crawled a few paces to the stream and took several large swallows of ice cold water. Sitting up, she looked around her again, not recognising anything. Then, looking back at the mountains, she saw a light blinking high up among the peaks.

It flickered out of a building that didn't seem to stay still, one that hurt her eyes as she looked at it, because it appeared to be moving.

For more information about forthcoming titles
please visit

www.amillionmilesfromanywhere.net

THANKS

Big thanks as always to those of you who provided help and encouragement. My proofreaders Nick, Jenny, Hazel, Kathryn and Lisa get a special mention, as does as always, my muse, Jenny Twist.

In addition, extra thanks goes to my Patreon supporters, in particular to Ann Bryant, Amaranth Dawe, Charles Urban, Janet Hodgson, Juozas Kasiulis, Leigh McEwan, Teri L. Ruscak, James Edward Lee, Catherine Crispin, Christina Matthews, Alan MacDonald, and Eda Ridgeway.

You guys are awesome.

Printed in Great Britain
by Amazon